Bree Wiley

Cover Photo by Igor Vetushko

Cover Design by Bree Wiley

Editing by Bree Wiley

Paperback ISBN 979-8-9918930-1-5

Contents

Foreword V

Soundtrack VI

1. Shilo 1

2. Ryann 9

3. Shilo 18

4. Ryann 27

5. Shilo 38

6. Shilo 52

7. Ryann 64

8. Ryann 71

9. Shilo 91

10. Ryann 103

11. Shilo 118

12. Ryann 136

13. Ryann 148

14. Shilo 171

15. Ryann 193
16. Shilo 203
17. Ryann 218
18. Shilo 237
19. Shilo 251
20. Ryann 271
21. Shilo 287
22. Ryann 296
23. Shilo 304
24. Ryann 312
25. Shilo 330
Epilogue 343
Afterword 349
Acknowledgments 351
Content Warning 352
About The Author 354

Foreword

Though Ryann and Shilo's story is considered moderate angst, they do deal with themes that may be triggering to some. For those of you who would like to know what you're getting into, please refer to the Content Warning in the back of the book.

Please, please always remember that your mental health matters and your experiences are valid. The world is a brighter place with you in it, and you are loved.

Soundtrack

Too Good – Breathe Carolina
soft boy – Robert DeLong
Waste My Time – Dance Yourself Clean
Find It – Breathe Carolina
Dream Boy (MC4D Remix) – Water parks, MC4D
Sweater Weather – The Neighborhood
I Want It – Two Feet
Make Me Feel – Elvis Drew
Perfect Strangers – Archers
Good Vibrations – MISSIO, Wes Borland
Sweet – Cigarettes After Sex
Anthem – Leonard Cohen

"There is a crack,
a crack in everything.
That's how the light gets in." – Leonard Cohen

Shilo

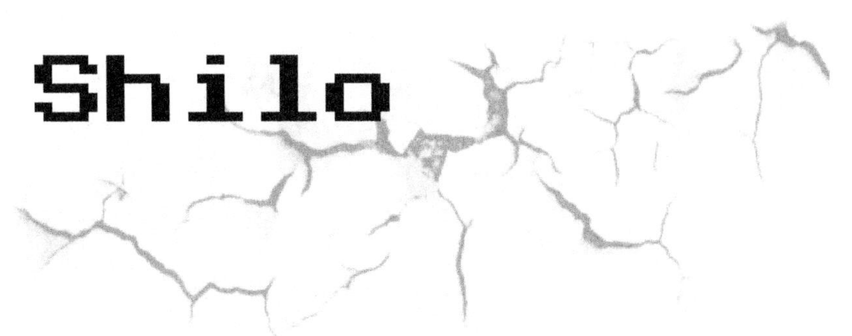

"Dude, I think... I'm gonna puke."

Cheezus Christ, again?

"Hang on, let me pull over," I grumble irritably, quickly pulling the car to the side of the street. Seriously, why does this keep happening to me? Why are so many people in downtown Seattle such lightweights?

Honestly, it's probably my own fault for sticking around a college area on a Friday night, but I'm trying here, okay? Can I get a break?

Drunk Party Bro starts to gag, not attempting to open the back door when we come to a stop, and I silently curse whatever powers that be for giving me my fifth wasted Uber rider of the night as I climb out and round the SUV. Freezing rain pelts my skin as I yank open the door, but I'm too late. Puke Face has already started vomiting up whatever noxious mixture he drank at the bar.

"You frickin' kidding me?!" Pulling him out so that he's hanging over the side, I barely jump back in time to avoid the backsplash on my fraying Chucks as he soaks the gutter. A good chunk of the stuff—emphasis on chunk—is pooling in the middle seat, but luckily, Dad went with the leather upholstery. Won't help with the smell, though.

As he keeps emptying his stomach, I push damp strands of purple hair out of my face and try to focus on the positives, like my therapist suggested.

Let's see...smelly car, cold wet hoodie, and a whole ten bucks from this ride, which won't even cover the detailing I'll need. And because I actually have a conscience, I still have to drive Pukey McGee another mile and a half.

Sooo many positives about leaving the house tonight. Look at me go, Doc.

"Sorry, man," the guy slurs, wiping his mouth on his sleeve, and I grimace as I grab a towel from the trunk.

"Just...wipe up as much as you can, please."

The rest of the ride is awful. He starts crying. By the time I drop him at his dorm at UW, he's a snot-nosed mess, and I couldn't be happier to pass him off to his friends. I wonder vaguely what classes he takes, if we're in the same program.

Not that it matters—my classes are all online, much to my parents' and therapist's dismay. But honestly, it makes sense. Why would a Computer Engineering student need to sit in a classroom instead of, you know, on a *computer*? Self-explanatory, right?

I barely have time to wipe down the backseat before another pickup comes through. Great. Another bar.

Why am I doing this again?

Because Doctor Iskar said I need to 'socialize' and Dad's charging me rent.

Oh, right. Still doesn't mean I have to put up with drunk asshats.

I'm about to decline the ride when I see the tip, and my eyes nearly bug out of my skull.

Five-hundred dollars? For a fifteen-minute drive over to the Belltown area?

Well, shit. That'll cover rent for a month. Or a new graphics card for my computer. Hell yeah.

Hitting accept, I pull back onto the main road, my wipers working overtime. August in the PNW is usually dry, but naturally, it's pouring on one of the two days I drive for Uber, lucky me. Not that I mind. Me and the sun? We have issues. My ghostly complexion should be a hint. Just call me Elmer, 'cause I'm muthafrickin' pasty.

Letting off the gas, I stop in front of the bar and double-check the address with a frown. This part of Seattle is sketchy at best. The building looks like something straight out of a horror film—square, concrete, one blinking neon window, and a nondescript door wedged between two abandoned storefronts. A dive, if I ever saw one.

I shoot a quick message to my rider, Ryann, asking them to sit in the front seat. There are a few people loitering outside, smoking and giving me looks that send a shiver down my spine.

Hurry the hell up, Ryann.

My hoodie is still wet and clinging to my small frame, so I turn up the heat despite the warm summer air outside. Shadows dance in the windows of the abandoned shops, tricking my mind into seeing monsters lurking in the dark, waiting to tear me apart. I must zone out because the passenger door suddenly opens, and I yelp in surprise.

My heart nearly leaps out of my chest as my rider slides into the seat next to me, frowning at my reaction, and I'm struck by the most intense hazel eyes I've ever seen. Green and gold blending together, swirling like a kaleidoscope beneath shapely dark brows and equally dark hair. Straight, perfect nose. Full lips. A stubbled jawline that could cut glass. All of this attached to a tall, muscled man in a fancy suit who's looking at me like I've sprouted horns.

Holy shit, he's frickin' gorgeous. Adonis personified. A god of a man, right here in my passenger seat.

He clears his throat, a deep, rumbling sound that sends a jolt between my legs, and the panic of popping a boner snaps me out of my stupor.

"Sorry," I squeak, throwing the car into drive and pressing too hard on the gas, causing the SUV to lurch forward.

The angel—uh, the man, Ryann...whatever—huffs in annoyance before grabbing the oh-shit handle. His legs spread to brace himself, and I catch a glimpse of his thighs stretching his pants. Jeez, they're like tree trunks. Bet he could squeeze my head with those bad boys and pop me like a watermelon.

"Watch the fucking road!" He snarls as the car bounces, and I jerk us back on track just before hitting a mailbox.

Ah, shit.

"Sorry!" I squeak again, my voice still sounding like my balls have retreated into my body, and I slap my chest to get a grip.

It's suddenly way too hot, so I tug on the front of my hoodie to fan myself. From the corner of my eye, I see him watching me like I'm one step away from a nervous breakdown.

Which... might be true.

I've found guys attractive before—hell, I've watched more gay porn than is probably healthy—but I've never actually *been* with one. I wasn't exactly popular in high school, and I haven't left the house much since the Great Graduation Disaster three years ago. Hence the 'socializing' therapy homework.

But this man? This...beautiful specimen of masculinity sitting in my dad's Subaru? I'm fighting the instinct to hump the steering wheel right now. How embarrassing.

I blame the meds. They say SSRIs affect the sex drive, so that's probably it. I'll have to call Doctor Iskar tomorrow and inquire further because my virgin ass has never felt this way before.

Eventually, he looks away, and I let out a breath. Weirdly, I kinda want him to look back at me, which is nuts because I'm usually trying to blend into the background. Contradictory to the purple hair, but you can blame my older sister for that.

As he pulls out his phone, I find myself talking without actually hearing the words. "So what's with the bar you were at?"

Am I hoarse? Why do I sound like a forty-year-old chain smoker?

He doesn't even look up from his screen as he responds. "What about it?"

Clipped tone. Baritone voice, smooth like honey. A hint of an accent. So frickin' hot.

"I mean...kind of a sketchy place for someone dressed as nice as you."

"Sketchy places are good for sketchy activities."

Well, that's... not ominous at all.

Cutting him a sideways glance, I lick my lips at his inked forearm. "And did you find what you were looking for?"

There's a beat of silence, rain pelting the windshield, and I feel his gaze slide to my face again. "No."

"Oh." I nod like a bobblehead. "Well, there's always next time."

Don't even know what the hell I'm saying, but look at me, Doc. An entire conversation with someone who isn't related to me. That's progress.

He doesn't reply, only drops his head back with a heavy sigh, and I force myself to keep from ogling. "So, Ryann, huh? Interesting. I've never seen it spelled that way before."

"It's Irish."

"Ah, that explains the accent." Glancing over to switch lanes, I fan myself again. His lap is just the perfect size to crawl into. Curl right up and make a home there, like a house cat. "Did you come from Ireland?"

"Obviously."

Wow, not much of a talker. I'm not usually one either, but I'm nervous as hell right now, and I turn into a real chatterbox when I'm anxious. Honestly, I hate it. It used to make things worse for me in high school because my brain doesn't know how to shut up. So I just bite my lip and nod.

After a few quiet minutes, though, he speaks, running a hand through his dark strands. "My family came stateside when I was a kid. We go back every few years to visit."

"Very cool," I give him a crooked smile. "My favorite actor is Irish. You know Cillian Murphy?"

He blinks those hazel eyes at me, unimpressed, and the sweat on my neck spreads to my palms.

I try again. "Uh, from the show Peaky Blinders? Inception? Batman Begins?"

Nope, not a single reaction other than a twitch of his lips.

Okay, then. See, Doc, this is why I don't try because I'm frickin' *weird*.

Luckily, we're pulling up to his destination, and I don't have to stew in my awkwardness for long. The address leads to a luxury high-rise, and I expect him to hop out here. Instead, he gives me a gate code.

We drive into a parking garage, and I park in his designated spot. As he opens the passenger door, I give a half-wave, relieved to finally escape.

But then he pauses and raises a brow at me. "Are you coming?"

"Wha-huh?" I gape at him in confusion.

Sighing heavily, he tilts his head back before reaching over to grab my junk.

"Do you want to get off or not?"

I jolt with a yelp, glancing down at his hand cupping my hard dick through my sweats. A flush creeps up my neck because, holy shit, I didn't even realize I had a boner.

Oh, jeez, what the hell?!

"Let's go." He climbs out of the car, his tall frame unfolding like some kind of Greek god, easily over six feet. I stare for half a second, watching those powerful legs stride toward the elevator, before my feet kick into gear and I follow, still in a daze.

Holy smokes. Well, Doc, you said I should do something unpredictable and spontaneous, right? Put myself out there?

I don't think this is what you had in mind, but... here we are.

Fingers crossed it doesn't blow up in my face.

Ryann

He's a fidgety little thing.

As the elevator slowly crawls up forty-one stories, the boy messes with his hoodie strings, sneaking glances at me from under long lashes. His purple hair keeps falling into his bright blue eyes, and he's standing way too close, practically pressed into my side. I shift away, needing some space.

He's cute, if I was into the whole shy guy thing—which I'm not. Especially not tonight. My patience is hanging by a thread, and I'm halfway drunk. All I want is to bury myself in a pretty twink, ride out this buzz, and pass the hell out.

Tossing him a sideways glance, I take in his smooth, porcelain skin and delicate features as he stares at his shoes. Definitely pretty, like a little doll with those soft pink lips. He seems younger than what I usually go for, but he has to be over twenty-one if he's driving for Uber. Old enough to drink, at least. And judging from the feel of his rock-hard dick under those sweats, he's definitely down for some action.

Perfect for a night of fucking away my frustrations. The bar had been a bust—no one caught my eye—so this couldn't have come at a more opportune time.

The elevator dings as we reach the penthouse, and the doors slide open to reveal the opulent entryway spilling into the dining room. Tossing my keys onto the console table, I glance over my shoulder to see him blinking up at the crystal chandelier like a deer in headlights. Still too close.

"Wow, this is your place? Are you rich or somethin'?"

I scoff. *Somethin'* is right.

"Wait," he continues, squinting up at me with one eye in a way that might be adorable if I could actually feel anything. "You're not like... a drug dealer, are you?"

"Do you want a drink?" Ignoring his question, I head for the bar in the corner of the living room, leaving him to scurry after me.

"Y-yeah. Sure."

He sounds overly nervous, like he's trying too hard, and I roll my eyes as I pour a finger of bourbon. When I was younger, that coy innocence might've been intriguing, but at thirty-seven, it just pisses me off.

We're both adults here. We know what we want.

The way he eye-fucked me when I got into the car earlier tells me he *definitely* knows what he wants, so he can drop the act. I'm not in the mood.

"What do you want? Scotch, bourbon, vodka?"

"Uh, yeah, sounds good," he answers distractedly, clearly not listening.

With a frown, I glance over to find him standing near a display case by the balcony, his attention fixed on the medals and trophies from my college basketball days at UDub. All that wasted success, before my father hit me with cold, hard reality.

Coming up behind him, I take a slow sip of my drink. "You follow college ball at all?"

He jumps, startled, as those blue eyes meet mine briefly. "My dad does. Do you play?"

"I used to."

Humming softly, he studies me sidelong like he's waiting for more, but I didn't bring him up here for story-time. He's here to fuck. Nothing else.

And I'm getting impatient.

"Come here, doll face." Draining the rest of my drink, I set the tumbler down before wrapping an arm around his waist, pulling him flush against my chest.

He squeaks, his palms landing on my pecs as his wide eyes dart up to mine. We stay like that for a moment, his quick breaths brushing my skin, before I weave my fingers into his hair and crush my mouth to his.

The boy goes rigid, stiff as a board, and I lick at those pretty lips until they part for me. The second our tongues touch, he melts, his body softening as his hands slide up to cup the back of my neck. That hard cock grinds against mine when he rolls his hips, and I groan as I reach down to squeeze his perky ass cheeks.

Kissing isn't something I normally do when hooking up, but damn, he tastes so sweet.

"How do you want it?" I murmur, backing us up toward my leather sectional. "Rough? Soft? I can go either way."

Rough is preferable, but I'm not a complete jackass. I always consider what my sexual partner wants, even if it's just for one night. Usually, there's a conversation beforehand to set expectations, but I've no patience tonight. The Uber driver will have to do.

A small voice in the back of my mind tells me I should at least ask his name, but I shove it aside. I really don't give a fuck.

"Uh." He breaks the kiss, pupils blown wide in desire as he ducks his head. "What—whatever's clever."

... *Whatever's clever?*

What the fuck?

Immediately, alarms blast in my head, telling me to slow down, halt, *cease and desist.* Bad idea. But then he sinks his teeth into his swollen lip as he peeks up at me from under silky waves, and I completely forget all thoughts other than getting this sexy piece of ass onto his hands and knees.

Fuck, I thought I was over the whole innocent role-play, but apparently not. It works for him. He's probably trapped plenty of victims with that look alone.

Keeping my gaze locked on his, I remove my suit jacket before slowly unbuttoning my shirt. "Take off your clothes."

He watches, enraptured, as I toe off my shoes and reach for my belt, his eyes widening at the apparent bulge in my crotch. A pretty blush spreads across his skin, turning it a deep red. His gaze snags briefly on the burn scar covering the side of my left thigh, and he inhales sharply, like he's about to comment. They always do.

But the second I slide my slacks down, leaving myself in nothing but a pair of Calvin Klein's, his focus shifts. The scar is forgotten, replaced by nervous energy as he pulls off his hoodie. He hesitates, bunching the hem of his t-shirt in his fists, his gaze darting around the room.

"Can I keep my shirt on?" he asks, his voice so small and uncertain that I once again pump the brakes.

That feeling in my gut intensifies, screaming at me to stop because something about this isn't right. I open my mouth to tell him that we shouldn't do this, but then the little vixen drops his sweats to the floor, no underwear, and I'm rendered speechless when his hard length springs free.

"Damn, doll." Little guy has a gorgeous cock.

Reaching for him, I slide off my underwear and wrap a hand around our shafts. The most musical sound leaves his throat, a breathy whimper that I swallow with a kiss, stroking us together while he thrusts into my palm.

His mouth is sloppy against mine, too much tongue, teeth clacking together. It's clear he needs some practice, but the eager way he's fucking my fist and digging his nails into my shoulders more than makes up for the lack of experience.

I'm about to push him down onto the couch when a sticky warmth floods my hand. Our lips part with a *smack* as I look down to see his cock erupting like a geyser, shooting onto his shirt while he moans. His eyes roll back, and I continue to jerk him through the orgasm until he sags in my arms once I've milked him dry.

It's a fucking beautiful sight, watching him fall apart, and my mind conjures up other ways of making him come before I shove those thoughts behind a steel door. This is only happening once, and only for tonight. As soon as I get off, he's gone.

Huffing a small laugh, I give in for just a second, resting my cheek on his hair. "That was, uh...fast."

"That's *so* embarrassing," he groans, still panting as he buries his face in my chest. The sudden urge to wrap myself around him is overwhelming, to hold him close, but I quickly take a step back instead.

I don't cuddle. Ever.

"It's fine." Spinning him around, I nudge the backs of his knees until he crawls onto the couch. "Bend over."

With a hand between his shoulder blades, I gently push him down, trailing my palm down the knobs of his spine until I get to his crease. As he white knuckles the cushions, I spread his bouncy cheeks, getting a delicious view of his little pink hole puckered just for me.

"Fuck, you're perfect," I murmur, rubbing a cum-covered finger around the rim.

"Whoa, that...what are you doing?" He chokes, thrusting slightly, and I snort at the cutesy act he's still playing—like he didn't know exactly what would happen when he followed me up here tonight.

"Just relax for me." Using his release as lube, I press a finger past that tight ring of muscle, groaning at the velvet heat that envelops me, my cock heavy and aching for a turn. His head drops forward, hair damp at the base of his neck from sweat, and I lean forward to lick the salt from his skin.

He shivers, crying out, his dick leaving a sticky trail of arousal on the leather of my couch as I palm his throat and fuck my finger into his ass.

"God, you're tight." Too tight. Like it's been a while since he's taken cock. Gritting my teeth, I suck on his earlobe, irritated at the extra time I'll have to spend stretching him. "You're going to need to loosen up if you want me inside you, doll face."

Another soft whimper spills from his lips as I spit down his crease before leaning over to dig inside the end table for a condom and lube. Most guys I take home are prepped and ready to go, all that's left to do is slide right in and come. I know it's not his fault—he was working and probably had no intention of getting fucked tonight. But still.

After the shit-show that was work, followed by a bullshit family dinner, I just want to take my pleasure and then go to sleep.

Using the lube, I insert a second finger, scissoring him open before searching for his prostate. When I nudge it, he yelps again, back muscles tightening as he falls forward, mumbling under his breath.

"Frickin'...gawd, what the hell..."

"That's it, baby," I chuckle as he rocks back on my fingers, a third one joining them. "I can't wait to pound this ass."

With my teeth, I rip open the condom packet and roll it onto my thick length while I continue to stretch him. There's still some resistance, and he could probably use more prep time, but the night is growing late. I have an early morning meeting, so I line myself up with his hole and grab onto his hips.

"Breathe out," is all the warning I give before pushing forward, barely breaching him with my crown when he gasps and digs his nails into my thighs to get me to stop.

"Ow, Jesus, that *burns*," he whines through clenched teeth, tensing up, and I glare down at the sight of his hole stretched to max capacity around me. Fuck, I'm not going to fit. He's too tight, too small for my size.

If we had the time, he'd probably need a few days to be ready for me, but all we have is tonight.

"Turn around," I growl in frustration, backing up to pull off the condom. "Open your mouth."

He obeys, eyes wide and cheeks flushed as I quickly jerk off against his tongue.

When the orgasm hits me, it's shallow and empty. There's only a few piddly spurts of cum that land on his lips, which he wipes away without meeting my gaze.

"Well, that was extremely unsatisfying," I mutter, stepping away to pull on my underwear. "Thanks for nothing, I guess."

A slight, choked noise leaves his throat, face brighter than a tomato. Clearly embarrassed.

Tough shit. If he's wanting sweet words, he came to the wrong place.

Tossing him his clothes, I turn my back and head for my bathroom to get ready for bed.

"The elevator will take you back down," is all I say before I shut the door behind me, pissed off that I have no time to text any of my hookups if I want enough sleep for tomorrow.

My father's criticisms from dinner echo in my ears as I step into the shower, harsh and berating, drowning out any wave of pleasure I might have been riding. The weight of my life crashes down on me without the high of sex, pulling me down until my knees hit the floor, and I let the scalding water burn away his voice until it's nothing but an echo rattling around my skull.

Briefly, the Uber driver's face flashes before me—pretty skin and silky purple waves, a smile that would have lit me up if it could.

God, I wish I could feel something.

Shilo

"I look like a goob. A goofy one."

Glaring at my reflection in the bathroom mirror, I touch the gel-slicked hair on my head. It's awful. Horrendous. Same with the dress shirt and pants I borrowed from Dad. "I look like I wear a fedora and go around saying *'milady.'*"

My sister snorts, rolling her dark eyes as she turns me around to fasten my tie. "No, you don't. You look nice."

"*Nice?*" Flapping my arms like a bird, I show her how the sleeves hang loose. "Paige, look at this. I'm about to take flight right out the window. And my pants won't stay up."

"Shilo," she sighs in frustration, grabbing my shoulders when I start to chirp. "Will you stop? I know you're nervous, but this isn't a big deal."

See, that's where she's wrong. This is a big deal. As in *half-my-grade-for-the-semester* big deal. As in, *if I don't land this internship, I fail the course and have to start again next year* big deal.

Big frickin' deal.

She rolls up my sleeves, her brows pinching with concern as her fingers circle my thin wrists. "Mom offered to take you shopping, but you refused."

"Yeah, because it's embarrassing. Nothing ever fits right. Why couldn't we just order something off Amazon like normal people?"

"You know why." Blowing brunette waves out of her face, she frowns at the pant legs pooling around my feet. "And things would fit you if you actually ate something."

I scowl at the top of her head when she kneels to fold the hems of my pants. "I ate breakfast."

"And before that?"

Okay, she's got a point. Before that, nothing. Not since breakfast yesterday—or maybe the day before. Honestly, eating takes a lot of brain power, and mine all goes to programming.

Once she's done, I step out of the bathroom into my bedroom, squinting in the black light as I dig through my dresser drawers. "Why can't this interview be online? Who even does in-person interviews anymore?"

"You can't live your whole life through a computer, Iggy." Paige flips on the light, startling my rat, who squeals in his cage by the closet. "CalTek does things differently."

"Yeah, well, you'd think they'd be all for it."

Seriously, CalTek is one of the most innovative software developers on the West Coast. They were on the list of companies my professor sent out in August, offering internship interviews, but... I dropped the ball. Kind of forgot about it, honestly. By the time I received a passive-aggressive reminder from my professor, interviews were closed.

Lucky for me, though, I've got a sister who happens to work at CalTek as Head of Security. And she's also dating one of the CEO's twins. Both of whom need an assistant.

Woo-frickin'-hoo.

Pulling out a pair of suspenders, I clip them onto my belt as Paige grimaces.

"Suspenders? Really? Are we seventy?"

"You're just jealous that you can't pull them off," I grin, flopping onto my bed to slip on my Chucks.

I need the suspenders to keep the pants up—my belt's too big now. But if I tell Mom or Dad I need a new one, they'll worry, and it'll turn into a whole thing. Yada yada. No thanks.

My sister rolls her eyes, glancing at her phone. "Are you almost ready?"

No. This is sucky, and I don't wanna go.

Giving her a noncommittal shrug, I move over to Master Splinter, my rat, to give him a treat. Then, I make my bed—*slowly*.

Next, I grab the watering can from my desk and tend to all my plants (there's a lot) before deciding now's a perfect time to check on my custom World of Warcraft server. Paige watches me the entire time, arms crossed, her heeled boot tapping against the floor. She has way more patience than I give her credit for.

It's not until I start fiddling with my 3D printer that she snaps, marching over to gently but firmly grab my shoulders.

"Iggy," she starts, using my childhood nickname. "Come on, what's the deal? This is a great opportunity to get your foot in with an amazing company. Even Doctor Iskar thinks so. Don't you want to work with me?"

"Of course I do." Guilt washes over me as I avoid her gaze. "I just... don't see why I can't do this from home. I really, *really* wanna stay home, Paige."

She studies me for a long moment, her fingers flexing on my arms. "I wish you'd talk to me. You were doing so well in August. Ubering, shopping with Dad, going on walks with Mom. But then everything just..." She trails off, and I shrink into myself, wishing I could curl up like an armadillo and roll away. "Two months, Igs. You haven't left the house in two months. Is it because of what happened with that guy?"

A pair of hazel eyes flash in my mind, the same ones that have haunted my dreams for weeks. I can still hear his deep voice, whispering sweet words before cruelly kicking me out. Just thinking about what we did—and where his fingers were—has me flinching with embarrassment.

Of course I told Paige the bare minimum. Besides the faceless strangers I game with online, she's my only friend.

Licking my lips nervously, I pull away and head into the bathroom. "It just... set me back a little. But it's fine, I promise. I'm fine."

Zig Ziglar once wrote, *'Repetition is the mother of learning, the father of action, which makes it the architect of accomplishment.'* The more I tell myself I'm fine, the more I'll believe it.

Paige watches me, unconvinced, as I dip my head into the sink, washing the sticky gel out of my fading purple strands.

I really hope that if I keep saying it out loud, eventually, everyone else will believe it, too.

CalTek sits smack in the middle of downtown Seattle's business district, with a breathtaking view of Elliott Bay. The building itself is made of silver glass and sleek metal arches, twisted in an artsy-fartsy way that probably cost millions. At the very top, there's a tower where the CEO supposedly reigns supreme while the rest of the peasants toil away in cubicles and labs below.

Paige leads me through the massive sliding glass doors, and the lobby opens into a sprawling atrium. A towering white oak tree stretches toward a glass ceiling, surrounded by lush greenery lining the curved walkways. I pause near a fern, brushing its delicate leaves, and Paige nudges my shoulder with a grin.

"They're all real," she says, gesturing to the glass ceiling above us. "The architects used smart glass that adjusts the light. It's tintable and controlled by an app."

I nod, falling into step behind her. "I read about that. CalTek developed the software, right?"

"Yep. It's our bread and butter."

She greets the security team at the front desk, introducing me briefly while I study the plants with my hands shoved into my pockets. The lobby buzzes with energy, the sound of voices and footsteps blending into a dull static in my ears. I feel bad for the plants stuck in this fishbowl of a building. You'd think it'd be hard to grow with hundreds of eyes watching you every day, but they're probably made of sturdier stuff than I am.

"Ronin Callahan must be, like, a gazillionaire," I mutter once we're alone again, referencing the company's CEO.

Paige huffs a dry laugh, grabbing a radio before leading me into a glass elevator in the middle of the lobby. "He's no Bezos or Gates, but he's definitely up there."

"And does his majesty ever come down from the ivory tower?"

She shoots me an unimpressed look. "Sparingly. I've seen him maybe ten times in five years. He handles the big-picture stuff and leaves day-to-day decisions to Declan and Ry."

"Right, the two princes looking for a lackey. Which is why I'm here."

"Shilo, enough."

As the glass elevator rises, I wish it would take us right through the roof, like in *Charlie and the Chocolate Factory*.

Just yeet me the frick outta here.

"You'll like Declan, he's super chill," Paige assures me, smoothing a wrinkle on my shirt. "Ry is... a little abrasive at first, but he grows on you."

I scoff, pointing at her. "That's just a nice way of saying he's a massive dick, but you get used to it."

She laughs as the elevator dings, opening up to a fancy lounge with bright furniture. "I'm still not used to hearing you swear. It sounds weird. Like a toddler cursing."

"You should hear what people say when I game online. It'd make your hair curl."

"No thanks, I get enough of that working with IT guys all day."

She leads me to a set of double doors labeled *Conference Room Alpha* before pausing to fuss over my appearance.

"You should've left the gel in. You need a haircut, Igs." She pushes a loose strand of hair back from my face and grins when I bat her hand away. "How about we put in some fresh dye this weekend?"

"Fine. And you'll repaint my nails?"

Paige grabs my hands, frowning at the chipped purple polish. "Only if you stop biting them. You're ruining my handiwork, jerk face."

"No promises."

With an eye roll, she releases me and slaps my shoulders before stepping back. "Alright, don't be nervous. I already told them we were coming, so they're expecting you. I'll wait out here, and afterward, we'll grab food at the café. Sound good?"

No. Hell no. But I nod because I really need this grade, and at least the internship is paid. Maybe they'll let me work from home. Emails, spreadsheets—I can handle that. I can *so* handle that.

"Good luck," my sister winks, swiping her security badge to unlock the doors before gently pushing me inside.

The first thing I notice is the floor-to-ceiling windows, offering a panoramic view of the coast and the Space Needle in the distance. Grey October skies stretch endlessly. A massive wooden table dominates the room, flanked by black office chairs, a gigantic TV screen built into one wall, and—more plants. I focus on the ferns, studying their leaves to avoid looking at the two men sitting at the head of the table.

Apparently, I take too long because one of them clears his throat.

"Shilo Reed?"

That deep, familiar voice hits me like a freight train, and I go rigid.

I know that voice.

It's the same one I hear at night, whispering things like *doll face* and *baby, that was unsatisfying, thanks for nothing.*

A voice I've jerked off to more times than I care to admit over the last two months, the weight of shame crashing down on me every morning after.

Like a magnetic pull, my eyes lift and lock onto his golden-green irises, burning into me like two hot coals.

Ryann stares at me, expressionless.

Next to him, his brother Declan smiles warmly, tilting his head in mild confusion. "Please, take a seat. We're excited to meet you."

But I can't. I can't be here. I can't speak. I can't do this.

As nausea churns in my stomach, bile rising from the pancakes Mom insisted I eat this morning, I do the only thing that makes sense.

I turn and run.

Ryann

"Our interview is here."

Declan's grating voice snaps me out of my concentration, grinding on my already frayed nerves. I shoot him a glare over the dual monitors I've been glued to for hours. Christ, I've got a headache.

"So go do it. I'm busy."

More than busy. Absolutely *swamped*, drowning in spreadsheets and endless conference calls. We soft-launched our secret project today, and there are way too many bugs for my liking. Add to that the fact that I'm hungover as hell, and it's a recipe for disaster.

"Nuh-uh, nope." Dec drops into the chair across from me, the 3D model of Seattle I've been working on hovering behind him like a holographic shadow. "You've been sitting there so long you're growing roots. Plus, we both promised Paige we'd meet her brother, remember?"

How could I forget? They roped me into this last week during lunch, when my dear fraternal twin's girlfriend used those big brown eyes to guilt us into hiring her little brother.

"He really needs this," she'd said. *"Not just for college. He's always been unique, super shy. He was severely bullied in high school."*

And somehow, the fact that he's newly out of the closet got brought up, Paige no doubt mentioning it as a way to sway me.

"His first time with a guy didn't go well... it ruined all the progress he made in therapy. Maybe having a gay influence would help?"

She said that to *me*, like I'm some shining beacon of queer mentorship. I'd scoffed at the thought. Me? Maybe as a cautionary tale of what *not* to do. Definitely not a positive influence.

"Paige is on her way up with him," Declan continues, smirking at the murderous expression I'm sure is on my face. "If you don't leave this office right now, I'll have IT lock you out of your computer."

He would, too. It wouldn't be the first time. Bastard.

Growling in frustration, I save my work and push out of my chair, trailing after him toward the conference room.

"Is an interview even necessary if we're just going to hire him anyway?"

Dec sighs, running a hand through his tawny curls. "Formalities. It looks good on paper in case Dad audits me, you know?"

Grinding my teeth, I glance down at the resume waiting on the table between us, shoving away my guilt.

Shilo Reed, age twenty-one.

Junior at UDub, Computer Engineering program. Perfect GPA. No work experience, but volunteered at the local humane society as a teen, with references to back it up. Honestly, his resume is almost identical to Paige's when we hired her five years ago.

The conference room doors open, and a flash of purple hair catches my eye. As I lift my head, all the blood drains from my face.

And rushes to my fucking dick.

Because the Uber driver from months ago—the one who's been haunting my subconscious—has just walked into my conference room like a waking nightmare.

He hasn't even looked at us yet, his light blue eyes fixed on the potted plants lining the shelf as his fists work nervously in his pockets.

Fists that had gripped my couch when I'd fingered his tight ass.

Faded purple strands fall over his brow, wavy locks that I know feel like silk—because my hands were tangled in them just weeks ago. His teeth sink into that bottom lip I kissed, and I have to shift in my seat, struggling to keep the raging hard-on in my pants under control.

Jesus Christ.

The whole experience had been disappointing, a sexual encounter that I should have forgotten by now, and yet nearly every night when I dream, it's about a pretty boy with cracked porcelain skin.

A broken, blue-eyed doll.

Declan kicks my leg under the table, throwing me a perplexed look as the silence stretches on. I quickly clear my throat.

"Shilo Reed?"

He freezes, his face going impossibly pale. Those wide, terrified eyes meet mine, and Paige's words from last week hit me like a gut punch:

"*He's always been unique, super shy.*"

Declan glances between us, confusion etched across his face. "Please, take a seat. We're excited to meet you."

Shilo's complexion turns sallow—almost green—and before either of us can say another word, he fucking *bolts*. Spins on his heel and slams through the doors like he's on fire, leaving behind a flurry of shouts from Paige.

"What the fuck just happened?" Declan mutters.

For a beat, we just stare at each other, stunned, before scrambling out of our seats to chase after him into the lounge. At first, he's nowhere in sight, but Paige's frantic voice directs us around the corner to the bathrooms, where she's pleading softly through the door.

"Shilo, please, come out. It's okay. Nobody's upset with you."

She turns when she sees us, her tear-filled eyes swimming with guilt. "I'm so sorry. He has horrible social anxiety. I thought if I stayed, he'd be fine."

"Hey, shh, it's okay." Declan leans down, pressing a comforting kiss to her nose and gently wiping away her tears. "Is he alright?"

"I don't know, I think he's in there throwing up. I just... I don't know what to do anymore. Everything's been a mess for him since August."

Her words snap my spine straight, a cold wave of dread curling in my stomach.

"What happened in August?" I ask, my frown deepening.

She sniffles, glaring at her feet. "That whole thing I told you about during lunch, remember? His first time with a guy. His first time *ever*, really. I think it messed him up."

The ground shifts beneath me, my head swimming.

No, it couldn't be... could it?

"What happened?" My voice is tight, and Declan throws me a sideways glance as Paige shakes her head.

"I don't know exactly. He wouldn't tell me all the details, just that the guy was an asshole. Treated him like shit afterward. Someone he picked up while driving for Uber."

The breath leaves my lungs as hazy memories from that night filter through my head.

Shilo's nervous tics. Fidgeting with his clothes, avoiding my gaze. His embarrassment when he came too quickly, the way he'd wanted to keep his shirt on. That sweet, nervous flush on his cheeks.

And my fucking irritation at not being able to fit inside him. Jesus Christ.

I thought it had all been an act. I thought he'd been just another hookup.

I was so very, *very* wrong.

It was me.

I'm the one who broke the doll.

"I'll go in and talk to him," Declan says, reaching for the door handle, but my hand stops him quickly.

"No. I'll do it."

Two sets of eyes snap toward me, and I vaguely register the differences between Shilo's appearance and his sister's as she blinks in surprise.

"No offense, Ry," Paige begins, curling her lips, "but... you?"

She's got a point. I'm the last person Shilo should be around. All I ever do is drag people down into my darkness, and he's already had a taste of that. But I need answers. Closure, or whatever the hell you want to call it.

Lifting a brow, I look between my brother and his girlfriend. "Isn't this what you wanted from me? A '*gay influence*,' you said?"

Declan makes a small noise, throwing me a knowing look, but Paige's expression softens. "Yeah, you're right. Okay. We'll stay out here."

Fighting back a heavy sigh, I give her a tight smile before pushing open the bathroom door. My ears are immediately assaulted by the sound of someone puking their guts out.

Guilt and shame swell in my chest as I lean against the row of black marble sinks, waiting for him to finish. It takes a while—his breathing ragged as he coughs and gags—but finally, the choking noises subside, leaving an uncomfortable silence.

"Shilo," I say quietly.

There's a whimper, followed by the scrape of a lock sliding back. The stall door creaks open a sliver, just enough for him to peek out. The moment he spots me, he slams it shut again.

How very fitting.

Trying again, this time more forcefully, I speak his name louder. "Shilo."

He squeaks in response, then cracks the door open, a strained smile plastered on his face.

"Oh, Mr. Callahan, I didn't see you there." His voice is rough, no doubt from all the puking. Avoiding eye contact, he steps up to the sink to wash his hands.

"Mr. Callahan is my father," I grit out, watching him closely. "You can call me Ryann."

Something in my tone makes him freeze. His shoulders stiffen under that oversized shirt he's wearing, looking thinner than he did two months ago.

"Why didn't you tell me?" My words come out harsher than I intend, but I don't care. I feel duped.

"Hm?" He shuts off the water, carefully drying his fingers, giving me a glimpse of chipped, purple nails. "Tell you what?"

What is it with people who like purple making it their entire personality?

"Why didn't you tell me that you're a virgin."

Well, close to it. Not that we did a whole lot, but...we did enough.

Shilo freezes again, his eyes widening, then narrowing as he pats his pockets like he's forgotten something. "I, uh, think I hear my phone."

With a frown, I take in the bright red flush on his neck. "I don't hear anything."

"Nope, that's definitely a phone call. I need to take it." He pulls his phone out before pressing it to his ear. "Hello? Oh, yes, I can talk right now. Sorry, Mr. Callahan, but this call is very important. I have to go!"

"Shilo, you didn't even unlock your screen," I call after him, scrubbing a hand over my stubbled cheek with a sigh as the bathroom door swings shut behind him.

Well, that definitely could've gone better.

Taking a moment to collect myself, I step out to find Declan and Paige by the elevator. Their attention shifts to me.

"What happened?" Paige asks, her voice tinged with worry.

"He ran out to take a call," I lie, and her brows shoot up.

"It could be Dad checking on the interview. I'll go find him."

She takes a step forward, but pauses, tossing Declan a worried glance over her shoulder.

"Don't look at me like that," he laughs, giving her an utterly unprofessional swat on the ass. "We're still going to hire your brother. Don't worry."

We're *what?!*

Her shoulders relax, a warm smile lighting up her face as she steps into the elevator. The second the doors close, Declan turns on me.

"What did you do?" he demands, pinning me against the wall by my shoulders, and I bare my teeth at him.

"*Me*?"

"Yeah, Ry. You. What did you do to that boy?"

"What makes you think I did anything?"

He scoffs, smacking the side of my head. "Because I know you, asshole. We shared a womb."

"Yes, and I wish I'd eaten you." Pushing him off me, I let out a breath as I pinch the bridge of my nose. "I didn't know who he was, alright? I thought...he seemed like he just wanted to fuck."

"*You fucked him?!*" His voice jumps five whole octaves. "Oh, my god. Paige is going to kill me. First, she's going to kill *you*, and then she's going to kill me because I'll have to avenge your death."

Dec starts to pace, pulling at his curls, and I roll my eyes before grabbing his wrist. "Calm down. We didn't fuck." Well... "Not really."

"Not really?" He blinks, eyes bouncing between mine. "What does that mean, not really? Either you fucked him, or you didn't."

"We..." I wince, dropping my gaze when the memories hit me all over again. "I tried to, but...well, he's small, and I'm a fairly large guy..."

He nearly chokes, looking completely petrified as he grips my shirt. "Did you *force* yourself on him? Is that why he's all fucked up?"

"*What!?*" It's my turn to shout, shoving him so hard that he nearly flips over a nearby chair. "Stop acting the maggot! Do you really think I'm capable of such a thing, Dec? Christ."

Declan holds up his hands, his suit now disheveled from our scuffle. "Alright, yeah, I'm sorry. That was too far. But seriously, Ryann, what *did* you do? Because Paige made it sound horrible."

Because it *was* horrible, wasn't it? I used Shilo for my own pleasure and then tossed him out like nothing. I took what should've been a sweet experience and turned it ugly. Twisted.

I broke something precious that wasn't mine to break.

"Whatever it was," my brother starts, studying me as I fight my own thoughts, "whatever happened, you need to fix it. Because Shilo's starting with us on Monday."

My head snaps up quickly. "What the fuck? Are you serious? You really think that's a good idea?"

"We promised Paige we'd help him, didn't we?"

"Aye, but—"

"No buts," he cuts me off with a pointed look. "We promised her, Ry. And Callahan men keep their promises."

"Don't quote Dad at me, asshole."

Heaving a sigh, I glare at the ceiling, knowing this can only end in disaster. I may be a lot of things, but I've always prided myself on not sleeping with employees—with one very regrettable exception downstairs. Unlike my father and brother, who have no qualms dipping their toes into the proverbial pond.

Not only will I be Shilo's boss, but we'll be working together, practically on top of each other—and not in the fun way. I'll have to interact with him constantly, twenty-five hours a week, five hours a day. Someone I've shared an orgasm with. Someone I'm pretty sure I traumatized.

How the fuck are we supposed to work together?

Declan slaps my shoulder, a smirk tugging at the corners of his lips before he heads back to his office. "Monday morning, brother. Be prepared."

Shilo's blue eyes flash in my mind—the way they dimmed when I left him half-naked on my couch, and the shame that's always simmering beneath my skin rises, tightening its grip.

There's no way this won't end with one of us in pieces.

Shilo

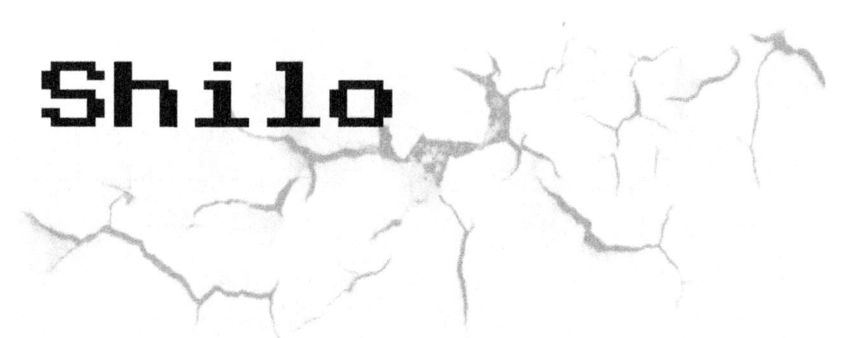

I hate this. Hate everything about this stupid assignment, this class, and the passive-aggressive professor who can go kick frickin' rocks.

But here I am.

At CalTek, bright and early at the butt-crack of dawn on a Monday morning, waiting at the security desk for my clearance badge.

The toast Mom practically shoved down my throat before I left sits like a rock in my stomach. Or maybe it's the thought of work today. Probably both.

After running out on Friday, Paige caught up with me in the lobby to give me the bad news—I got hired—before dragging me into the HR office for onboarding. She was completely oblivious to the fact that the guy from August is her boss. Well, now *my* boss. And don't even get me started on yesterday's shopping spree, where Dad bought me dress clothes, made me promise to pay him back, and then told me how proud he was. That was probably the hardest part of all.

Besides Paige doing my hair, I haven't had a moment to breathe. Relax. Hang out with my rat and play WoW.

"Here's everything you need," the security guard says, handing me a badge and a binder. "Company directory, building map, daily schedule, and employee handbook. Executive offices are on the thirteenth floor. Good luck."

Mumbling a thanks, I flip through the binder as I walk, studying the map. Some areas are marked as *restricted* in red, others as *limited access* in yellow. Apparently, my badge won't get me into places I'm not supposed to go. For now.

Snickering at the thought, I glance at my badge photo and my smile fades into a grimace. I look shell-shocked, worse than my driver's license. Like a crackhead who just spotted the cops.

Reaching the elevator, I'm about to step in when I hear my sister's voice.

"Shilo! Hang on a sec!"

She's out of breath, sweaty strands falling into her face as she hurries over. I can't help but laugh at how haggard she looks.

"Rough morning?"

"You've no idea," she groans, tightening the messy bun on her head. "I've got three high school tours on the roster today, a career seminar, and emails coming out of my ass."

"That sounds painful. You should see a doctor."

"Hardy-har, smarty pants." She ruffles my hair and fixes my shirt collar. "Ry texted me. He wants you to bring coffee and doughnuts to Conference Room Delta for their morning startup."

My shoulders slump, sweat forming on the back of my neck at the thought of dealing with the baristas in the Café. "He can't get it himself?"

Paige gives me a funny look, pulling me aside as a group of employees step out of the elevator. "Probably not, considering he's in the middle of a meeting. That's kinda why he hired a personal assistant."

"To fetch his coffee?"

I shouldn't even be surprised. It sounds exactly like something an entitled rich asshole would do. And honestly, I wouldn't mind so much if it were Declan asking, but *Ryann*?

The last thing I want to do is cater to the guy who jizzed on my face and then kicked me out like...like some kind of prostitute or something.

Now that I think about it, though, the five-hundred dollar tip he gave me seems highly suspicious.

Oh, my god, does he think I'm a prostitute?!

"Igs, it's not that big of a deal," Paige huffs, steering me toward the Café. "Just drinks and snacks. You've ordered food before. I'd go with you, but I need to get back to my desk. I'll text you the drink orders, okay? Just swipe your badge to pay."

I can't even respond, still reeling from the embarrassment as I shuffle up to the counter in a daze.

"I like your pin," says the barista, a younger guy with long blond hair tied back and a dimpled chin.

I glance down at the Horde logo from World of Warcraft on my shirt and blink at him, mumbling off the orders Paige sent me. When I get to Ryann's, I scoff because, of course, a soulless jerk like him would drink his coffee black.

An idea has me grinning stupidly as I finish ordering, and once everything is ready, I make a mental note to bring my backpack tomorrow. Balancing eight cups of coffee on top of a doughnut box is a bit of a struggle. Somehow, by the grace of the gods, I manage to get it all up the elevator without spilling a drop.

But then I just stand there, bouncing my gaze between the door handle of Conference Room Delta and my full arms, wishing I had telekinesis like Jean Grey from X-Men because how am I supposed to open it?!

After a few seconds of deliberation, I set everything on the floor to open the door. When I do, eight pairs of eyes swing my way, including two familiar hazel ones. My cheeks burn as I pick up the coffees and set them on the table, keeping my gaze down.

"Everyone," Declan clears his throat from where he stands next to the wall-length TV, "this is Shilo Reed, our new intern PA. He'll be helping us out a few hours a week while he's in school. Shilo, these are all of our department heads."

There's a chorus of hellos, and I nod awkwardly, hands shoved in my pockets. I'd hand out the coffees, but I don't know anyone yet, so Ryann stands up from the head of the table to do it for me.

I try not to look at him. I really do. But when he steps close enough for me to smell his cologne, I can't help but notice how nicely his dark grey suit clings to his tapered waist. Or how the material of his slacks stretches over those thick thighs that I grabbed onto when we—

Oh hell no, we are not doing this here.

"Shilo's actually a student at UDub in their Computer Engineering program," Ryann says to a woman with frizzy hair as he hands her a cup. "Maybe he'll be one of yours soon."

The woman raises her brows, smiling at me. "Oh, is that right? And how do you like it so far?"

It takes me a moment to form a response under all the attention. I shrug, fighting the urge to bite my freshly painted thumbnail. "It's... fun."

"Fun?" Her smile falters, and I immediately regret speaking.

"Programming is fun." And safe. Computers never judge me for being weird or for how I look. Numbers and codes make sense. Unlike people, who confuse the ever-loving shit out of me.

Thankfully, Declan calls the meeting back to order, and Ryann tells me to take a seat, tossing a notepad and pen onto the table. I have no idea what I'm supposed to write, so I just jot down everything. Daily metrics, production goals—stuff I really don't care about, but it keeps me focused. Apparently, they're having issues with a new product launch. That's how I learn the frizzy-haired woman is Liza, a Project Manager over the software developers.

Out of my peripheral, I catch Ryann grimacing at his coffee, and it takes everything in me not to laugh.

Hope you like ungodly amounts of sugar, asshole.

His hazel eyes flick up to mine, and I quickly drop my gaze to the doodle I'm drawing in the margins of my notes.

The meeting drags on for an hour, and when it finally ends, I gather up the empty cups to toss. Everyone filters out, including Declan, leaving me alone with Ryann, who pushes the nearly empty doughnut box across the table.

"Eat," he demands, pointing to the last one.

I scowl down at the glazed doughnut. "That's yours."

Gabbing it, he huffs and shoves it into my hands. "I don't do sweets. Eat the doughnut, Shilo."

"I'm not a prostitute," I blurt out, wincing at my own stupidity. Ducking my head, I stuff as much of the doughnut into my mouth as I can.

Ryann goes still, his broad shoulders tightening. We stand there in silence as I chew slowly, the weight of his stare pressing down on me. He waits until I swallow before speaking.

"Shilo. Look at me."

Um, no.

As I move to eat the rest of the doughnut, his hand shoots out, pinching my chin and roughly tilting my face up to his.

"Where did that come from?" He asks, his eyes searching mine so intensely that I feel like ants are crawling on my skin.

"Y-you gave me five hundred dollars," I stammer, heat rising under his touch. "And then we... and you... not that there's anything wrong with sex work, but I'm not... I want to pay it back."

I don't know how, but I will. I'll work for free if I have to—because no way am I selling the new disk drive I just bought.

Ryann stares at me for a long moment, jaw clenched. His dark hair catches the morning light from the window, looking soft, almost like raven feathers. I kind of want to touch it.

He seems to choose his next words carefully. "That money was just a tip for driving me home, Shilo. I don't pay for sex."

A small noise escapes my throat at his words, the reminder of what we did. His gaze darkens as it drops to my mouth.

"You've got frosting here," he says thickly, swiping his thumb across my bottom lip. "Open."

My jaw drops, and an electric jolt shoots straight to my groin when he presses the pad of his thumb against my tongue, the sticky-sweet flavor exploding on my taste buds. Instinctively, I close my lips around him and suck, drawing a deep, rumbling groan from his chest that shouldn't sound that sexy.

But as quickly as it happens, it's over. His thumb slides out of my mouth, and he steps back, leaving me feeling oddly empty. And embarrassingly hard.

Jesus, why does this always happen around him?!

He grabs my notebook and binder, gesturing toward the door. "I'll show you to your work area."

All calm and collected, cool as a frickin' cucumber, while I subtly try to adjust myself the moment he turns his back.

What the hell just happened?

He holds the door open, waiting somewhat impatiently, cocking a brow when I just stand there, gaping.

Okay, then.

I try to keep some distance between us as I follow him down a hallway lined with glass windows showcasing the Seattle skyline. We pass multiple offices—some empty, some not—before he leads me to a small alcove with a counter-height desk in front of a bay window.

So many windows. So much glass.

"This is where you'll sit most of the day," he says, rounding the desk to show me how to log on. "After our morning meetings, you'll enter the notes into this diary. The same process goes for any other meetings Declan and I have during your hours."

I mutter a vague acknowledgment as he spends the next twenty minutes showing me how to work the systems. I'll be managing their schedules, answering phones and emails, gathering office supplies—basically a glorified secretary and gofer.

Yippy.

"My office is here," he points to the left, "and Declan's is to the right. If you need anything urgently, use the work chat. Any questions?"

Clipped, precise, to the point. No-nonsense. Not even a hint of a smile.

I shake my head, climbing onto the chair, my legs dangling awkwardly. Ryann sweeps his gaze over me briefly before turning toward his office.

"Oh, and Shilo?" He glances back with a glare. "Tomorrow morning, I expect my coffee order to be correct."

With that, he shuts the door behind him, and I don't see him for the rest of my shift.

Finally, five long, boring days are over, and my first week is done. It wasn't so bad, honestly—except for the phone calls. I hate talking on the phone, it's weird not being able to see facial expressions. Makes me nervous.

Declan had a bunch of conference calls I had to notate. I guess he handles the financial side while his brother does...e verything else. They're so different for being twins, like night and day. They don't even look alike.

Where Ryann is all hard edges and scowls, Declan's soft-er—sunnier, with jokes and dimples. He had me run down to the Café for him multiple times this week, which I didn't mind because he's just so nice. He even offered to buy me lunch. Paige has only been dating him for a few months, but I get what she sees in him. I think he'll be a good boss.

It's his brother I'm going to have issues with.

Since Monday, I've done my best to avoid being alone with Ryann for more than a few seconds, running out of his office as soon as he finishes whatever task he gives me. Take notes, make copies, order office supplies, pick up his frickin' dry cleaning—yeah, I'm still annoyed about that. The most excit-ing part was getting more filament for the 3D printer in his office, and I had to physically restrain myself from talking his ear off about it since I've got a small one at home.

"What are your plans for today?"

A voice startles me, and I turn from the maidenhair fern I've been studying in the lobby to see the Café barista grinning at me—the guy with long hair. It's loose now, tumbling around his shoulders like sunshine. He's been trying to talk to me all week, but I never know what to say, so I usually just shrug and escape.

But now he's in my space, watching me like he's expecting something. It takes me far too long to realize he's waiting for a response.

My plans. He's asking about my plans.

"Uh, homework," I answer slowly, taking in his paint-splattered leggings and tight shirt.

His smile widens, bright eyes twinkling as he holds out his hand. "Hey, me too. Maybe we can do it together. I'm KC. Just the letters, like Kansas City."

"That's a weird name." The words slip out before I can stop them, and I brace myself for the inevitable offense as I shake his hand.

Only, it doesn't come. He just laughs.

"I blame my parents. They weren't very original. My brother's name is DJ."

I squint at him, suspicious. "Really?"

"Swear to God. And my little sister? Guess her name. Go on, guess."

All I can do is shake my head, unsure what to make of him.

He grins, flashing white teeth. "Aribellianna."

I just stare at him for a second, completely at a loss for words, before a snort of laughter escapes me—a real one that makes my stomach clench and my face scrunch. "That... is terrible."

"I know." He flops down next to me on the bench, our knees bumping, and I can't help but marvel at him.

"Why so many letters for her, and so few for you?"

"At least mine's easy to remember." He nods toward the badge hanging from my lanyard. "But so is Shilo. I like it. It's pretty."

That comment catches me off guard. I tilt my head, feeling my cheeks heat as I look back at the fern. No one's ever called my name *pretty* before.

KC continues, "So, what do you say? Wanna do our homework together?"

I glance up at him from behind my purple hair, frowning. "Like... at the same time? With each other?"

Like hanging out?

He laughs, reaching out to touch the pin on my shirt. "You're too cute. Yes, with each other. And then maybe we can play some WoW or something."

That's... well, I haven't done that in a long time. Hung out, I mean. With anyone other than my parents or Paige. I had a few friends back in elementary school, but then we moved constantly for Dad's job until junior high, and... well, friends got hard to make after that.

I gaze at him as he fiddles with my pin, my thumbnail finding its way between my teeth. Doctor Iskar would want me to say yes.

But I did that last time, and what did it get me?

Covered in cum and a sore ass, that's what.

Okay, but why does that not sound as bad as it should?

Sounds downright amazing, if you ask me—

Shut up, brain, no one asked you.

Gah, why is this so hard? I've never been this unsure about computers. They don't have ulterior motives—they don't have any motives, really, other than what I tell them to do.

I open my mouth, ready to say no thanks, when a deep voice straightens my spine.

"Shilo."

Ryann stands a few paces away, arms folded, wearing that ever-present stony expression. It pisses me off.

"What?" The word comes out harsher than I intended, and his perfect brows jump while KC twiddles his fingers beside me.

"Hi, Ry," KC says sweetly, almost flirtatiously. Ryann spares him a brief nod before those golden-green eyes lock back onto me.

"What are you still doing here?"

"Waiting for Paige to go on lunch," I snap, and I don't miss the way his lips tighten—like he doesn't appreciate my tone.

Well, too bad. I'm off the clock, Boss, and you don't need to know my business.

He nods, a crack forming in his composure as he runs a hand through his styled hair. "How did your first week go?"

KC bounces his gaze between us, some funny expression on his face, while I shrug and study my shoes.

"Fine."

A beat passes. "Good. That's good."

And then he's walking away, the soft thud of his dress shoes fading. I don't look up until he's gone.

KC whistles low, his eyes on Ryann's back as he disappears into an office. "Well, that was interesting."

"What was?"

His glittering eyes swing toward me. "I'm sensing some tension between you two."

I blink, suddenly sweaty, wiping my palms on my pants. "No, no tension. Just, uh..." *Quick, make something up*. "I've gotten his coffee wrong all week. I think he's mad about it."

Okay, not quite a lie. He *is* pissed about that.

KC seems to accept it, nodding sympathetically. "Ah, yeah, that'll do it. Ry's a total coffee whore."

His words make me choke on my spit, and I slap my chest, coughing as I stare at him, red-faced. "Why do you call him Ry?"

He shrugs, glancing furtively to the side. "He asked me to."

Well, that's... huh.

My fists clench when I think about how he told me to call him *Ryann*.

Asshole. And here I was, planning on getting his coffee order right on Monday.

"Igs!" Paige calls from her office, waving me over, and I turn back to KC, giving him an apologetic grimace.

"I'm kinda busy today, but, uh... rain check?"

I'm not. Not really. I just want to get my schoolwork done, work on my PC, and crash.

"Sure," KC waves, flashing me a dazzling smile. "See you Monday, Shilo."

Paige's eyes widen as I step into her office. "Were you talking to the Café guy?"

"His name is Kansas City."

She snorts, wrinkling her nose. "Well, I'm glad you made a friend."

I glance back, about to agree, but KC's no longer on the bench. He's over by the elevator, stepping inside while Ryann guides him in with a hand on his lower back.

Something ugly burns in my stomach at the sight.

It sizzles, churning as I catch the look they share before the doors close, and I can't eat the food Paige offers me. It'll probably come back up anyway.

I don't know if KC's my friend or not, but something tells me he's more than that to Ryann.

And I don't like it.

Shilo

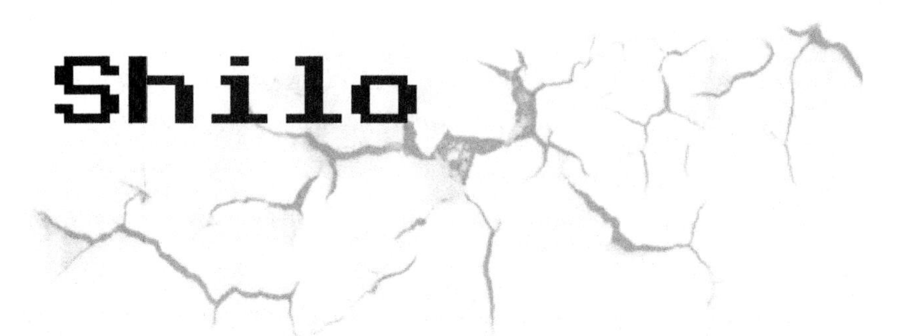

Another week nearly passes, and by Thursday, I'm irritated. Peeved. Whatever the word is for *more* than annoyed but not quite pissed.

I've been getting Ryann's coffee right every day, and he hasn't said a damn thing. No "Thank you, Shilo," or "You're doing great." Nothing. Just a stiff nod as he goes about business like he hasn't seen my butthole—which I try *really* hard not to think about during work hours.

His lack of emotion bothers me.

So this morning, I ordered him an extra-sweet espresso with pumpkin spice, because I know how much he loves sweet things. Which is not at all.

KC laughed when I ordered it. He's been pestering me to hang out in person, and I'm running out of excuses. We've been gaming together online, but since Friday, I can't shake the weird resentment that flares up every time I see him. The way he acted with Ryann has been on my mind all week.

There's no startup meeting today since everyone's losing their heads over that secret project, so I drop Ryann's coffee off at his desk and turn to leave. He's so engrossed in work that he doesn't even acknowledge me, not that I was expecting him to.

It's not until an hour later that I hear him gag loudly, and a grin spreads across my face.

"Goddammit, Shilo."

He storms out of his office, hazel eyes blazing as he slams the cup down in front of me. "This is *not* what I ordered, and you know it."

"My bad, Boss." I duck my head to hide my smirk, taking a sip of the coffee. It's gross—I hate pumpkin—but I keep my eyes on the screen. "We'll try again tomorrow."

"No, you'll try again *now*."

I glance up at him briefly, noticing the dark circles under his eyes. He looks like he hasn't slept. Maybe I'm playing with fire, but after a week of being ignored, I feel bold. Pulling up an email, I start typing away. "I'm very busy."

"You're—" He cuts himself off, pinching the bridge of his nose as he exhales slowly. "I'm not in the mood for this. It's the easiest coffee order on the planet. Medium grind, black, no sugar. Do I need to write it down for you?"

"No. What you *need* to do is say please."

A muscle jumps in his jaw as he stares at me, emotions flickering across his face before he spins around and disappears into his office without another word.

I slump back in my seat, honestly disappointed. I don't know what I was expecting, but I thought I'd get *something* out of him. Guess I'll have to try harder.

The phone rings, and I spend the next few hours busy with work, adding things to Ryann's schedule that are meant for Declan, canceling his car dealership appointment, and forwarding him spam emails. I get so into sabotaging his day that I don't notice someone sneaking up on me until it's too late.

"What are you doing?" KC's voice makes me jump, and I yelp, fumbling with my keyboard.

"N-nothing!" I try to hide my screen for some reason, which only makes me look guilty, and KC cackles.

"Watching porn on company time, huh? Nice." He grins, waggling his brows.

"I am *not*."

"Sure." He turns toward Ryann's office, holding up a cup of coffee. "Just bringing Ry his order since *someone* messed it up this morning."

Wait... what?

I frown, something pinching in my chest as KC shuts the office door behind him, giving them privacy.

A few more emails trickle in, but I can't focus. My eyes keep drifting to the office door, and the longer they're in there, the hotter my gut burns. After twenty minutes, I push away from my desk, the frustration bubbling over.

Swiping my badge, I shove open the door, expecting to find them in a compromising position. Instead, Ryann looks aggravated at his computer while KC lounges in a chair, scrolling TikTok. They glance up at me, eyebrows raised, and I freeze.

"Did you need something?" Ryann asks, clearly annoyed, so I do the only thing I can think of.

I point at KC. "Him. I need to talk to *him*."

Without waiting for a response, I march over and drag KC out of the office while Ryann mutters something like *thank fuck* under his breath.

"What's up, cutie?" KC reaches up to pinch my cheek, but I swat his hand away.

"Don't ever do that again." Licking my lips nervously, I stare down at my shoes, hating the words about to come out of my mouth. "Do you, uh... wanna hang out today? With me?"

A delighted smile splits his face as he bounces on his feet, instantly making me regret all my life choices. "Hell yes! Your place or mine?"

"Yours," I respond quickly. "Definitely yours."

No way am I letting Dad meet him. I don't need the bigoted lecture, thanks.

"Cool. Let's exchange numbers so I can text you the deets."

Reluctantly, I hand him my phone, already cringing. But it's too late now, and I've somehow agreed to dinner at his place. Mom's gonna be thrilled. So will Doctor Iskar, I guess.

Look at that, Doc. I made a friend. *Sort of. Reluctantly. Against my will.*

God, this blows.

"See you after work, bestie." KC throws me a wink before skipping off, leaving me grimacing as I slump back into my chair. I momentarily forget about sabotaging Ryann—at least until I hear him shout my name, and I make a beeline for the bathroom to hide for the next half-hour.

After that, I wander around the building, exploring places my badge will let me access. This place is huge—a whole fourth floor dedicated to a gym, a rec room with video games, and an outdoor garden. But the Research and Development department? Not on the map. Bummer.

It isn't until a text comes through that I realize my shift is over.

YourNewBFF:

Hey, it's KC :) meet me in the lobby and I'll drive you to my apartment.

Scowling, I change his contact name to Kansas before shoving my phone into my pocket. Maybe I can sneak out the back. Make up an excuse—family emergency, or something.

As I tip-toe back to my desk to grab my bag, I glance into Ryann's office and find it empty, a breath of relief leaving my lungs.

I'm almost home-free... until the elevator doors open downstairs, revealing my boss standing there with an outraged expression.

"I've been looking for you for an hour," he snaps, glaring as he steps back to let me out.

"Uh... couldn't find the paper clips," I mumble, trying to dart around him. His arm shoots out, enveloping me in the warm leather scent of his cologne as he leans down.

"My patience only extends so far, Shilo. Disappear like that again, and there will be consequences."

A shiver runs down my spine at the low rumble of his voice, my blood thrumming as I peek up at him. "Like what?"

Ryann's eyes flash, nostrils flaring as he searches my face. His breath flutters the purple strands of my hair when he leans in, sending goosebumps over my skin, his lips brushing my ear when he parts them to speak—

My name being called has him straightening quickly.

"Shilo, you ready?" KC appears next to us, his eyes twinkling as he looks from me to Ryann. "Oops, am I interrupting?"

"Nope, let's go." Grabbing KC's wrist, I practically run for the front doors, calling over my shoulder. "Have a good night, Mr. Callahan!"

It isn't until we reach the parking lot that I let go of his wrist and breathe, immediately freezing from the October wind cutting through my sweater. What the hell was that?! Not the reaction from him I'd wanted, that's for sure. I meant to make him mad, not...not whatever *that* was.

"My car's this way." KC jerks a thumb over his shoulder, gesturing toward an old pink Volkswagen beetle. "Passenger seat's a little messy though, so you might have to move some stuff."

Dammit. I should've made up an excuse.

The 'stuff' is mostly paint supplies—canvas, brushes, a foldable easel. Apparently, KC's an art major at UDub, in his senior year. The Café is his second job. His first? Yoga instructor at CalTek's gym, where he met Ryann. Great. He's got two roommates, and they all rotate making dinner. I guess tonight is his night.

"I make the best risotto, swear to god. It'll taste like an orgasm in your mouth."

I choke on the water bottle I'm sipping as he leads me up the steps of a small brick apartment building fifteen minutes away from work, nearly tripping on the rain-slicked surface. A flush heats my cheeks as he chuckles, stopping before a rusted metal door that reads '#9'. The hinges groan when he shoves it open by a shoulder, echoing loudly, and I rub my chilled hands together as I step inside reluctantly, considering texting Paige to get me out of this.

The space is small—barely enough room for a saggy-looking sofa and coffee table. Shelves of succulents line brick walls, a skylight reflecting off industrial cabinets in the kitchen. A grated spiral staircase leads to the loft, where someone about my age with jaw-length dark hair leans over the railing, blinking at us groggily.

"Mornin', gorgeous," KC chirps, using his shoulder to shove the door closed. "Shilo, this is Tina, one of my roommates. Pronouns are they and them."

"Another boyfriend of yours?" Tina asks, yawning as their lip piercings glint in the light.

KC rolls his eyes. "He's a boy, and he's a friend, but he's not mine. No offense." He shoots me an apologetic grin. "I'm not into twinks."

I blink, unsure how to respond as Tina laughs and retreats back into the loft.

"But *you* are a twink."

"Yes, thank you, and I don't want to fuck one. I like my men with more meat on their bones." He saunters into the kitchen after throwing his bag onto the couch, and I can't stop the words from flying out of my mouth.

"Men like Ryann?"

Shit. Why, brain? Why?

KC pauses mid-motion, pulling out a pot, his back to me. His response is slow. "Muscle men, I suppose. Working in a fitness center has done wonders for my sex life. You'd be surprised how many closeted gym bros there are."

A snort comes from upstairs, but I stay silent, shuffling awkwardly as I scan the room.

He glances over his shoulder at me, rifling through the fridge. "Anyway, feel free to make yourself at home. Bathroom's down the hall, my room's next to it. Our other roommate, Carpenter, crashes on the couch but won't be back til later."

Without much else to say, I just nod, following his directions to his room, where a computer setup similar to mine rests on his desk. Clothes cover the pink platform bed, and there's a large window with a view of the fire escape. The walls are covered in paintings, and I laugh when I spot lewd drawings of various male superheroes, some fully naked.

What would Dad say if I had stuff like this hanging in my room? Probably nothing good.

While KC and Tina banter back and forth, I pull my laptop out of my backpack and settle into the desk chair, content just to listen while I catch up on some assignments I've been avoiding. Every once in a while, he'll shout a question at me, keeping me included while giving me space, and even though I don't know if it's intentional, I appreciate it all the same.

When dinner's finally ready, I leave his room and perch on the arm of the sofa with my plate while KC sits cross-legged on the counter, Tina swinging their legs from the loft.

"So, what's your story?" Tina asks between mouthfuls. "What made you want to work at CalTek?"

I shrug, taking small bites of food even though I'm not hungry—despite how good it tastes. "Needed an internship for a class, and my sister runs security there. Seemed like a good idea."

It's not entirely untrue, but it's not the whole truth either. I hated the idea when Paige suggested it. We fought about it, but of course, Mom and Dad took her side. Like always.

Tina sighs. "Ah, siblings. Wish I had some."

"You can have mine," KC pipes up, wrinkling his nose. "Well, not my sister. Take my brother. He's a homophobic asshole."

"Hmm, no thanks. I'll pass."

I glance up at him, curious but cautious. "He doesn't accept you?"

KC rolls his eyes. "DJ likes to pretend he does, but the little comments slip out. It used to hurt when I first came out in high school, but now I'm over it."

"My dad is kind of the same way. He doesn't know about me. That I'm gay, or anything. He's an Air Force guy, so...yeah."

Tina groans, throwing their head back while KC points at me with his fork. "See? I *knew* you were gay. My gaydar is never wrong. Tina, you owe me twenty bucks, bitch."

"My sister knows, though," I continue, smiling despite myself. "And my mom. They're cool with it."

"Same. My dad's not around anymore, but he would've loved me no matter what."

"You both are lucky," Tina sighs again, setting their plate aside. "I'm from small-town Missouri. My family is religious. They all but disowned me when I brought home my girlfriend for Christmas last year."

I frown, glancing up at them. "That's... messed up. I don't know if my dad would go that far."

"Now we just need Carpenter to bat for the other team, and we'd have a whole club going." KC stands on the counter, reaching up for Tina's empty plate as his roommate laughs.

"If your booty shorts haven't enticed him yet, I don't think it'll happen. That boy is straighter than an arrow."

"I am nothing but persistent."

They chatter away, making jokes, while I try to eat the rest of my food. And I really do try, forcing down a few more bites, until KC asks me a question that has my stomach souring.

"So, you got a boyfriend, Shilo?"

Nausea floods my system. I shake my head as I stand, handing him my plate. "No."

"Whoa, what was *that* reaction about?" His eyes widen, blond strands brushing his face as he tilts his head. "Is it my cooking?"

"No, your cooking is amazing." I wince because I'm terrible at talking to people. "I've only had one experience with a guy, and... it wasn't good."

Well, it was. Until it wasn't.

Tina grips the railing, eyes blazing. "What happened? Did someone hurt you? Was it at one of the clubs here in Seattle? We're not afraid to hunt down a motherfucker if we have to."

Jesus. "No, it was some guy I picked up for Uber. He didn't hurt me, not exactly. He just kind of made me feel used. Worthless."

Well, that was unsatisfying. Thanks for nothing.

KC's expression shifts, a flicker of something I can't place, before he grabs my shoulders firmly. "Fuck that guy. We're taking you out and finding you someone better to erase that memory."

"Here, here!" Tina cheers, raising a sippy cup, which makes me blink in confusion before refocusing on KC's determined smirk.

"Wait, huh? Take me out?"

"Yep. Halloween's this weekend, and we're going dancing. We'll be your wingpartners."

My heart jumps into my throat, and I step back, shoulders hunched. "That sounds awful and I'd rather die."

Frickin' hell. Why didn't I just say I have other plans?

"Oh, stop. You'll love it," KC laughs. "There's a costume party, and I've got the sexiest outfit planned."

"I highly doubt I'll love it," I grumble, tugging at my hair with clammy fingers. "Pretty sure it'll suck because me and crowds don't mix. Learned that lesson the hard way when I showed up to my high school graduation and Bobby Crawford pantsed me in front of everyone to prove I wasn't a guy, which I am. And everyone saw it because I don't wear underwear. *I don't wear underwear, Kansas.*"

There's a beat of silence where I can feel both of their eyes on me, and I duck my head, biting my lip to stop the word vomit that wants to spill out. They don't need to know how I ran off the stage with my pants around my ankles and tripped down the stairs onto my bare ass. Or how everyone laughed. Even my dad.

KC exhales slowly. "Well, we won't let that happen again, will we, Tina?"

"Hell no. Promise. And since it's a costume party, you can wear a mask if it makes you feel safer."

That...actually does make it seem better. Anonymity and all that. If something goes wrong, nobody will even know it's me. I even have the perfect cosplay to wear.

Even though my instincts are screaming at me to refuse, make up a lie, or run for cover, I find myself speaking before I can stop.

"Fine. When and where?"

Ryann

The goddamn boy is trying to kill me.

Shifting in my seat, I try to stay present as one of our analysts discusses quarterly budgets, but one—it's fucking boring.

Two—this meeting isn't supposed to be for me, but a certain PA put it on my schedule.

And three—said PA is *killing me.*

Three weeks. Three fucking weeks now, and Shilo's been a thorn in my side. If he's not purposefully messing shit up just to fuck with me, he's keeping me distracted by putting things in between those soft lips. Pens, paperclips, his thumbnail. He seems to need his mouth filled constantly for someone who doesn't eat much, and it's driving me insane.

"Shilo!" I bark, realizing that I'm thankfully on mute. "Cut it out, or I'll give you something else to suck on."

Shilo jumps in the chair across from my desk, blue eyes widening as he gapes at me. "W-what?"

His bottom lip is shiny from spit, and I can't stop thinking about what it would feel like to wipe it off with my cock. Jesus Christ, I'm hard.

"Take the thumb out of your mouth."

He squints incredulously but obeys, a flush turning his cheeks pink as he drops his gaze and focuses on his notes, hiding behind purple waves. That bothers me just as much as the thumb chewing, only in a different way.

"What are your thoughts on that, Ryann?" The analyst asks, and I focus back on my screen with a frown. Fuck if I heard anything he just said.

Unmuting myself, I clear my throat. "I'll have my PA make a note for Declan, and he'll send a follow-up email when we've discussed everything."

Did that sound professional? God, I hope so because Shilo now has a pen in his mouth, and I'm about ready to lose my mind. It's been so long since I've fucked, my balls are aching.

The analyst, whose name I cannot be assed to remember, nods before moving on to his next topic. "Now, about last quarter's profit margins. I think we have some areas for improvement."

Kill me now.

As he launches into numbers, I try with all my strength to pay attention, but once again, my gaze slides over to Shilo and that damn pen. The way his lips mold around it like two soft pillows, warm and inviting, with just the right amount of suction—

Fuck.

"Shilo, come here," I command, rolling my chair back as I spread my legs.

His head snaps up, eyes flashing as the pen leaves his mouth. "Why?"

Suspicion layers his tone, and I give him a stern look. "Because I said so."

Scoffing, the brat scoots his chair farther away from my desk before crossing his arms. "That's not a good enough reason."

We stare each other down for a long moment, listening to the conference call. Thankfully, this analyst is a yapper. When Shilo doesn't move an inch, I point at the space between my knees. "I want you to sit right here, silently, while you take notes. Is that reason enough for you?"

The delicate column of his throat flexes with a swallow, and he tilts his head, interest sparking in those baby blues. Sliding cautiously off his chair, the flush spreads to his neck when he crawls over to me, avoiding the camera. He stops too far away, however, so I crook my finger for him to move closer. After a brief moment of hesitation, he finally settles in between my legs.

"Now, was that so hard?" Flicking my gaze up to the screen, I focus on the boy kneeling at my feet. The sight of him looking up at me curiously has my length twitching, and it damn near waves when he drops his gaze down to it.

Fuck, has he ever sucked cock before?

No. No, I will not think about an employee in that manner.

Even one who's partially had my dick in his ass.

Christ.

"Do you want to tell me why you keep chewing on things?" I ask, keeping my eyes on the analyst and nodding like I know what the hell he's talking about.

Shilo shrugs, shoulders warming the sides of my thighs. "Helps me concentrate, I guess."

"Hmm." Drumming my fingers on the desk, I consider the appropriateness of my next move for all of five seconds before deciding to hell with it. He's already on his knees for me. "Open your mouth, doll."

His pupils blow wide, jaw dropping in confusion, and I cup his cheek before sliding my thumb onto his tongue. "There. Now we both can concentrate."

Not fucking likely.

Automatically, his lips close around me, just like they did that first morning in the conference room. He sucks gently, testing out the feeling, and I bite back a groan at how velvety soft his mouth is. So fucking perfect.

We sit like that for a while, Shilo suckling my thumb and taking notes as I answer more questions. It's hard to think, slightly stuttering over myself, my cock so hard that I palm it over my pants for some relief.

A whimper draws my attention. Glancing down, I find the little doll eyeing my bulge hungrily, his hips moving as he rubs himself. I click my tongue, kicking away his hand to press my foot into his crotch.

"Now, now, none of that."

"P-please," he whispers around my thumb, humping the sole of my shoe, "I really...please, Mr. Callahan."

A flair of annoyance has me lifting my foot away and removing myself from his mouth. "What did I tell you?"

Shilo huffs angrily, honestly adorable as he chases my thumb with his tongue like he can't bear to part with it. "*Ryann*. Okay?"

"Mm, better." Placing my shoe back on his hard length, I withhold my thumb as I speak with the analyst for a few painful moments. He writhes against me the entire time, and when I put myself back on mute, I find his attention once again on my obvious erection.

"My thumb isn't quite doing the job, is it, baby?" I murmur, my hand moving toward my belt. "I think you need something a little more filling."

"Y-yeah," he nods eagerly, his hot tongue poking out, and I finally let out a groan when I undo my buckle.

This is wrong. This is so fucking wrong.

God, I'm going to hell.

His eyes widen to saucers when I pull out my cock, already sticky from edging myself for the past half hour. Giving it a few lazy strokes before aiming it at his mouth, I gently hold him still when he dives for it.

"No sucking. No licking. Just let it rest on your tongue, understand?"

He nods, purple strands falling over his brow, and I slowly ease my cock between his lips. His lashes flutter, lids falling shut, the urge to thrust down his throat so strong that I grip the edge of my desk until the wood cracks.

"Take your notes," I grit out through clenched teeth, immediately regretting this idea but so far lost to the pleasure that I can't back out now. He feels absolutely divine.

A content sigh leaves his nostrils as he rests his cheek on my thigh, using the other one for his notebook while moving under my shoe. He does what he's told, warming my cock without sucking, only swallowing when the saliva gathers in his mouth. Every instinct screams at me to snap my hips forward and take what I want, but I force myself to remain still. This is for Shilo, not me. To help him concentrate.

What a bunch of bullshit.

"So, that about sums it up," the man on my screen smiles, utterly oblivious to the fact that I'm defiling one of my employees before his eyes. "Is there anything else we haven't covered, or do you have any questions?"

As soon as I open my mouth to answer, Shilo shudders against me, letting out a filthy whine as his cock pulses against my shoe. The fact that he's coming has me seconds away from spilling my own release, so I pull out of his mouth before I choke him with a throat full of cum.

"Uh." Clearing my throat, I gaze at the screen, gripping myself tightly to stave off the orgasm. "No, I think we're all set. I'll have my PA," *—who's currently falling asleep as we speak—* "upload those notes as soon as possible. Thank you."

Once the Zoom call ends, I slump back in my seat, chest heaving while I take a minute to collect myself.

Fuck, what the hell did I just do? Have I gone insane? Am I really that desperate to get my dick sucked that I resort to this?

Soft snoring reaches my ears, and I tuck myself away, jostling Shilo awake. He leans back on his knees, wiping drool from his lips as he blinks at me, and we both glance down at his crotch simultaneously—where a large wet spot has started to form.

He squeaks in embarrassment, slapping his hands over himself before jumping to his feet.

"I...I need to go home," he stammers, spinning to hightail it out of my office, and concern has me launching after him.

"Shilo, wait, it's alright—"

"See you tomorrow, Mr. Callahan!"

My office door slams shut behind him, leaving me in deafening silence. The reality of what just happened hits me like a fucking Mack truck, and I lean against my desk for support.

I just made an employee warm my cock while on a conference call. An employee sixteen years younger than me. *And the door was wide open.*

Scrubbing a shaking hand down my face, I slowly sit in my chair. One word from Shilo, and I'd be fired on the spot. Ronin would probably do it himself—the fact that I'm his son holds no consequence. That actually makes it worse.

Jesus Christ, what have I done?

Ryann

Wiping the sweat from my brow, I dribble the basketball, slipping past Declan to toss it from the free-throw line. It bounces off the backboard, and Declan snickers. I shoulder-check him hard as I jog past to grab the ball, irritation coiling tight in my chest, fueled by weeks of pent-up energy.

It's been three days since the cock-warming incident, and I've been on edge, waiting for HR or Paige to show up and march me out of the building. So far, things have been quiet.

Too quiet.

Miraculously, my schedule has been wide open, Shilo assigning every meeting to Declan. I should be happy about this—it's what I wanted, after all. Instead, I'm annoyed by it. My PA has been avoiding me at all costs, and it bothers me. Fucking hell.

Did he not like it? Did he feel pressured?

The way those blue eyes had widened as a blush darkened his pretty skin flashes across my mind. He's so damn responsive to me. Too perfect. Too tempting.

Maybe it's for the best that we avoid one another, but...I don't want to.

"What's got that irritated look on your face, man?" Declan laughs, grabbing the ball after I miss another shot. His wild curls drip with sweat as he leaps away. "You're playing like shit today."

Don't I fucking know it.

We've been going for hours now, aggressively pushing each other on the court after a grueling workout, and I'm still strung tighter than a bowstring. I need to *fuck.* Or drink. Either sounds great right now. Or both. Anything to get my mind off the dinner coming up in a couple of weeks, where our father will make his big *announcement.* The one Declan is entirely unaware of but will change the course of our relationship, for better or worse.

I'm betting on the latter.

"Okay, that's it," he breathes, dropping the ball to place his hands on his knees, panting heavily. "I'm done. You've worn me out, and I still have to get ready for my date tonight."

Right. It's Halloween.

I scoff, picking up the ball to take another shot, this one making it into the net. I'm not as well-trained as I was in college, but I keep myself sharp. The coach for the Adult Basketball League has been pestering me to join his team for years, but when would I have the time? Work consumes me. Maybe tonight would be the perfect opportunity to get laid—it's been a few weeks. "Where are you going?"

"Some club Paige is dragging me to. Not my original plan, but her brother's going too, and she wants to keep an eye on him."

That has me missing my next shot. "Shilo?"

"The one and only," he chuckles, pulling off his shirt to wipe at the sweat on his face. "And that barista from downstairs, KC. I guess he and Shilo have hit it off."

My grip tightens on the ball until my knuckles ache. I've noticed they've been getting chatty, but *hitting it off*? I didn't know they were that close. KC can get super handsy, and the thought of him touching Shilo just...well, it makes me want to break something.

The ball flies out of my hands as Declan smacks it away. "No."

"No, what?"

He gets in my face, finger jabbed into my chest. "You leave that boy alone, Ry. He needs friends his own age."

"Christ, you make it sound like we're old men," I growl, shoving him back. "He's a legal adult."

"I know that look on your face, and I'm telling you that *nothing* good can come from this," Dec warns, narrowing his eyes at me. "He's your subordinate."

"Pot, meet fucking kettle. How many of our employees have you slept with?"

He smacks his lips. "None since I started dating Paige, thank you very much."

"Between you and Dad, we might as well send out a monthly NDA with the company newsletter, I swear."

"Hey, the horndog bug bit us both, or did you forget that I know about your weekend sexcapades downtown?"

"Just tell me what club you're going to," I sigh in frustration, eyes aimed at the beamed ceiling.

Declan purses his lips stubbornly. "No."

Fine. I throw him a glare and pull out my phone, thumbing a text to KC.

Me:

What club are you and Shilo going to tonight?

His response is almost immediate.

KC:

Well, hello Ry. Long time no text. I've missed you.

Me:

The club, KC.

KC:

I love it when you're bossy. We're going to Kintsugi, they're having a costume party.

Kintsugi. Not my usual scene, but I've been there. They have a VIP section, themed drinks, and a decent-sized dance floor. Not that I usually go there for dancing—unless we're counting the horizontal kind.

Me:

What are you wearing?

KC:

Right now? Nothing. Wanna see? ;)

Heaving a sigh, I ignore him and shove my phone back into my shorts pocket. We were only together a handful of times, but even though I ended it months ago, KC's still pushing. I should've known better.

"What costumes are you wearing to Kintsugi?" I ask Declan, smirking when he stops mid-sentence, gaping at me.

"How did you—" He stops himself, waving it off with a huff. "Never mind. It's a *Marvel vs. DC* theme, so Paige is dressing as Catwoman, and I'm Batman."

"Very original." I frown, thinking about where the hell I'll get a costume on such short notice.

"Ry," Declan steps forward, placing a hand on my shoulder, his green eyes—so much like Mom's—searching mine. "Why do you even want to go? And be honest. I know when you're lying."

I stare at him, trying to come up with an answer. The truth is, I don't know. Shilo confuses me. That shy innocence he radiates like sunshine draws me in. I want it. And yeah, the idea of anyone else seeing that side of him—the side I saw in my condo—sets me off.

"Oh, shit," Declan whispers, pulling me out of my thoughts.

"What?"

He pulls his lips back, shaking his head incredulously. "You *like* the boy."

"So what if I do?" Shaking him off, I spin around and head toward the locker room. "Both you and Dad are dating employees. Why does everyone make a fuss when I decide to do it?"

"*Dating* being the keyword there, bro," he follows close on my heels. "You don't date. You mess around and use people, then throw them away when you're done. And this is my girlfriend's baby brother we're discussing here."

I rear back, turning to glare at him because *ouch.* After the history we've had, those words burrow deep.

He holds up his palms. "I'm not judging you. Just stating facts. Thirty-seven years I've known you, and you've never so much as had a single boyfriend. Only fuck buddies and one night stands."

"And that's not about to change," I find myself saying, entering the locker room to tug off my shirt. "I just...want to make it right, what happened between us. He thought I *paid* him for sex, Declan."

"Jesus Christ."

"I know." Grabbing my gym bag, I head toward the showers. "So, just let me try and fix this, alright? Fix it my way."

He quiets momentarily, both of us taking shower stalls next to each other as we scrub up.

"Okay. I understand, but Ry...just don't break it more than it's already been broken."

I have no response to that because I can't promise shit.

All I've ever done is take people apart, but who's to say this time won't be different?

Maybe the longer I lie to myself, the more I'll believe it.

Kintsugi is a nightclub in the industrial district, housed in a renovated warehouse across from a boatyard. Even with the relentless downpour, the line to get in stretches around the corner, the thumping bass echoing off the steel surroundings as searchlights sweep the stormy sky.

I tip the bouncer and slip inside, bypassing the line. Paige and Declan are already here, somewhere up on the mezzanine overlooking the dance floor, where—according to my brother—Shilo is currently planted dead center. I have no idea what costume he's wearing, and Declan hadn't known either. But I know KC's dressed as Harley Quinn, so I search for that first, even though it feels like half the crowd has chosen the same outfit.

Fuck.

I don't even know what I plan to do when I find them. I just want to get Shilo away from the grinding, groping sea of bodies moving around me. After several minutes of futile searching, I give up and head to the bar, ordering a whiskey neat. The burn is smooth, warming me as I sweep the room again, eyes scanning for a flash of purple hair.

The costumes are typical: Spidermans, Supermans, a few Poison Ivys, and Captain Americas scattered throughout the crowd. Strobe lights flash overhead, illuminating veins of gold snaking up the deep blue walls, glitter flecking the floor like shards of broken glass. Tassels hang from the ceiling, and the air is thick with smoke and the unmistakable scent of marijuana. Private rooms line the back, an area I've grown familiar with over the years.

The thought of Shilo inside one of those rooms with KC—or anyone—has me grinding my molars. It's irrational, I know. But I can't stop the simmering rage that flares every time I think about it. After searching for another twenty minutes, I give in and head toward the private rooms, forcing my way through the crowd.

Then I spot him. A shorter figure in a black and white checkered bodysuit, purple hair, masked in white. It's a character I've never seen before. KC dances next to him, dressed in tight shorts and a crop top that reads *Daddy's Little Monster.* He's shaking his ass while Shilo stands mostly still, bobbing his head, but he's clearly uncomfortable. Without thinking, I shove my way through the crowd, stopping right in front of him, his face still tilted toward the floor.

KC presses into my side, shouting over the music. "Well, don't you look sexy."

Shilo's head snaps up, and I'm momentarily stunned at the cracked doll mask covering his face, like he's reached right into my head and brought my nightmares to life.

"Who are you supposed to be?" I ask, my voice catching in my throat as my hands find his waist.

He tenses, standing on his tiptoes to answer. "Rag Doll. My favorite DC villain. Who're you?"

His words are slurred, muffled beneath the mask, and I pull back with a frown. "Are you drunk?"

"S'what if I am?"

KC sidles up behind Shilo, trapping him between us. "He only had two shots. Guy's a lightweight."

My jaw tightens as I lift the mask, revealing wide, unfocused blue eyes blinking up at me. "You didn't eat today, did you?"

He scoffs, dropping his gaze. "You're not the boss of me."

"I beg to differ." Grabbing his chin, I hold him in place, our noses nearly touching. "Who do you think signs your paychecks?"

"But I haven't even gotten paid yet," he mumbles, scrunching his face in confusion.

Exasperated, I roll my eyes and tug him toward the stairs. He latches onto KC, dragging him along, and the three of us push through writhing bodies up to the mezzanine, where it's mercifully less crowded.

"What's going on?" Paige and Dec suddenly appear, both looking a hot mess, hair mussed and lips red like they've been devouring each other.

"Your brother needs to eat if he's going to continue drinking," I bite out as I pass, making my way to the VIP booths, where I all but shove Shilo into a seat.

Everyone else piles in when I leave to order bottle service, and I have to force myself in between KC and Shilo upon returning. I can feel Paige's eyes narrow in my direction, but I ignore her, turning in my seat instead to face the boy next to me whose delicate features are twisted into a grimace.

"Why Rag Doll?" I ask, watching as he stares down at the mask on his lap.

"He's...misunderstood," Shilo answers with a small shrug. "Not the original, but his son. And non-binary. I don't know, I've just always liked the character."

I tilt my head, processing that information as the cocktail waitress appears, and I order myself another whiskey as well as some cheese fries for Shilo.

He blinks up at me, brows furrowing. "What about Kansas?"

"What?"

Pointing over my shoulder, he gestures to KC, who wiggles his fingers while my brother smirks from the other side of the booth.

"I'm pretty famished myself," Declan chuckles, looking ridiculous in a Batman suit next to Paige's dominatrix-worthy Catwoman costume. She's still eyeing me warily, so I order food and drinks for everyone just to get them off my back.

KC loops his arm with mine, grinning as he taps my thick-rimmed glasses. "So, who are you supposed to be, Ry?"

"Clark Kent. Can't you tell?"

In an instant, my vision blurs as my glasses are lifted off my face, and I turn to see Shilo slide them on.

"Are these real?" He snorts, squinting around the dark booth. "Wow, you're really blind, Mr. Callahan."

Declan chokes on his beer as Paige barks out a laugh, and I have to force myself to breathe.

"It's Ryann," I growl, plucking my glasses off his face, "and I'm well aware, thank you."

"You'd think someone as rich as you could afford lasik."

An edge to his tone has me lifting a brow, wishing he'd meet my eyes instead of focusing them on everything else.

"Oh, no," KC interjects, leaning over to address my broken doll. "If Ry ever got rid of the glasses, I'd riot. They make him look sexy."

Fuck off, KC.

Paige knocks her knuckles on the table, drawing our attention as she points between us. "So, are you two a thing?"

Shilo tenses as KC's lips roll inward, and I unloop my arm from his.

"No. KC's just a friend who has no semblance of personal space."

He smiles apologetically, twirling a strand of hair around his fingers while the cocktail waitress arrives with our orders. I turn back to Shilo, intending to ensure he eats, when he reaches across my lap and snags KC's drink like a brat.

Bringing the straw to his mouth, he sucks on it with a glance at me from under his lashes, an innocent gesture that shouldn't tempt me as much as it does. He drains the entire glass, licking his lips when he's done, and I take it from him before replacing it with the basket of fries.

"I'm not hungry—" he starts to complain, but I cut him off by shoving a fry between his teeth.

"I don't care."

Paige makes a noise as Shilo glares at me, chewing and swallowing with clear reluctance. I'm about to offer him another fry when he slaps my hand away and begins feeding himself, a flush creeping up his neck. I want to run my hand through his soft strands and praise him, but I hold back, not wanting to risk a kick in the balls from his older sister. Next time he refuses to eat, though, I'll make sure he does, Paige be damned.

I'm not oblivious. I've noticed how he avoids food, skipping breakfast at work and guzzling water like his life depends on it. I don't know if Paige has picked up on it, but I have—and I'm not letting it slide. He's my employee, my responsibility.

"So, I hear you're having troubles with AVA," Paige says, smiling innocently as she bites into a burger, and I shift my gaze over to my brother's very guilty-looking face.

"Now I wonder where you could have heard that."

Declan groans, throwing his head back. "Can we not mix business and pleasure, please?"

"What's AVA?" KC looks between us, and I glare at Dec as I steal one of Shilo's fries.

"Something our developers are working on that we're keeping under wraps for now."

"Ah, top secret. Gotcha."

Paige hums, giving her boyfriend a smirking sideways glance. "So the rumors that we're unveiling a new product at IntelliCon in January aren't true?"

"Fucking better be," Declan mutters into his food. "All the overtime hours we've spent getting this shit ready—"

"Declan!" I snap, warning him with my eyes to keep his fucking mouth shut. He simply grins around his beer.

"What's wrong with it?" Shilo's quiet voice draws my attention, and I turn to see him chewing on a nail, food more than half-eaten.

"Nothing you need to worry your pretty little head about," I tell him, pressing my whiskey glass to his mouth.

He stiffens as he takes a sip, eyes darting up to mine, the color leeching from his lips as he dips his head. Mumbling something about needing to use the restroom, he slips from the booth, and I watch him go with a frown.

Have I said something?

KC continues to press about AVA, momentarily distracting me as Declan and I argue back and forth over what we can and cannot disclose. Paige finds it highly amusing, bouncing her brown eyes between us while her and KC giggle like teenagers.

It takes me far too long to realize that Shilo isn't back yet. A heavy feeling settles in my gut as I make my way to the bathroom, chest tightening. As soon as I step inside, I'm hit with the smell of vomit, and boiling anger has me clenching my fists until my knuckles turn white.

There's only one stall, which is shut tight, plus three other urinals, and two of them are occupied. I go about my business, taking a piss and washing my hands while I wait for the other men to leave.

When the bathroom is finally empty, I pound on the stall door, Shilo's familiar yelp bouncing off the walls.

"H-hang on, I'm almost finished," he chokes, a sniffle from his nose making me bite the inside of my cheek.

He barely has the door cracked before I shove it open, crowding into the stall before slamming it shut and throwing the lock.

"What are you doing?!" He shouts angrily, falling onto the toilet as my body takes up most of the space, and I lean back against the door with my arms folded.

"I think the question is, what are *you* doing?" I glare at him, watching his frantic gaze bounce around the stall. "How long has this been going on?"

The bridge of his nose wrinkles, his hair a mess, far too cute for the discussion we're about to have. "What do you mean?"

A sharp breath leaves my nostrils as I count to ten slowly, reigning in my temper. This boy has been testing all my limits over the last three weeks, and I'm ten seconds from snapping. "The vomiting, Shilo. And the binge eating, followed by a lack of appetite. Don't think I haven't noticed your suspicious absence every time I've seen you take a bite of something."

"Y-you..." His face scrunches, small hands fisting at his sides as his face turns bright red. "You don't know what the hell you're talking about!"

"Don't lie to me. This is the second time I've caught you throwing up in a bathroom."

He scoffs, swallowing as he focuses his gaze somewhere to my left. "Maybe it's *you* who makes me puke, did you ever think of that?"

My mouth opens, but nothing comes out, somewhat stunned by the words he just said. An uncomfortable feeling claws its way up my throat, talons digging deep until they draw blood, and the stall suddenly feels too small for the air punching out of both our lungs.

A group of guys filter into the bathroom, loudly rambunctious as they use the urinals, and I keep my eyes on Shilo until they finish up. He still won't look directly at me, studying the paint chipping on his nails instead, and I'm reminded of the smile he gave me in the car that first night we'd met. There'd been an unguarded softness that's no longer present, and it kills me that I'm the reason for its absence.

"Doll, listen," I start once we're alone, and his eyes snap up to clash with mine.

"Don't call me that," he nearly snarls, catching me off guard once again with this new display of teeth. "I'm not...not a doll. And I'm not *pretty*. I'm not anything, so stop with the names and just call me Shilo. Or Reed, like everyone in school does."

That has me tilting my head, brows knitting together with a frown. "You don't like it when I call you doll?"

A beat passes before he answers.

"No." He suddenly deflates, wrapping his arms around himself as he whispers so low I barely hear. "I like it too much."

I push off the door in an instant, reaching down to cup his face between my palms. "Shilo, listen to me. What happened between us back in August was a mistake. It shouldn't have happened as it did, and I'm sorry if my actions made you feel anything less than the gorgeous boy you are."

There. I said it. It's done.

So why is the guilt still eating me alive?

And why does he still look so broken?

How do I fix this?

Shilo licks his lips, wrapping cold fingers around my wrists. "If you think I'm so gorgeous, then why did you kick me out like I was nothing?"

God, and that just...

Guts me.

Fucking spills my insides onto the floor as I let my hands drop away from him, not missing how he tries to cling onto my fingers, a small noise leaving his mouth.

This is why I don't do relationships. Why I don't get involved, and why I definitely don't mess around with baby gays. Feelings make shit complicated. With the type of life I lead—a demanding workload, and an even more demanding father—a complicated love life is the last thing I need.

"I'm not a good person, Shilo," I sigh, leaning back against the door once again. "I could tell you that I was having a rough night after receiving some bullshit news, that I was wasted, that I'd worked eighty hours in one week. All of it would be true, but it's not an excuse because the truth is, that's just who I am. You asked me that night if I found what I'd been looking for at the bar, and I'd told you no, remember?"

His brows furrow as he nods, fingers twitching where they rest in his lap.

"Sex is something I use as a...release. A way to unwind after a long week. I'd been looking for a hookup, and you happened to be in the right place at the wrong time."

It's harsh and cruel, but the truth usually is.

Shilo tilts his head, blue eyes searching my face. "Is that what you're doing with Kansas?"

"Who?"

"KC," he waves his hand impatiently, and I stiffen out of instinct.

"Did he tell you that?"

"No. Just guessed."

Forcing myself to relax, I choose the truth instead of a lie. "I was, but I ended it months ago."

"Why?"

Releasing a breath, I let my head fall back against the stall door. "Because I couldn't give him what he wanted." Honestly, I'd been a little sad to let him go. KC's quite bendy and actually entertaining once you get past that irritating personality, but he started asking for *more*. Wanting to stay the night, have sex in my bed instead of on the couch—which I never do—and touch in public. Intimacy. "Things that just aren't in my nature to provide."

Shilo seems to understand, nodding slowly as he lifts his thumb to his mouth, features far off and pensive.

"Do you..." He starts to speak but loses his nerve, dipping his head while muttering something under his breath. All I catch is the word '*frickin*'.

"Just spit it out, Shilo," I bark, no patience tonight, and he glares up at me from under his hair.

"Maybe we could...help each other," he says, once again shifting his gaze around the stall, and my brows slam down.

"Help each other, how?"

"Well, you need to get off, don't you?"

I don't answer, choosing instead to wait and see where the hell he's going with this because I've lost the plot.

He smacks his lips, flinging a hand at me. "You definitely do because you're grumpy."

"Maybe I'd be happier if my paid intern actually got my coffee right every morning."

"Irrelevant." Chewing his thumb, he bounces his head from side to side as he picks apart whatever he's trying to say in his brain. "I'm not...confident in myself or my body. The kids in school were jerks, and...well, anyway. Maybe you can help me see myself the way you do?"

Trying to follow along, I gaze at him for a few perplexed moments. "The way I see you? Pretty?"

He nods slowly, wringing his fingers together.

"And how would I do that?"

"By..." Shilo stalls again but shakes himself out of it and pushes forward. "By getting each other off...together?"

Now, *that* was the last thing I'd expected to come out of his mouth.

Consider me speechless because, for my life, I cannot think of a single answer to that proposition.

We stare at each other, music thumping from the club around us, and even though I can see his pulse running wild on the side of that slender neck, Shilo doesn't drop my gaze.

Just as I think of a response, the door to the bathroom opens, and Declan's voice calls for me.

"Hey, Ry? You in here?"

"Aye," I shout, my voice rough like gravel as I take in the boy in front of me, all soft skin and tender bones.

"Have you seen Shilo? We thought he had gone to the bathroom, but he wasn't in the other one. Paige is losing her marbles."

My jaw tenses as I swallow thickly. "He's right here."

And offering himself to me on a silver fucking platter.

A beat passes before Dec sighs heavily. "What the fuck am I supposed to tell his sister?"

"Tell her I got sick," Shilo squeaks, clearing his throat. "Ry. ..uh, Mr. Callahan was just helping me through it."

A scoff answers back. "Yeah, alright. Helping you with his dick, maybe."

"Get the fuck out, Declan," I growl, ten seconds away from leaving the stall to kick his ass.

Once the bathroom door snicks shut, I kneel down, gripping Shilo's thighs tightly in my hands.

"Do you understand what you're asking, Shilo? What you want from me?"

His throat flexes as he squirms under my touch. "Just sex. Right?"

"And *only* sex. No dates, no cuddling, no cutesy good morning and goodnight texts. Just one or two good fucks a week, and that's it. I don't think you can handle that."

He rears back, lips curling over his teeth when he shoves me away. "I can handle whatever the hell I say I can. I'm shy, but that doesn't mean I'm weak. You don't frickin' *know* me."

Well, shit. Consider me put in my fucking place.

My mouth twitches as I fight a smile, raising my palms in surrender. "You're right. I just want to make sure we're on the same page if we're going to do this."

Crossing his arms, Shilo squints, pursing those pretty pink lips. "Just don't treat me like a trash can afterwards, and we'll be fine."

With a wince, I lift to my feet, reaching down to offer him my hand. "I think I can agree to those terms."

As I pull him up, he stiffens, blue eyes flying wide. "W-wait, are we starting right now?"

I give him a blank look. "You just puked, and your sister is probably waiting right outside that door, so I'd say no."

"Ah." He bobs his head, stepping out to the sink. "Yeah, you're right. She's a real boner killer."

Yes, and probably *my* killer when she finds out what I plan on doing with her little brother.

"Tomorrow, come to my condo around eight. I'll text you the address and the gate code in case you forgot."

Everything about this is wrong. I'm his boss, sixteen years older, and my brother is dating his sister. He's young and inexperienced. There are so many red flags being raised, but fuck if I can bring myself to say no. Because I'm a selfish bastard, and the memory of Shilo's tight little hole stretching around my cock has been replaying in my head for weeks.

Fuck, what have I just gotten myself into?

Shilo

The last time I was in this elevator, I was so nervous I almost passed out.

Thinking back to that night in August, I recognize now how extremely reckless it was. God, he could have been a serial killer or something, but I followed a stranger up to his penthouse because I was horny?

In my defense, all my blood was busy fueling the wrong head. Much like it is now. As I watch the numbers tick up on the elevator to Ryann's condo, I palm my dick over my sweats.

I've been annoyingly hard since that day in his office when I humped his shoe—which I'm still embarrassed about, by the way. Never thought he'd *actually* agree to my offer of getting each other off. Together. Mutually. Yeah...I may or may not have jerked it last night and this morning to the idea.

As the elevator stops at the penthouse floor, doors opening with a resounding ding, I swallow my nerves and step into the foyer. Other than a text asking if we were still on for tonight, which Ryann sent a dry *yes* to, I haven't heard from him all day. It makes this even more daunting because I'm unsure what to expect. Will he...try to have sex with me again? Will it burn like last time? Do I want it to?

Bare feet pad over the tile to my left, and Ryann steps out of the living room dressed in nothing but joggers, inked torso on display.

"I wasn't sure you'd show," he says, dragging a hand through his dark hair as he leans a hip against the entryway, and I take a moment to admire his tan exposed skin. It's jarring to see him in something other than the suits I've gotten used to over the last few weeks.

"I almost didn't," I find myself saying, mouth dry at the sight of his tattooed abs, a thick line of hair leading from his belly button down to the hem of his pants. Last time, I hardly got a chance to study his body. Examine that burn scar on his leg.

"What changed your mind?"

Glancing up briefly, I twist my lips at the bulge currently tenting my crotch. "It's been hard for almost twenty-four hours, and I think I'm getting lightheaded."

Ryann snorts, pushing away from the wall as he strolls toward the kitchen with his hands in his pockets. "Come on, I'll make you something quick to eat."

"But I already ate." Following him with a frown, I stop short just before an island, taking in the white granite counters and dark wooden cabinets.

He pauses, turning to throw me a skeptical glance over his shoulder. "Recently?"

"Yes, Dad." I roll my eyes, feeling my cheeks heat when a rumbling hum hits my ears.

"I think you mean Daddy."

Inhaling sharply, I choke on my spit, coughing as I meet his amused gaze. "I am *not* calling you Daddy."

Nope, hell no.

"I guess 'sir' will have to do."

"How about I just call you Boss?"

He gives me a ghost of a smile, barely twitching his lips, as he leans against the counter and crooks a finger. "Come here."

God, that's sexy.

Heartbeat ramping up, I make my way over to him slowly, a surprised squeak leaving my throat when he grips my waist and spins, lifting me onto the counter before stepping in between my thighs.

He pushes my jacket off my shoulders as his thumb swipes my bottom lip, minty breath brushing my face when he tilts his head thoughtfully. "Was I your first kiss?"

"Not technically." I eye his abs, trailing my palms along the ridges, muscles flexing under my touch. "I kissed Samantha Rawley in the sixth grade, just a peck, and then I gagged after."

He lets loose a small laugh. "Is that when you realized you were gay?"

"Kinda. My obsession with Zuko from *Avatar: The Last Airbender* should have given it away, though."

"I have no clue what that is."

The tip of my finger slides over his nipple, causing him to inhale sharply. "Then you're missing out on probably one of the greatest shows ever."

"Shilo, look at me." He circles my throat, angling my face to softly press his lips to mine while his golden-green eyes keep me trapped. With his free arm, he pulls me closer, sealing our bodies as our tongues slide together, hot and slick.

My lids sink closed when he slips a hand under my shirt, lightly grazing his nails down my spine, the friction of my dick between us so good that I have to break away and pinch myself at the base over my sweats to keep from embarrassing myself *again*.

"We need to work on your stamina," Ryann chuckles when I groan, lifting me off the counter. My legs wrap around him automatically, arms locking behind his neck when he tries to set me down, and he gives me an exasperated look before walking us toward the living room. "Don't tell me you're a clinger, doll face."

That pet name lights me up, exactly like it did the first time he called me it.

"I don't know what I am. Never done this before, remember?"

He huffs, prying my arms off to toss my body onto the couch, where I bounce with an *oomph*. And then he's climbing on top, pinning me to the cushions with his thick thighs while he buries his face in my neck. "Other than the last time you were here."

"That doesn't count," I squirm, the feeling of his stubble tickling my skin. "You were drunk, and I was, uh...distracted."

"Distracted, hm?" He bites down on my throat, eliciting a squeak from me before leaning back. Dark strands of hair fall over his brow, a stark contrast to the carefully styled way he wears his hair at work. I think I like him better this way.

His hands find their way under the front of my t-shirt, causing me to tense, and he pauses as he studies my face intently. "Can I take this off?"

Dropping my gaze, I shake my head, not brave enough for him—or anyone—to see me like that yet. Or ever.

Ryann stays quiet for a long moment, so I explore his body with my hands to mask the anxiety knotting my stomach. He's so much bigger than me, shoulders wide and chest broad. We're both hard, his solid cock poking my stomach from underneath his pants, and I boldly squeeze my fingers around it.

"Fuck," he breathes, dropping his head as he thrusts slightly. "We shouldn't be doing this."

My eyes fly to his face, alarmed, and I try to sit up. "What, why? D-did I do something wrong?"

"Relax, I just said that we shouldn't." He puts a hand on my chest to push me back down. "Not that we won't. I'm an evil son of a bitch, and you're too tempting." Bending to steal another kiss, he sinks his teeth into my bottom lip. "God, I want to corrupt you. Take that innocent light in your eyes and turn it dark. I'm going to hell."

"I'm not that innocent," I argue against his mouth, growing irritated when he throws me a disbelieving glance. "I'm *not*. I...watch porn and stuff."

He lifts a brow, trailing his hands down my torso before hooking his fingers under the waistband of my sweats. "And stuff? What kind of stuff?"

"Um..." My brain short circuits when he slowly pulls down my pants, releasing my dick. "Chatrooms."

"And what are you doing in these chatrooms, doll?" He strokes me firmly, swiping a thumb over my leaking tip, a soft whimper leaving my throat.

"T-talking. Sometimes swapping pics or videos." I try to thrust up into his fist, but he still has me pinned, working my length so slowly that my legs tremble.

"Mm, you naughty boy. I don't think I like that." Moving down my body, Ryann pauses with his face inches from my shaft as he meets my gaze, eyes flashing. "From now on, while we're doing this, you don't talk to anyone else like that except me. Understand?"

My first instinct is to scoff, tell him that he doesn't control me, but then his warm mouth envelopes my cock, and every word leaves my brain except—

"Oh, god," I moan as he takes me to the back of his throat, swallowing and swirling his tongue in a way that has my balls tightening instantly. It feels better than I've ever imagined, the sight of my length disappearing into his wet lips so damn hot that the whole thing ends pretty quickly.

I'm coming before I can even warn him, my back arching off the couch as I shoot onto his tongue with a strangled cry, fingers gripping the cushions so hard I'm surprised the leather doesn't rip.

He takes it all, humming in approval while I fill his mouth. When I'm finally finished, because I swear it goes on forever, he leans up to pull out his cock, dipping his head to spit all over it.

"Holy fuck," I murmur dazedly, watching him work his dick with my cum as lube, and he glances up bemusedly.

"Watch your mouth, or I'll have to put something in it."

Pursing my lips, I squint up at him. "Prove it."

He freezes, hazel eyes blazing with fire, before hauling me up by the back of my neck.

"Let me be perfectly clear," he bites out, gripping my jaw with one hand until I'm forced to open it, "I don't make idle threats, Shilo."

When his cock presses between my lips, I accept it eagerly, tasting myself on his skin as he slowly pumps in and out of my mouth. My jaw aches as I widen it to accommodate his size, and a gag takes me by surprise when he hits the back of my tonsils.

"You're gorgeous," he groans, running his knuckles down my face as he holds me in place by my hair. "God, you're doing so good. Suck in your cheeks for me. Breathe through your nose."

I do as he says, my eyes starting to water as my dick swells again. Reaching down, I stroke myself, whimpering around his length, the taste of his precum mixing with mine. Ryann thumbs away the tears spilling onto my cheeks, smiling wickedly as he drops his gaze to where my hand moves up and down my shaft.

"Definitely not innocent." He pulls out, allowing me to inhale a deep breath. "You going to make yourself come again while you suck my cock, doll face?"

Nodding eagerly, I lick my lips, feeling suddenly empty without him in my mouth, and I grab onto his hip to bring him back to where I want him. He doesn't let me, though, keeping himself inches away with a small laugh, and I lift my eyes pleadingly.

"Please," I beg, close to spilling over a second time, and Ryann takes a ragged breath.

"Jesus, the way you look right now," he says thickly, easing himself back into my mouth. "So fucking sweet and dirty all at once. It's killing me."

A sigh of relief leaves my nostrils, his heavy weight on my tongue like a blanket to the senses, and I lean back against the armrest while he takes control. The way his body vibrates tells me that he's measuring his movements, careful not to thrust too far into my throat, but a piece of me wants to see him let go. Fall apart. Lose that disciplined demeanor he wears like a mask and just use me.

My second orgasm slams into me, covering my hand and shirt with the sticky mess as I moan around his cock, and his thrusts falter.

"I'm going to come. Will you swallow?"

Closing my eyes, I nod and brace for it. He coats my tongue with a growl, cradling my face, thick ropes of cum flooding my throat. It's not the slightly bitter taste that makes me choke—I've tasted my own before—but the *amount* that has me coughing so hard I swear sperm starts to seep out of my nose.

"S-so sorry," I gasp after he leaves my mouth, slapping at my chest while I hack up a lung. "Think I inhaled some. Might die."

Honestly, I'm expecting him to roll his eyes and get annoyed. Maybe even snort. What shocks me, though, is the laugh that bursts out of him. Just one, a deep guffaw that seems to take him off guard from how his lips immediately tighten.

"You're fine. I should have warned you that it would be a lot." Climbing off the couch, he tucks himself away before stepping over to the sink behind the bar in the corner, turning it on to dampen a rag. He brings it to me, and I wipe up my hands and shirt as best I can while I eye him curiously.

"You didn't come that much last time."

Ryann says nothing, only watches me with folded arms, and I put my dick away before standing. His words from two months ago replay in my mind, causing me to shift on my feet awkwardly, which makes me realize I didn't even take off my shoes. Jeez.

"Is..." Biting my lip, I turn toward the island in the kitchen, where my jacket still rests. "Is that why you didn't...have sex with me tonight? Because it wasn't good before?"

A heavy silence follows the question, making my skin crawl as I zip up my jacket to hide the stain on my shirt. The longer it stretches on, the worse I feel about what just happened, which makes me mad because he told me I wouldn't be able to handle this. But I can. I know I can, and I won't let him see otherwise. Even if the thought of him not liking my body makes me want to run home, climb under the covers and never come out.

"Makes sense." I clear my throat, tucking a loose wave behind my ear, forcing my voice to remain steady. "I'm sure you've been with guys more experienced than me. Kansas was probably better at it."

Ryann sighs heavily, a sound I've come to hate over the last few weeks, and his bare feet slap on the tile somewhere behind me. A sliding glass door opens, followed by a cold chill that blows into the room.

"When you're done feeling sorry for yourself, join me on the balcony," he barks, slamming the door shut behind him.

Tears prick my eyes, but I blink them away, feeling like an idiot for letting my insecurities show, essentially proving him right. Sure, he called me gorgeous, but only because I was sucking him off and I was fully clothed. He didn't mean *me*. Just what I was doing for him.

Jesus, Shilo, pull it together. Or this whole thing will end before it even starts, and I'll probably never get to experience this again with someone I'm actually kind of comfortable with.

Blowing out a breath, I take a few extra seconds to gather myself before following Ryann onto the balcony. He's still shirtless, leaning against the railing as he gazes at the ocean beneath the moonlight, somehow not shivering as the wind stings my cheeks.

"How are you not frozen solid?" I chatter, tugging my jacket tighter as I step up next to him, reeling slightly from the view forty-six stories below.

His lips quirk. "Ireland's summer months are usually this cold, maybe a tad warmer. It feels like home."

"Do you miss it?"

"Sometimes, I do," he shrugs, running a hand through his hair. "But it's only the memories of my mother that make me miss it."

Warming my hands with my breath, I glance at him sideways. "Does she still live there?"

"She's dead." His tone is flat, practically screaming *I don't want to talk about it,* so I tell him I'm sorry despite wanting to know more. He shrugs again but doesn't answer.

Okay...awkward.

We stand in silence for a long while, him eyeing the horizon while I study his profile, taking in the outline of his slightly crooked nose, and the breeze mussing his hair. He's literally the most stunning man I've ever seen.

Eventually, he does that irritating sigh again before scrubbing a hand down his face. "It's getting late, and tomorrow comes early."

Even though I knew it was coming, I still can't help the way my stomach drops at the fact that he's kicking me out. Again. Maybe not in the rude way he did last time, but the insinuation is there.

With a nod, I turn to head back inside. "Yeah, I'd better get going."

"I'll walk you out."

Well, aren't you a gentleman. I chew my cheek, fighting to keep those words inside my brain, feeling exhausted from biting my tongue.

Ryann places a hand on my back, directing me toward the elevator, and though I craved his touch just moments ago, I don't want him touching me right now. So I put some distance between us, stepping ahead to make it the rest of the way myself, and as I spin around to press the button, I catch him watching me with an unreadable expression. Blank. Back to being a brick wall.

So this how it's going to be, then? I mean, I shouldn't be surprised. He did warn me. Doesn't mean I have to like it. And it doesn't mean I won't show him that I'm upset.

Giving him a forced grin, I throw up two fingers in salute. "See you bright and early, Mr. Callahan."

The flash of outrage in his eyes just before the doors close is almost satisfying.

Almost.

Ryann

"Shilo, get in here."

I've had it with him. *Had it.*

He showed up at the start of the week with a petulant attitude for whatever reason, and it hasn't gone away since. Not only did he drop the wrong package off at the post office—which I suspect was just to get extra time away from the desk—but he's misplaced my dry cleaning, uploaded the wrong notes from a dire meeting with a client, and filled my schedule with a bunch of useless shit.

> 9am: Bathroom Break
> 1030am: Smiling Lessons
> 12pm: Practice Saying Thank You

Miraculously, Declan's schedule is fine. Everything he asks gets done right.

Oh, the boy has pushed me to my breaking point. He wanted to know the consequences, and he's about to find out. The little brat is in for an attitude adjustment.

Shilo glances up from behind his monitor, widening his eyes before ducking back down. "I'm, uh, ordering more copy paper right now if that's what you need."

I needed that yesterday.

"It's not. My office. Now."

He hesitates for a second, going still. "Well, would you look at that? Declan's got a meeting in five minutes. Sorry, Boss, but I've got to notate."

"No, he doesn't." Losing patience, I step around the desk and into his line of sight, waiting until he meets my gaze. "Did you not know we can see each other's schedules?"

His fingers twitch on the keyboard, lips parting as he flounders for something to say. Giving up, he hangs his head with a huff before sliding off the chair. Passing me silently, he makes his way to my office with shuffled feet, and my attention drops to his pert ass behind those dark slacks. He looks absolutely delicious today in a white button-down tucked in and rolled at the sleeves. All pressed and neat. So unlike the baggy clothes he wears outside of work. I want to make him messy.

"Are you going to fire me?"

Shutting the door and throwing the lock, I turn to see him standing in the middle of the room with his gaze on the floor, fists working in his pockets. Purple strands hide his face. I hate when he hides from me.

"Do you think you deserve to be?"

Sucking in a deep breath, he shrugs, peeking up at me as I make my way to my desk without a word. Once seated, I lean back, spreading my thighs and crossing my arms. "Why don't you tell me what you think you deserve?"

He swallows hard, tongue poking out to wet his lips. "T-to be punished."

Mm, my thoughts exactly.

"And how should I do that?"

As he lifts his head, a flush spreads across his cheeks, pupils expanding. His breath catches, but he loses confidence and shakes his head before looking away.

The sight makes me angry. Who did this to him? Was it me? Did I mess up so badly that he has no trust in himself? No, Paige mentioned bullies in high school. He also moved from place to place every few years for his father's job.

Fuck, but why do I care? He's just a hookup. He agreed to no feelings attached. Just fucking.

Except we haven't even fucked yet.

"Come here." I point at the spot between me and my desk, watching as he slowly approaches while biting his bottom lip. When he comes to a stop several paces away, I reach out to pull him closer by his shirt before gazing up into his narrowed eyes. "Is there a reason you've been acting out all week? Have I done something?"

Or, didn't do, rather.

Shilo scoffs, backing away, but he doesn't get very far because the edge of the desk is right behind him. "I haven't been acting out. I am not a toddler."

"No, you're a damn brat who's making my life hell," I growl in exasperation. "This is because I didn't fuck you on Sunday, yes?"

He sputters, squinting in that adorable way he does while tripping onto my desk so that his ass hits the keyboard. Luckily, the computer is locked, and I watch him squirm while I wait for a response. All he does is get redder, suddenly finding something interesting about a blank spot on my wall as he avoids my gaze.

Heaving a sigh, I lean forward to reach into a drawer, pulling out the object I planned to give him at the end of the day. "Do you know what this is?"

Blue eyes swing to what I'm holding in my fingers before widening comically. "A butt plug?"

The nervous squeak in his voice has me fighting a smile.

"You asked why I didn't fuck you, and the reason is that you're too tight." I can't even believe those words are coming out of my mouth. "When we tried the first time, I couldn't fit even after stretching you with my fingers. So, we'll start with this one and then go up a few sizes."

He points at the plug. "You're going to put that thing in my ass?!"

It's on the tip of my tongue to say *no, you'll do it yourself,* but then the idea of glimpsing his little pink hole again has my cock swelling in my suit pants. Judging from his reaction, it's clear he's never used one of these before, and it sends something incredibly possessive through me. Of being the first person he tries it with, showing him how to put it in and make himself feel good.

Fuck, it's powerful. Too powerful.

"Stand up," I command, voice thick with desire. "Turn around and drop your slacks. Hands on the desk."

Hesitating for all of five seconds, Shilo scrambles to do as he's told, muttering curses under his breath as he fumbles with his belt. When two pale ass cheeks fill my vision, I force myself to bite back a groan. He bends forward slightly, breathing heavily, and I take a moment to appreciate the view before my hand comes down on his ass with a smack.

"Ouch," he yelps, jerking forward before glaring over his shoulder. "You just spanked me!"

"Mm, I did. And I'm going to do it again. Bad boys get spanked, doll."

A red mark appears on his skin, so damn beautiful that I have to give it a twin on the other side.

This time, when his cheek bounces from the force of my slap, a choked moan claws its way out of his throat. He hangs his head, arms wobbling slightly, and I tug on his hips until he has no choice but to bend over for me, elbows resting on the desk surface. Using both hands, I spread his crease, not even hiding the sound that comes out of me when I glimpse that puckered ring of muscle for the first time in months.

"Fuck, that's what I needed to see."

He's smooth and hairless, my mouth watering to dive right in and feast on him while my cock leaks in my briefs, but I don't. I have self-control.

Instead, I pull a bottle of lube from the drawer and open the cap, pouring some onto my fingers.

"Have you touched yourself since Sunday, Shilo? Be honest."

He whimpers when I gently rub around his hole, feeling it flex under my touch. "Y-yes."

"Starting right now, you will not masturbate until we meet again Friday night. Understand?"

"But that's three whole days," he nearly shouts, turning to gape at me over his shoulder, and I raise a brow at him.

"Do you do it every day?"

The flush on his skin is so deep it's visible on the back of his neck. He turns around to bury his face in his arms, mumbling incoherently, and I press the tip of my finger inside him.

"What was that? I didn't hear you."

With a huff, he raises his head. "I said I sometimes do it...more than once a day, okay? Like maybe twice. In the shower and before bed."

"My horny little doll." Pressing in up to the knuckle, I finger him slowly, loving those small noises of pleasure he's making. "No jerking off unless I give permission. Say it."

It takes a moment for him to respond, and it isn't until I've got two fingers inside his tight pucker that he finally agrees.

"Kay, not til you say. But...mm god, but why?"

He's rocking back now, thrusting his hips to fuck himself on my fingers, and the strain in my pants is almost painful. It's been so long since I've been buried inside a tight ass. All I want to do is pull my cock out to slam into him.

"Because you need to learn some restraint."

And maybe the thought of anyone other than me touching him is unacceptable—even himself.

I want all of his orgasms to belong to me.

Fuck, what am I doing?

"Can I come right now?" He whines once I've got three fingers stretching him open. "Please, Ryann, can I come?"

God, the sound of him begging is going to kill me.

"Not at work. You'll have to wait." Biting back a smile at his muttered curse, I take the plug and lube it up before positioning it at his entrance. "This is a beginner plug. Tomorrow, I'll put one slightly bigger inside of you and then another size up on Friday."

He squeaks when I slowly push it in, glancing at me with watery eyes over his shoulder. "I have to wear this for the rest of the day? And all night?"

"You can take it out before bed, but be gentle."

Once it's in place, I press on the base, Shilo crying out when the plug nudges against his prostate.

"How...." He breathes hard, rutting against the edge of my desk. "How the frick am I supposed to wear this all day and not come? I'm gonna have a perma-boner."

"Self-control, doll face. If you so much as touch your dick before Friday, I won't fuck you."

Growling in frustration—which is honestly cute—he spins around, glaring down at his swollen, angry cock dripping all over my floor. Actual tears run down his splotchy cheeks, bottom lip marked from where he bit into it. He looks absolutely wrecked, and all I did was finger him.

"Please, Ryann, just—" His whole body shudders, fingers gripping the desk so hard his knuckles jut out, eyes squeezing shut. "Make me come. Just once, to hold me over. I can't..."

Jesus Christ, he's beautiful. Literally perfect. How I didn't see it that night in August is beyond me, but I see it now.

"You're so close, aren't you?" I muse, reaching out to lightly trail a finger up the bottom of his length. "I bet this is all it would take to—"

A whimper is my only warning before he explodes, and I barely have time to lean forward before he's spilling into my mouth. Thick, hot cum coats my tongue, salty-sweet as I hold his hips to keep him still.

"Oh, god, oh, god," he moans, clutching my shoulder through waves of pleasure, head thrown back in ecstasy, a sight that'll forever be burned into my memory. I swallow him all, tonguing his slit to catch anything left when he's finished before releasing him. My own cock is so stiff that it aches, but I love the feeling of edging myself, so I focus instead on the boy in front of me slumping forward with relief.

Shilo buries his forehead into my neck, shivering through an aftershock as he hums contentedly. The scent of his shampoo tickles my nostrils, something floral and slightly fruity. The urge to press my face into his hair is so strong that I find myself pushing him away gently, playing it off by helping him pull up his pants and tuck his shirt back in.

Once he's decent, we stand in momentary silence, neither of us looking at the other, and I clear my throat.

"As I said, tomorrow you'll come in here, and I'll put a new plug in."

"Okay." A beat passes. "I'll add it to your schedule."

"Don't you fucking dare." I reach for him with a growl, but he's already gone, pumping his legs toward the door. Without another word, he exits my office, leaving me to seethe as I get up to wash my hands in my private bathroom, still rock hard. When I log back into my computer to finish what I really shouldn't have paused working on, a notification warns me that my schedule has been updated for tomorrow.

830am: Learn To Say Please

Little shit.

I change the plug out for Shilo on Thursday and Friday, letting him come each time because the sound of him pleading does something feral to me. The taste of his cum wakes me up better than the coffee he keeps getting wrong.

By Friday night, I'm so keyed up that I nearly orgasm while washing myself in the shower, head filled with thoughts of his ass clenching around my cock. I've been eager for this all week, surprisingly, and now that the time is almost here, I find myself pacing around my living room, waiting for him like a pathetic schoolboy.

Six o'clock rolls around, and I'm antsy, glaring at my watch because I have to pull overtime in the morning, one of many Saturdays in a row. It's been so long since I've had an entire weekend off.

Without much else to do other than watch the Krakens lose yet another hockey game, I pull out my phone to text Declan while I wait for my little doll to show up.

Me:

What are you up to?

Dec:

Poker night with the lads. Want to join?

A slight resentment has me frowning. Unlike myself, Declan gets his forty hours and that's it. No extra responsibilities, never on call. I know it's not his fault—I can never repay what he did for me, but I can't help wishing it didn't all fall on my shoulders. We're twins, after all. Both our father's sons. It should be split equally between us, the future of CalTek a joint responsibility, but it's not. It's all me. I've known this for quite some time. You'd think I'd accept it by now.

As I'm typing out a response to him, Shilo texts me, and I tap it quickly, feeling myself deflate as I read the words on my screen.

Shilo:

Hey, I'm sorry but I can't make it tonight. My dad kinda sprung something on me last minute and I'll be gone til Monday. Sorry again.

Blinking down at the message, an exasperated sigh leaves my throat as disappointment has me tossing my head back to glare at the ceiling. Part of me wants to call him and demand to know what the hell he's talking about, while the other half shrugs it off with a vague indifference and pulls up my contact list to search through my hookup options. Just as I'm about to pull one up and give them a call, though, something has me pausing with my thumb over the button.

As much as I need a good fuck...I don't want any company right now.

Not unless it involves a pair of light eyes and purple hair.

I dismiss that thought immediately, figuring my workload must have made me more exhausted than I thought as I pull up Declan's message to decline his offer of poker night. I can't stand his old college friends—a bunch of straight guys with wives, kids, pets. *Shudder.*

Me:

I'll pass. No Paige tonight?

Dec:

Nope. She's going hunting with her dad and brother I guess.

Me:

Hunting?

My brain conjures up an image of Shilo dressed in camo carrying a rifle, and it's so ridiculous that I snort to myself.

Dec:

Yeah, they hunt their own turkey every year. The trip was supposed to be next weekend but their dad had work stuff come up.

Well, shit. There goes my weekend plans, I suppose. Casting one more glance at the hockey game, I turn off the flatscreen in disgust before pushing off the couch to head for my office. Maybe if I get a head start on some work, I can plan on at least only eight hours tomorrow instead of ten. Jesus. Hiring an assistant was supposed to help *lighten* my workload, and here it is, just as chaotic as before, having to correct everything that Shilo fucks up. If he were just someone we'd hired off the street, I'd have fired him after that first week. I still probably should. It would make my life a hundred times easier, and yet...

Ignoring that train of thought, I sit at my desk in front of the floor-to-ceiling window, trying to lose myself in writing a document for Ronin. The unfinished draft stares back at me when his name suddenly appears on my screen via video call.

Grinding my molars, I hesitate, staring at the blinking icon. It's been months since we last spoke face-to-face, and I can already feel the tension coil in my chest. The last time we talked, he'd barely acknowledged my existence, and the memory of that disastrous dinner back in August still hangs heavily in my mind—right before I invited a certain Uber driver up to my condo.

With a resigned sigh, I click the accept button and lean back as Ronin's face fills the screen.

"Father," I greet him with practiced indifference. "To what do I owe the pleasure?"

"Ryann," he acknowledges curtly, the background of his study at the Manor house coming into view. "I expected the operations review this morning."

"I'm doing well, thanks for asking." I smile tightly. "It was just getting typed up when you graced me with your presence."

His hazel eyes, a mirror of my own, narrow slightly, but he doesn't engage. "Good. And the diagnostic report for AVA?"

"In progress," I reply, even as my stomach knots at the thought of the delays. Two months until launch, and AVA is still riddled with bugs. But I keep that to myself. "You'll receive an update by Monday."

"Sunday morning at the latest." His tone leaves no room for negotiation.

I clench my teeth, nodding through the tension. "I'll do my best. Anything else?"

"Yes," he says, reaching off-screen to accept something from his secretary-turned-wife. "Have you had dinner with Olivia yet?"

The mention of her name feels like a sucker punch.

"Not yet." My chest tightens with frustration. "I still don't see why Declan can't be the one to—"

His stern look cuts me off. "Declan won't be the one running everything next year."

No shit. "But doesn't that make him better suited? He has less on his plate. I don't understand why—"

"Your job isn't to understand, but to do as you're told," he snaps. "Unless you want to inherit a sinking ship in six months."

I want to argue that he's exaggerating, that CalTek's stocks have never been higher, and that our operating system's revenue is through the roof. But truthfully, the bitter man is retiring in the spring, and he's made it clear that if AVA fails, it'll be my fault, just like everything else.

He murmurs something off to the side before pressing his phone to his ear, signaling the end of our conversation. "We'll discuss this further at Thanksgiving. See you in a few weeks."

Just like that, the call disconnects, leaving me staring at a blank screen. The taste of bitterness floods my tongue as I bite down hard on my cheek, and the composure I'd been clinging to begins to crack. My knee bounces anxiously under the desk as my fingers grip the mouse until it creaks from the pressure.

I need a distraction—something to take the edge off and quiet the roiling storm of inadequacy that's been brewing since I was fifteen. A stiff drink, a mindless hookup, anything to numb the weight of expectations pressing down on me. Anything to dull the ache of a father's approval I'll never earn.

I need Shilo.

That thought alone has me inhaling sharply, shoving away from my desk to stomp into the living room, angrily grabbing a bottle of bourbon off the bar. Pulling the cork with my teeth,

I spit it onto the ground and take a hefty swig, glaring around my empty condo.

I don't *need* anything, least of all a single person. There's an entire phone in my pocket full of hookups I could call if I wanted. They'd all answer. They always do. KC definitely would. The fact that I don't feel like speaking to any of them right now means nothing. I'm just tired. Overworked. Burnt out.

Lonely.

With a scoff, I chug a few more swallows, taking the bottle with me to my bedroom, where I crash into a cold king-sized bed and drink myself to sleep.

It's probably for the best that Shilo had other plans.

Because I don't need him. I don't need anyone.

Shilo

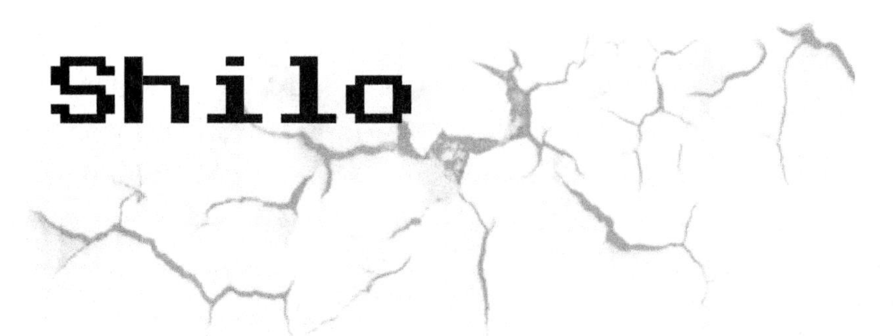

By the time we get back from our trip Sunday night, the fall chill has settled deep into my bones, and I'm sick—shivering, feverish, and puking up all the Budweiser Dad forced on me.

Real men drink beer, he'd said, handing me can after can while I silently begged Paige with my eyes to make it stop. Eventually, she started drinking them for me when Dad wasn't looking, but it didn't save me from the final shot he insisted I take—the one that secured our Thanksgiving dinner. I threw up after that, too. Honestly, I didn't keep anything down all weekend. I hate this time of year.

The only silver lining was prying the truth about Ryann and Declan's mom out of Paige. She died in a house fire, apparently. How sad is that? They were home when it happened, too, which explains Ryann's scars. No wonder neither of them ever talk about it.

I'm so drained that I call off work Monday and Tuesday, stuck in bed with chills and a crushing mood that leaves me unable to move—even to use the bathroom. I hold it until the pain in my bladder is unbearable, finally dragging myself to the toilet with tears in my eyes. I can't even bring myself to do schoolwork.

Mom and Paige check on me regularly, but I can't help myself—I keep glancing at my phone, hoping Ryann might have messaged to ask if I'm okay. He never does. He didn't even respond when I told him I couldn't make it on Friday, and we haven't spoken since that morning when he gave me a blowjob in front of his office window.

I wish he would text me.

By Wednesday morning, I'm feeling a little better—but not much. The hollow ache in my stomach only deepens when Ryann ignores me during the morning meeting, even though I got his coffee right. Declan, on the other hand, claps me on the shoulder, says he's glad to have me back, and asks if I need anything. But not Ryann. He doesn't even spare me a glance.

Whatever. I'm sure he hooked up with someone over the weekend since I wasn't available, so he's probably satisfied for now. That thought has my insides boiling, and I'm angry at myself. Angry at my dad. Angry at the world.

The rest of the week passes in a haze. I move through the days like a zombie, robotically following orders without a second thought. Every minute is a countdown to getting home, where I collapse into bed and hide under the covers. KC keeps pestering me to hang out or hop online for a game, but I can't muster the energy to talk to anyone. Even work calls feel like too much, so I've started letting them go to voicemail and responding with an email instead.

Another Friday rolls around, and I have two hours until I'm off, sitting at my desk with my head resting on my arms. Just breathing. For once, I finished all my tasks quickly, if only to hide in the shadowy cocoon of the hoodie I chose over dress clothes today. Ryann barely reacted, just raised a brow as his indifferent gaze swept over me this morning. Fine by me. I didn't want a reaction from him anyway. I just want the day to end so I can spend the weekend watching Master Splinter run around my room while Attack on Titan plays on repeat. Maybe, if I feel up to it, I'll finally install the new CPU I bought with my first paycheck—

"Shilo."

His deep, rumbling voice brings me out of my thoughts, and I tense, lifting my head to peek at Ryann from under my hood. He's wearing a navy blue suit today with a pale green tie that compliments the gold in his eyes. Tastefully handsome. A strand of hair falls over his forehead when he tilts his head down at me, a cup of coffee in his hand.

"Was the coffee cold?" Frowning, I straighten in my seat. "I can ask Kansas to heat it up if you want. Or get you a fresh one."

He blinks, opening his mouth to say something before closing it. Then he opens it again. "Are you alright?"

"Yeah. Why?"

That only confuses him, and he sets the cup down with an odd glance. "The coffee is perfectly fine."

"Oh." I squint up at him. "Do you need something from me?"

He crosses his arms, staring at me for a long moment before exhaling slowly. Something flickers in his eyes—an emotion I can't quite place—before he mutters under his breath and kneels in front of me.

"What's wrong, doll? And don't tell me you're fine because I haven't had to fix a damn thing for you this week."

My brows slam down as his palms settle on my thighs. "You... you're mad at me for doing my job *right*?"

"I'm not—" He inhales sharply. "I'm not mad. Just concerned you're plotting something."

I don't know how to respond, so I shrug, dropping my gaze to play with a frayed hole in my hoodie pocket. His fingers flex on my legs before a hand moves to tilt my chin up.

"Tell me," he demands roughly, intense eyes searching mine as warmth from his touch thaws the ice that's taken residence under my skin. Like all I needed was his hands on me to melt.

"I just..." Biting my lip, I try to contain my words, but they spill out against my will, tangling together in one breath. "I hate camping, and I hate beer because it's gross and makes me bloated, and I hate *hunting*. I don't want to hurt things. I want to take care of them, but my dad makes me go every year because it's what my grandpa did with him, and he thinks it'll toughen me up or something, but all it does is make me wish I'd been born different, and I don't even *like* meat anyway, and—"

"Hey." He cuts me off by tugging off my hood, tangling his fingers into my messy waves. "Take a deep breath. Slow down, it's alright."

But it's *not.* It's not, because I am who I am, and I'm pretty sure my dad wishes I wasn't. But instead of saying that, I nod, swallowing down the rest of my tangent while balling my fists in my sleeves. Ryann studies me for several seconds before standing abruptly.

"Come on." He leans over to log me out of the computer. "Grab your bag, and let's go."

Uh, what?

"Go where?" I squeak, clearing my throat as he checks his pockets before locking up his office.

"Lunch." Pausing briefly, he throws me a glance over his shoulder. "I'm taking my employee out as a reward for his performance. A work lunch."

Ah...got it. Strictly professional. So that's how he wants it between us, then.

Despite the sharp pang in my chest, I shoulder my backpack before following him to the elevator, where we descend to an underground parking garage that I didn't even know existed. Apparently, I've been parking Mom's car in the customer lot this whole time.

He leads me over to a sleek white electric car, cocking a brow over the hood at me when I scoff and roll my eyes.

"Figures you'd drive something this pretentious," I mumble, glaring down at the passenger door because the handle is flush with the car. How the hell am I supposed to get in?

"If conserving energy and shrinking my carbon footprint is pretentious, so be it," he bites back in response, sliding into the driver's seat. The windows are so tinted that I can't even see inside.

Standing there for a moment, I shift on my feet, waving a hand over the handle like a frickin' magician. "Open sesame."

Nothing happens, of course. Ryann leans over to open the door for me, lips twitching, but I avoid his gaze as I settle into the soft leather and put on my seat belt.

It's a rare sunny November day when we exit the garage, shining so bright that I flip my hood up as Ryann slips on a pair of fancy sunglasses while steering one-handed. From the corner of my eye, I trace the lines of his inked forearm—thorny vines winding up from his wrist like veins, twisting and curling before disappearing beneath the sleeve of his suit jacket. I know the design stretches all the way to his elbow, forming roots of the Tree of Life that spreads across his bicep and shoulder. I want to ask when he got it, and why. But instead, I stare out the window, my mouth watering because damn, it's impossible not to notice how ridiculously sexy he looks when he drives.

The silence is awkward as he takes us toward the coast, tension thick enough to make my stomach ache. After how he's ignored me the past few days, I don't even know how to act around him anymore. Last week, it felt easier—I knew where we stood, or at least I thought I did. Now, I'm just... confused. Does he still want to have sex with me? Or has he found someone else?

Bothered by the quiet, Ryann reaches out to turn up the radio as he navigates through Seattle traffic. An upbeat, melodic tune filters through the speakers. He taps his thumb against the steering wheel in time with the beat, mouthing the words. When he catches me staring, he cuts me a sideways glance, and I quickly turn toward the windshield, my cheeks heating. It feels like that night in August when I couldn't take my eyes off him, only this time, he's the one driving.

We play this game for a while—me stealing glances from under my hair and quickly looking away whenever our eyes meet. Eventually, a laugh escapes me, and his lips curve into a reluctant smile, the heaviness between us easing.

"Where are we going?" I ask, reaching out to change the station when the song ends, causing him to smack his lips in annoyance.

"A coffee shop I used to frequent when I needed to relax in college."

"You get all the free coffee you want at work, but we're going somewhere to *pay* for it?"

He rolls his eyes, glancing over his shoulder to switch lanes. "It'll be worth it."

I hope so because, truthfully, I'm not the biggest coffee fan. But I don't tell him that as he steers us down a street lined with storefronts, their backs to the ocean. He pulls into a roadside parking spot, and I blink out the window at a charming blue shop framed by a picket fence and a cozy covered porch. A wide bay window sits next to the door, where several cats lounge and stretch on the sill, basking in the sun.

I turn to stare at Ryann with parted lips. "A *cat* cafe? Really?"

He narrows his gaze as he undoes his seat belt, shutting off the car. "Why not? Who doesn't like cats?"

"My dad," I murmur, bouncing a little in my seat as my hand reaches for the door. "He's not a fan of any animal, honestly. We had a Labrador that he took everywhere when I was little, but she ran away, and we never got another one. I think it broke his heart."

Practically jumping out, I bound up the steps, rocking on the balls of my feet excitedly as Ryann takes his sweet ass time unfolding those long ass legs before joining me. For someone so tall, he sure moves slow. His hazel eyes spark with humor when he shakes his head, opening the door where tiny meows and loud screeches hit our ears.

An older woman with gray hair greets us pleasantly from the counter, a glass case full of various pastries and sandwiches on display. Behind her, there's a chalkboard detailing different drinks that are all cat-themed, and of course, my boss orders the most boring one on the menu. I get a fruit smoothie, declining any food, which he scoffs at and orders me a bagel anyway.

The place isn't too busy, so she seats us in a corner where a huge orange tabby is sprawled across the table. The cat grumbles as we slide into the benches but makes no effort to move. As Ryann pulls out his laptop, a small white cat jumps into his lap, curling up as if it's the most natural thing in the world. He surprises me by not pushing it away, instead petting its soft ears while it covers his suit in fur, the sight filling my chest with unexpected warmth.

I set my own laptop on the table, careful not to disturb the sleeping tabby as I start on my homework, trying not to get distracted by the man across from me. A skinny black kitten makes a grab for my bagel, but I scoop it up, cradling it in my sleeves. The kitten purrs and bats at my hoodie strings until it eventually falls asleep.

After a long, comfortable silence—so much better than the awkward tension in the car—I give in to temptation and sneak a glance at Ryann. He's frowning at something on his screen, completely oblivious to the cat perched behind him, rubbing its head against his in lazy affection.

A giggle slips out before I can stop it.

He looks up, dazed, and his frown deepens when he catches me grinning. "What?"

"You just..." Another laugh bubbles out. "You look so serious in your suit, surrounded by cats. It's like two puzzle pieces that don't fit."

Reaching up to pet the cat messing up his hair, he gives me a small smile. "I always wanted one growing up, but Ronin forbade it. And you can't have pets in the dorms in college. I'd come here to study when my roommate brought back girls."

"What were you like in college?"

"Much the same as I am now."

"Ah," I nod, petting the kitten in my arms. "Boring."

He chokes on his coffee, glaring as he coughs loud enough to scare the sleeping tabby away. "I'm not *boring*, Shilo."

With a shrug, I set the kitten down on the bench beside me. "You're a workaholic. Do you have any other hobbies besides being Chief of Operations?"

"I play basketball and go to the gym, thank you very much. Do you have any hobbies besides being a pain in my ass?"

My gaze meets his, and I straighten in my seat. "Can I watch you play sometime?"

That surprises him, his head tilting. "I thought you said you don't watch basketball."

"I don't, but..." Trailing off, I focus on my laptop, hesitating.

"But what?"

A flush creeps up my neck as I duck my head. "I bet you look really good...when you play."

Jeez, that was awkward. He probably thinks I'm weird now. Probably thinks he dodged a bullet by not taking things further, because I don't even know how to flirt. I can't even tell a man I want to see him all sweaty and out of breath without sounding dumb. I suck. I suck so much.

Gentle fingers brush the bottom of my chin, lifting my face to catch Ryann's devilish smirk. "Are you saying you want to eye fuck me while I shoot hoops, doll?"

Yes. God, yes. Unable to voice the words, I swallow hard and nod, tongue poking out to wet my lips.

"I think we can arrange that." His thumb swipes at my bottom lip, pulling it down, and I suck it into my mouth on instinct. A deep noise rumbles in the back of his throat, eyes darkening when I swirl my tongue over the pad of his finger. Heat instantly shoots down my spine, tightening my balls as my dick starts to swell, and I whine slightly with a squirm of my hips.

"I haven't touched myself," I breathe, his thumb leaving a wet trail of spit as it falls from my mouth. "Since you told me not to. Not once."

Ryann goes completely still, grip on my jaw tightening as a tangible energy crackles between us. "You haven't came since Friday last week?"

Shaking my head, I clench my hole. "No. And...and I'm wearing it. The plug. Right now."

"*Jesus Christ.*" He lets me go, sitting back in his seat to run a hand down his face before leveling me with a hard stare. "You've been wearing it this whole time?"

"Every day this week." My voice drops to a hoarse whisper, every part of me aching for release. I couldn't exactly do anything all weekend while sharing a tent with Paige, and I wasn't in the mood when we returned. But when I started feeling better...and I *still* couldn't jerk off? I don't even care how it makes me look. I'm desperate. Need it, or I'll die.

He mutters a curse under his breath, slamming his laptop shut before pushing to his feet. "Come on. We're leaving."

Gathering up my things, I tug the hem of my hoodie down to hide my boner and follow him back to the car. Ryann opens the passenger door for me before rounding to the driver's side, taking off once we buckle in. I have no clue where he's taking us, but I let out another whine as I press my palm against my cock, crying out when he snatches my hand.

"Hush, none of that," he chastises, turning onto some empty back road toward the beach. "We're almost there."

By *almost there,* he means seven ridiculously long minutes until an abandoned parking lot comes into view. The asphalt is cracked and crumbling in places where vegetation has begun to reclaim the land, sand encroaching as the ocean reaches for the horizon. There's no soul in sight since the bluffs off to the left entirely separate this part of the beach from the rest.

Throwing the car into park, he unbuckles both our seat belts and leans over the center console to wrap his hands around my waist, hauling me onto his lap while I squeak in surprise. My back hits the horn, blaring it loudly, but he doesn't seem to care as he fists my hair and crashes his lips to mine, groaning when our tongues glide together. His hard length presses into my ass, and I grind against it, clinging tightly to his suit jacket.

"Fuck, baby, you've been so good," he growls against my lips, reaching between us to undo my jeans. "Let me feel you."

"Please, Ry, I-I need...need..." *Need you to make me come.*

Sliding a hand down my back, he dips below the hem, fingers brushing my crease. "Shh, I know. I know." When he finds the base of the plug between my cheeks, a moan vibrates his chest, his teeth grazing my jaw as he kisses his way to my throat. "Climb into the back and take off your pants. I need to see it."

With blood roaring in my ears, I do as he says, crawling between the front seats to kick off my shoes and scramble out of my jeans. After carefully folding his suit jacket and undershirt, he follows me back shirtless, my breath catching at the sight of his hard muscle and golden skin. It's a bit cramped for his long legs, but he kneels over me and wraps his fingers around my shaft, stroking me slowly.

"Oh, God." Shuddering, I thrust up into his fist, needing more, but he forces me still with a wicked smile.

"Now, now. We both know how soon this will end if you don't stop, and I want you coming on my cock. Not my hand."

On his...

Oh, shit. *Oh shit, oh shit.* It's finally happening.

"On your hands and knees, doll," he commands, releasing me to lick my precum from his fingers. "Lay that pretty face on the seat and show me what's mine."

My teeth clench, every muscle taught as I flip around and fight the urge to touch myself. I've been so damn horny I nearly humped the pillow this morning, reasoning that it wouldn't actually count because, technically, my hands weren't around my dick. Still might do that, honestly, if this keeps up. He won't know. Can't tell me what to do.

Humming in approval, Ryann presses on the plug, causing me to jerk forward when it nudges against my prostate. "Fucking beautiful."

Moaning into the leather fabric, I try to get some much needed friction against the seat, but he lifts me up with a strong arm under my waist, slowly removing the plug. Once it's out, he replaces it with his fingers, easily sliding three of them in with a sinful groan that has goosebumps spreading along my heated skin.

"There's so much lube, it's leaking out. Have you been wet like this all week for me, baby?"

"Mm-hmm." Turning to glance at him over my shoulder, I catch the way he bites his lip, slacks pushed down to his knees as he strokes himself, fingering me slowly.

"Goddamn." A dark strand falls over his brow as he scoots closer, flicking his gaze up to mine when he pulls a condom from his pocket. "You ready to take me?"

With a nod, I whimper as I watch him roll it on, needing to feel his length fill me up. I've thought of nothing else since August, and I'm done waiting for it.

When he notches himself at my entrance, though, a thought has me asking him to wait. He goes still, shoulders tensing.

"Last weekend, did you..." Swallowing nervously, I turn away. "Were you with...someone else?"

There's a long pause that has my arms trembling, but then he turns my face to his. "No, Shilo. There's been no one else since we started this."

Hazel eyes hold mine intently, his voice steady and firm. So I nod again, leaning into his touch as I press my ass against his tip. "I'm ready. Please?"

"Fuck," he mutters under his breath, dipping his chin to watch as he pushes inside me slowly.

Like last time, it burns at first, but not nearly as bad. No, this time, the ache is almost pleasant, especially when he seats himself fully, hips resting flush against my skin. A soft moan leaves my lips when he shivers, leaning forward to trail kisses down my spine.

"You're doing so well, doll. How do you feel?"

"So full," I whisper, his length filling me up and calming the nerves twisting my stomach to knots. "So good."

Ryann chuckles, slipping his fingers under my shirt. "Let me take this off. I want to touch you."

Despite my earlier sentiment, doubt rushes in, causing me to drop my forehead and mumble into the seat. He still hasn't moved, content just to warm his cock inside of me, and I can't say I hate it.

Actually kind of like it.

His lips find the back of my neck, tongue lapping at the sweat, his hand snaking around to play with my limp dick. I hadn't even noticed I'd gone soft.

"Shh, it's okay," he whispers, nuzzling against my nape. "You're beautiful, baby. So perfect."

I hear his words. I do. And yet, there's that vile voice in my head, hissing that he's only saying these things because he's currently buried inside of me. That he wouldn't be saying them, or even thinking them, if we weren't having sex.

So I shake my head, reaching back to feel the hair on his thick thighs. "Can I turn around?"

My arms feel empty, an odd ache in my chest to hold onto something. Anything.

He hesitates, breathing unevenly against my neck before letting go of my shaft to pull me up. "Here, we'll do it like this, okay?"

With my back to his chest, he sits down so that I'm straddling him backwards. The new position has his crown hitting me just right, and I buck my hips, crying out in pleasure.

"Mm, fuck," he growls, wrapping his arms around my waist from behind. "Just like that. Ride me, Shilo."

Gripping the front seat, I bounce on my knees, hard cock now leaking profusely, sounds coming out of me I've never heard before. Desperate, needy, incoherent. He thrusts up, pounding into me so deep that I fall forward, my eyes stinging with some unnamed emotion when he places a hand over my erratic heart to hold me up. I'm so close, legs trembling as my head falls back against his shoulder, and just when I'm about to tip over that edge, he reaches down to grip both my length and balls in one tight squeeze, effectively cutting off my orgasm in its tracks.

"What the *hell?*" I snarl, tears spilling over my lashes as I try to move, but he's got me pinned.

"If you come right now, so will I, and I'm not done with you yet." His hot breath in my ear makes me shiver, the windows fogged from our heavy breathing as he gently wraps his free hand around my throat. "Slow down, baby doll. Nice and slow."

God, when he calls me that...

Releasing my dick, he uses my waist to lift me gently before pushing me back down, sliding inside at a pace that has a sob breaking past my lips. It feels too good. *He* feels too good. His strong arms cage me, lap as broad and comfortable as I knew it would be, the scent of his cologne mixed with leather and sweat.

Too much, too much.

I don't even realize I'm holding his hand until his fingers flex against mine, helping me ride him leisurely, his tongue licking at the tears tracking down my face. He's whispering words that I barely believe, sweet lies that make my throat close and chest tighten with desires that I'm too scared to acknowledge as I give myself over wholly and completely.

He said this would just be fucking. He told me I couldn't handle it.

As both our orgasms slam into us, my cum shooting onto my neck and chin as his release fills the condom inside of me, I can't help but think...

This didn't just feel like fucking.

And he was absolutely right.

I wanted to fall asleep after we finished, but Ryann wouldn't let me. Once the high faded and we caught our breaths, he pulled out of me silently. Tied off the condom and stashed it in a grocery bag while avoiding my gaze, the air between us thick while we pulled on the rest of our clothes.

Without him inside of me, I feel almost empty, my hole twinging when I slip back into the passenger seat with a wince. Either he doesn't notice or just doesn't care, because he says nothing as he puts the car in drive and merges back onto the main road toward CalTek. Silence stretches between us the entire ride, unbroken until he pulls up next to Mom's Corolla. Clearing his throat, he finally speaks.

"I leave Sunday to meet with a client and won't be back until next week. We'll be closed for the holiday then, so I'll see you after Thanksgiving."

Frowning, I peek at him from beneath my hair. "Where? I didn't see anything about it on your schedule?"

His jaw ticks at the corner, gaze locked on the windshield. "Florida. It just came up today."

Something tells me he's lying. Who is he meeting? What's the reason? But it's not my business, right? So I simply nod and mumble a goodbye as I stiffly grab my bag and exit the vehicle. The moment the door shuts behind me, he's gone, headlights blurring when I gaze numbly after him with watery eyes.

Everything hurts. My legs, from balancing on him. My throat from breathing and moaning too hard. My asshole. My heart.

As I limp to the car with my head bowed, uncomfortable from the lube drying between my legs, I make a decision that'll probably affect my grade and degree, but I don't care.

I can't do this.

I didn't know before, but I do now.

Casual sex is not for me.

I'm quitting. As soon as Thanksgiving ends, I'm done.

Ryann

The Miami sun beats down on my exposed skin, its warmth welcoming after the torrential downpour I'd left behind in Washington. A cool breeze rustles the palms above my head, salty Atlantic air clearing my senses. The beach is crowded, vast ocean teeming with bodies, a stark contrast to Seattle, where the coastal waters are only warm enough for swimming one month out of the entire year.

Would Shilo like it here?

Sighing in exasperation, I lean back in my seat and glare at the glass of whiskey on my table. It's been three days now since I took his virginity in my backseat, like a fucking teenager, and I haven't been able to get him out of my damn head.

Lord, have I tried.

The look on his face when I practically kicked him out of my car—after promising him I wouldn't treat him like that again—has been keeping me awake every night since Friday. But after what we did...the sex we had, the emotions tied to it, I couldn't look him in the eye. It's why I had him sit with his back to me after he'd asked to fuck face to face because that's something I've never done before. Never plan to.

But then I'd wrapped my arms around him, *held his hand,* talked him through it. Something shifted between us in that moment, and I don't like the vulnerable way it made me feel.

Raw. Exposed. Guilty.

I couldn't handle it.

"Callahan! As I live and breathe."

A booming voice jolts me from my thoughts, and my gaze snaps up to the towering figure of Darius Hunt, forward-center for the Miami Heat and my former college teammate.

His grin is wide and easy, flashing straight white teeth against skin a shade darker than the last time I saw him. Before I can react, he hauls me up into a hug, and I find myself grinning back just as earnestly.

"How long has it been since you visited me? Three, four years?"

"About that, yeah." With a few slaps on the back, we take our seats, gesturing to the waitress for his order while I take a hefty swig of my drink. "How've you been?"

"Same, same." He runs a hand through light brown curls, eyeing me up and down with an assessing gaze. "You seem to be keeping in shape. I thought desk life would have turned you soft by now."

"In your dreams. I can still run circles around you on the court."

He barks a laugh that could always be heard over the cheering crowd. "And yet, one of us is a professional athlete while the other makes spreadsheets."

The jab hits a tender spot, but I mask the sting with a scoff. I was never popular on the team, thanks to my charming personality, but Darius never let that bother him. Much like a certain purple-haired boy I know, he annoyed the hell out of me until I begrudgingly tolerated his friendship. As far as he's concerned, I wasn't lucky enough to be drafted like he was, and I've never told him the truth—that I was forced to turn down a guarding position with the Celtics to help Ronin run CalTek.

"So, what brings you to my neck of the woods?" He asks, casually sipping a tequila sunrise that the waitress sits in front of him. His eyes spark with interest when she smiles, and I'd bet a thousand bucks that he has her number by the time we leave.

Shrugging, I fold my arms over my chest. "Just needed to see an old friend."

I wasn't lying when I told Shilo that I had a meeting with a client. Some new company out here is partnering with us to utilize our tech, so Liza and I will be helping their IT guys set it up all week.

"Uh-huh." He gives me a knowing look, licking sugar from the rim of his glass. "And what's the *real* reason?"

Lifting a brow, I watch him smack his full lips. Darius has never been my type, but I can't deny his features are striking. Back in college, I used to proposition him regularly—half as a joke—but he's as straight as they come. Not that it ever stopped him from teasing me about it.

Setting down his glass, he snickers with a devious smile. "Come on, Ry, I know you. Social visits aren't your thing. Spit it out. What's up?"

Fuck, here we go.

Blowing out a breath, I avert my gaze, focusing instead on the sun kissing the horizon. Words tumble from my mouth before I can second guess them. "I have to get a girlfriend."

Out of my peripheral, I see his jaw drop while I casually lift my whiskey and take a gulp.

"I'm...confused," he says slowly. "Last I heard, you were gay. Unless that's changed?"

Snorting, I shake my head. "Of course not. I still like dick. And *only* dick."

"Then what the hell do you mean you have to get a girlfriend?"

I bite the inside of my cheek, mulling over how much to say. Darius owns part of CalTek stock, and as an investor, there's only so much I can divulge without venturing into insider trading territory. Legally, Dad could sue me if I say too much, and the bastard has no qualms about dragging his own son to court.

"There's a business merger we're working on with a security company," I finally say, keeping my tone measured. "My father wants to use me to ensure its success. He's also retiring next year, and he won't leave the company to me unless this deal goes through."

A few moments of silence stretch between us before Darius lets out a low whistle. His narrowed gaze pins me in place. "And this girlfriend thing ties into all that... how?"

"The woman in question happens to be the owner, and she currently has the rights to software that I... need."

"Ah." He leans back, studying me. "So, essentially, your dad wants you to lie? Sweet talk her until she agrees to his terms?"

Bingo.

I nod, gritting my teeth as I drain the rest of my drink and motion the waitress for another.

"Why does it have to be you? Isn't your brother straight?"

Sighing, I scrub a hand down my face. "All valid questions. But this isn't the first time he's pulled something like this. Declan's not the one taking over next year, and besides, Ronin's never approved of my sexuality. This is just another way for him to control me."

Darius drops his gaze, shifting uncomfortably as his shoulders tense. "That's heavy, man."

"I know. I'm supposed to have already taken this woman out on a date, but I've been dragging my feet for obvious reasons."

"Right, right." He rolls his lips thoughtfully. "But this relationship doesn't have to involve anything sexual, does it?"

My brows jump at that. "Definitely not."

"Then what's the issue?"

"The issue—" I cut myself off, inhaling sharply as another whiskey slides in front of me. I wait until the waitress steps out of earshot before continuing. "The issue is that I'm... seeing someone. And it's a delicate situation."

Understatement. Everything with Shilo is more than delicate—it's damn near fragile. And I'm not sure if I've completely shattered it already after what happened on Friday. The thought alone makes the liquor in my stomach turn sour.

Darius chokes on his tequila, staring at me like I've grown a second head. "*Seeing someone.* Like, dating? A relationship? You?"

"Not a relationship," I snap, my lip curling in irritation. "But we are... exclusive."

Jesus Christ.

He bursts into laughter, clutching his abdomen and slapping his knee like it's the funniest thing he's ever heard. I shoot him a withering glare.

"So, there's this river in Egypt," he begins, and I nearly slap a hand over his mouth.

"I'm not in *denial*, Darius. It's not a relationship. We have a mutually beneficial understanding."

His eyes sparkle with humor. "Ah, a *situationship*, then. Got it. And this exclusive guy of yours isn't happy about sharing you with a fake girlfriend, I take it?"

"That's the thing. He doesn't know. No one knows it'll be fake."

And there it is. The kicker. After being out and proud since junior high, I now have to convince everyone—including my twin brother—that I'm suddenly into women. It's all so fucked.

Darius's grin slowly fades, his expression softening into something almost sympathetic. "But you just told me?"

I sigh heavily, turning to watch a couple stroll along the beach with their dog, feeling heartsick. "I had to get it off my chest. Besides Declan... you're the closest person I have. And you don't work for me, so there's that."

My brother and a guy I've barely seen twice in the last decade. That's the entirety of my social circle. Pathetic. Maybe Shilo was right, I really *am* boring.

"Oh." Darius nods, then his eyes widen, lips parting. "*Oh.* Wait, you're involved with an employee? Are you serious, Ry?"

"Technically, we got involved *before* he became an employee. It just kind of... happened."

"Well, this is some shit." He chuckles, raising a hand to get the waitress's attention. "I'm not drunk enough for this."

"You and me, both."

We order another round of drinks, and while he flirts with the waitress, I stare at the table, turning over my next words.

"Truth is, I could use your help. Women have never been my forte, and I have no idea how to date one."

He grins, winking at the waitress as she walks away. "And you think I do?"

"You're handsome and charming. Women flock to you."

"Holy shit! *Playboy Callahan* needs a wingman?" He doubles over in laughter again as I scowl.

"Fuck off. Forget it."

Sobering quickly, he claps a hand on my shoulder with a genuine smile. "Of course, I'll help you, man. Remember when my momma kicked me out for throwing that party, and you let me crash in your dorm?"

"I didn't *let* you do anything. You broke in and made yourself at home."

"Yeah, but you didn't kick me out, so it counts."

Rolling my eyes, I stifle a smile and take another shot. "Whatever. So how would you go about something like this?"

He leans back, lifting the napkin under his drink. "Depends. How long you in town for?"

"A week."

"I can work with that." He smirks, holding up the napkin, which has a number and the waitress's name scrawled across it. "Come by my place tomorrow. We'll shoot some hoops, and I'll scare you straight. Literally."

I snort, shaking my head. Of course.

Called it.

Unfortunately, I never made it to Darius's place the next day—or the rest of the week, for that matter. On top of everything I already had to deal with out here, Dad threw even more shit my way. If I wasn't with our client making sure everything ran smoothly, I was glued to my laptop or phone, stuck on back-to-back calls. By the time I collapsed into my hotel bed every night, I was too exhausted to even think about meeting up again. With the holidays upon us, everyone's scrambling to cram everything in. Declan's schedule has been just as hectic, so I know it's not Shilo piling on extra tasks just to fuck with me.

Speaking of which...

I haven't heard from him all week. Not that I've texted, either. As much as I fucking hate to admit it, I miss my little doll. I miss seeing his face every morning at work, hearing that cute squeak he makes when he's surprised, and the way he acts out when he's craving attention.

Now that I've had several days of space to reflect, I'm beyond appalled with myself for the way I acted after we fucked. It wasn't right. He didn't deserve that, and I intend to make it up to him the second I get back to town. Aftercare isn't exactly in my wheelhouse, but maybe we could have dinner together post-sex or something, just... a way to make him feel less used.

I fucking hate that I probably made him feel that way. Again.

When the week finally ends, I'm irritable and downright antsy. Chomping at the bit to get home.

It's raining when my flight touches down in Seattle, the skyline painted with orange hues of autumn leaves. As much as I enjoyed Florida's warmth, there's something about Washington's seasons that call to me. The crisp, damp air carries a memory of my mother's smile and the warmth of her hands back in Ireland, before Dec and I were separated. Before everything turned to shit.

It feels like a home I lost long ago.

Riding the elevator up to my condo, I pull out my phone and fire off a quick text to Declan, letting him know I'm back. My fingers hover for a moment before I send one to Shilo as well.

I need to see him. Feel him. Apologize.

Me:

Just flew back in. If you're not busy tonight, swing by my place around nine.

He doesn't respond right away, which isn't a big deal—or so I tell myself. Declan keeps me distracted for a while as we message back and forth about the trip. I busy myself unpacking, tossing clothes into the wash, and grabbing a quick shower to scrub off the airport grime.

By the time I've dried off, though, Shilo still hasn't replied. Blinking down at the screen, I brush my teeth slowly, unease coiling tighter with each passing moment.

Is he upset with me?

Of course, he is asshole. You kicked him out of the car after he cried during sex.

Fuck. I don't know why it didn't register that he'd been sobbing until this very moment, but now, I...

God, I'm the most selfish son of a bitch on the planet.

Grabbing my phone, I quickly type out another text, toothbrush hanging loosely from my lips.

Me:

Look, about last Friday. I'm sorry for the way I acted. Things just got a bit deep, and it messed with my head. I promise it won't happen again.

Can I promise that, though? I don't know. But I can try. Fuck, I'll try.

He reads it almost instantly and responds a second later.

Dollface:

Going out with Kansas, Tina and Carpenter tonight.

That's it. That's all he says. No acknowledgment of my apology, no explanation. Nothing.

Who the fuck is Carpenter?

With a growl, I pull up KC's number and ask him that very question.

Me:

Who the fuck is Carpenter?

KC:

My roommate, why? Also hi :)

Me:

Where are you going with Shilo?

Tossing my toothbrush into the sink, I swish and spit some mouthwash, absolutely livid.

KC:

Hmm, this is the second time you've asked that, and I'm starting to catch a vibe. Swear to God, if you're the reason he's looked like a kicked puppy all week, I'll put laxatives in your coffee.

Me:

Where, KC?

KC:

Work is closed and we don't have to answer to you.

We?

Goddammit. Little shits are ganging up on me.

Deciding to give it a rest for the night, I flop onto my back in bed and seethe at the ceiling, visions of Shilo and whoever this Carpenter guy is flitting through my head. I know I deserve this, but it still pisses me off. Every night for the last week, I've thought of nothing else but having him again, and my cock is aching for it.

Maybe that's the problem. You want to fuck him, not keep him.

With a frustrated growl, I roll over and press my face into the pillow, willing my mind to shut the fuck up so I can sleep.

Tomorrow. I'll make it up to him tomorrow. For now, let him be angry. My little doll can't avoid me forever.

Ryann

It turns out that Shilo *can* avoid me forever. And is hellbent on doing it, too.

Not once in four days has he texted me back. With work being closed until Monday, I haven't been able to see him, either, and it's pissing me off. It pisses me off that I'm pissed off.

Standing in front of the mirror in my closet, I scowl at my reflection as I adjust the silver cuff-links on my sleeves, ensuring my sleek black suit is pressed and wrinkle-free. There's no hair out of place, my green silk tie shimmering, and my dress shoes are shined to perfection. Just the way my father expects it. We have appearances to keep up, after all, and God forbid my fucking pocket square be one inch too far to the right.

Heaving a sigh, I dial up Declan as I fasten a Rolex from my collection onto my wrist. He answers on the third ring.

"Happy Turkey Day, brother," he snickers, sounding muffled, but I'm not in the mood for jokes today.

"When will you be at the Manor?"

A beat of silence follows. "The Manor?"

"Yes. Thanksgiving dinner at Dad's, remember?"

There's a harsh swear on the other end, and my brows shoot up as I flick off the closet light and stride back into my room.

"Shit, Ry. I forgot to tell you. Paige decided it's time for me to meet her parents, so I'm having dinner with them instead."

I freeze in the hallway, hand hovering over my office door handle as my chest tightens. "Does Dad know?"

"I sent him an email," Dec says quickly. "He wasn't happy about it, but gave me his blessing."

Of course, he fucking did.

Instantly deflating, I slump against the wall as I reach up to rub my forehead furiously. As if tonight wasn't bad enough, now I'll have to endure the entire charade alone—surrounded by people I barely know, nodding through pointless small talk, and pretending to care about Ronin's wife, who's somehow *younger* than both of us.

"You're mad, aren't you?" My brother's voice cuts through the spiraling thoughts, and I grit my teeth, letting my head fall back against the wall with a dull thud.

I don't answer. I don't need to. He can probably hear me silently pleading through the phone, begging him not to *leave me to deal with this shit alone.*

"Look," he says after a moment, "why don't you come with me?"

Straightening away from the wall, I frown at the phone as if Declan can see me. "To Paige's house?" *Shilo's house.*

"Yeah, why not? I'm sure they won't mind. You're my twin. We're a package deal."

An unfamiliar yearning stirs in the pit of my stomach, and suddenly, there's nothing I want more than see Shilo in his natural environment, surrounded by his family. He won't expect to see me, either, which makes the idea more appealing.

Clearing my throat, I pretend to deliberate, even though I've already decided. "Dad will flip if I cancel this close to dinner."

My brother scoffs. "So what? He'll get over it."

Maybe for you. I'm always held accountable when it comes to Ronin's expectations, but I keep that thought to myself as I grab my wallet and keys. "What time should I be there? And text me the address."

"I'm heading over now."

Twenty minutes later, after a quick trip to the store for wine, I pull up in front of a charming Victorian-style home in the Queen Anne neighborhood. The house is made of brick, with a covered porch and small spire that showcases several lit windows.

Declan's already parked outside, leaning against his Lexus, and he chokes out a laugh when I step onto the curb.

"Are you trying to show me up or something?" He gestures down to his loose button-up as I roll my eyes.

"I was preparing for dinner at Dad's, remember? There was no time to change."

"Yeah, well, they'll probably like you better than me now. And you even brought the good wine."

"It felt wrong to crash someone else's family dinner empty-handed."

We make our way up a set of concrete steps lined with neatly trimmed bushes, a garden full of autumn flowers blooming beneath a large bay window. Dec rings the bell, his fingers twitching at his sides. I notice the telltale sign of nerves immediately, and when he catches me looking, he shoves a hand into his pocket with a crooked grin, his green eyes distant.

Much like me, he was never the relationship type—though there *was* a girl back in college who broke his heart. He didn't even get close to meeting her parents, so this feels like a pretty big deal for him.

Firing off a quick email to let Ronin know I won't be making it tonight, I shove my phone into my pocket just as Paige flings open the door in a tan sweater dress that hangs off one shoulder. When she sees Declan, her gaze lights up, but widens in surprise as it swings toward me.

"Oh." She pauses, a confused smile tugging at her lips. "You brought a plus one?"

Dec jabs a thumb in my direction. "Yeah, hope that's alright. Big baby Ry didn't want to face our stepmother's family alone."

I shove his shoulder as Paige snorts.

"The more, the merrier," she says, spinning on the heel of her black boots. "Come on in. I'll let Mom know to set another spot at the table. Dad's going to be thrilled."

We step into a large sitting room, hardwood floors covered with a deep red oriental rug. Flames crackle beneath a white brick hearth decorated in autumn decor, and framed photographs hang above a curved-back Chesterfield sofa. A staircase leads up to the second floor on our left, steps covered in a gold runner that casts a warm and inviting glow. Delicious scents of food tickle my nostrils.

My phone buzzes in my pocket, no doubt my father's response, but I ignore it as my curiosity pulls me toward the pictures on the wall. They appear to be family photos, taken several years ago, somewhere in the Grand Canyon, maybe?

Furrowing my brow, I lean in closer to one frame. A teenage Shilo stares back at me, looking... very different. Instead of his familiar shaggy purple waves, his hair is buzzed short and dark, his cheeks round and reddened with a sunburn. He's scowling at the camera, standing beside a broader man who bears a strong resemblance—his father, I'm sure.

Other photos show school portraits, and the boy in them is robust, with a fuller build and softer features. It's undeniably Shilo, the pale skin and blue eyes are unmistakable, but he's not the petite little doll I've come to know.

Paige mentioned bullies in school.

Is this the reason he won't take his shirt off?

"Well, I'll be damned." A deep voice snaps me out of my thoughts, and I turn to see the larger man from the photos striding toward me, his wide grin a mirror image of his daughter's. "Ryann Callahan, in my house? Is this Christmas?"

He bypasses Declan entirely, thrusting out a meaty palm for me to shake. I blink at it momentarily before clasping my hand around his firm grip.

"Mr. Reed, I presume?"

"Please, call me Mark." He claps me on the back, hard enough to sting, brown eyes twinkling. "I used to watch your college games. Couldn't believe you didn't go pro."

Right. Shilo mentioned his dad was a fan of college basketball. I'd forgotten.

I open my mouth to respond, but Paige interrupts, placing a hand on her father's shoulder. "Before this gets too out of hand..." She pulls an uncomfortable looking Dec to her side. "Dad, this is Declan."

Mark's attention shifts to my brother, his gaze appraising. He reaches out to shake Declan's hand. "You play ball too, son?"

"Lacrosse, sir."

The man flicks his hand at that, dismissing them both before steering me away to God knows where. Over my shoulder, I lock eyes with a smirking Paige and silently mouth *help*. She ignores me, tugging Declan into what looks like a kitchen, at least from what little I can see, before I'm swallowed up inside a study.

Mark proceeds to pester me about my basketball career for nearly forty minutes.

It's not that I don't enjoy talking sports, because I do. Get me going on a good night with a few glasses of bourbon, and I'll chat anyone's ear off about hockey or Huckslee Davis, the star running back for the Baltimore Ravens. But tonight? After the week I've had? Knowing I'm under the same roof as my little doll after not seeing him for nearly two weeks?

It's maddening. Every muscle in my body is coiled tight, and it's taking all my strength not to kick down every damn door in this house and demand to know where he is.

This... this isn't like me at all.

Apparently, Shilo's father is a full-time Aviation Officer stationed at the base. The family moved around almost every two years until Shilo was about thirteen, when they finally settled here permanently. Mark is midway through showing me his impressive collection of medals when we're both called to dinner.

The dining room matches the rest of the house, warm and inviting with a sizable six-seater table covered in food. A woman in a flowing blouse, who I assume is Shilo's mother, greets me with a pretty smile. She pulls me in for a hug that I return stiffly, feeling Declan's amused gaze on my face. She's petite, about Shilo's height, with golden blonde waves and those same pale blue eyes I've grown fond of.

"You must be the other boss I've heard so much about," she sing-songs, throwing me a knowing glance. "It's nice to finally meet you. I'm Sheila, Shilo's mom."

My brows shoot up at that, though I force myself not to tense as I take the seat she directs me to. "Oh? And what exactly have you heard?"

"Apparently, between you and your brother, you're the one who gives my son a hard time," she chuckles, reaching into a curio cabinet for some wine glasses while I fight the urge to bristle.

I'm fairly certain he's the one giving me *a hard time.*

Mark grunts, taking a seat at the head of the table. "Boy could use a firm hand every once in a while. It won't hurt him."

The memory of Shilo's reddened, spanked ass pops into my head, but I shove it away quickly. Not the time or place.

"Where is he, anyway?" Paige strides over to the stairs, shouting at the top of her lungs. "*IGGY, COME EAT!*"

She and Declan take their seats across from me, and I tilt my head curiously. "Iggy?"

"Oh, gosh." Sheila sets the last of the wine glasses down before sitting at the opposite end of the table. "We got a pet iguana when the kids were little that liked to bite. Shilo was just a toddler then and picked up the habit, so Paige started calling him Iggy whenever he'd chomp at her. The name stuck, I guess."

A snort escapes me just as someone comes stomping down the stairs.

"Stop telling embarrassing stories about me."

The sound of his voice sends a pleasurable jolt through me, and my eyes dart toward the staircase as he comes into view.

The first thing I see is feet. Pale, delicate feet with painted nails and cute toes that make me wonder what sound he'd make if I sucked on them. Have I seen them before?

I've never been into feet, but Shilo's toes are doing something to me.

He pauses at the bottom of the stairs, and my gaze drags up his bare legs, lingering on the sleep shorts and backwards hoodie he's wearing. Before I can make it to his face, my attention freezes on something else entirely.

I blink, frowning incredulously. "Is that a *rat* on your shoulder?"

His eyes widen the moment he notices me sitting at the table. "What are *you* doing here?!"

The animosity in his tone is unmistakable, and it stuns me for a moment.

Mark's head snaps up, his expression stern as he scolds his son. "Shilo! Manners. And where the hell are your pants?"

"Those are pants, Dad," Paige chimes in, rolling her eyes as if this is a regular occurrence.

Shilo ducks his head, muttering something under his breath as he shuffles toward us. The only open seat is next to me, so he hesitates for a fraction of a second before dropping into it with a huff. Immediately, my cock perks up at his presence, remembering what it felt like to be inside of him, and I surreptitiously cross my legs under the table as I look down into his rat's beady black eyes.

"Is that supposed to be a pet?"

Shilo scowls at me from beneath messy purple bangs. "His name is Master Splinter, from *Teenage Mutant Ninja Turtles.* Why are you dressed like you're going to a funeral?"

I narrow my gaze, letting it drift over his fraying sweater as the rat burrows into the hood hanging across his chest. "Why are you dressed like you live under a bridge?"

A beat of silence stretches between us, both glaring, until a reluctant smile tugs at my lips when he bursts into laughter. The sound warms the space between us, and my eyes drop to his lips. They look pink and soft, more inviting than I remember, the urge to lean down and taste them hitting me hard.

Declan's pointed cough jerks me back to reality, snapping my attention to the table. Everyone is staring.

Fucking hell.

My twin raises an enigmatic brow, his gaze flicking to Mark, who claps his hands loudly.

"Alright, let's get this show on the road. Shilo, grab the turkey carver."

My little doll stiffens, discomfort written all over his face, but before I can step in, Paige beats me to it.

"I'll do it this year," she offers, reaching for the carving blades in the center of the table.

Mark shakes his head firmly. "He's the one who shot and plucked it, so he gets to carve it. Them's the rules, Paige."

A sick churning twists in my stomach as I watch Shilo's shaking fingers reach for the carver. The memory of his words—what he looked like and how he acted after that hunting trip—echoes sharply in my mind.

I don't want to hurt things. I want to take care of them.

Without thinking, I take his hand, gently prying the blades away before getting to my feet. "Here, allow me. As the guest who invited himself, I insist."

The room visibly relaxes, both Paige and her mother exchanging grateful glances. As I slice pieces of turkey breast, I load up everyone's plates, minus Shilo's since he doesn't like meat. When I peek at him, his expression shifts slightly, surprise flickering in his blue eyes as he watches me cautiously.

Mark, oblivious, turns to Paige and Declan. "So, tell us the story. How did you two kids meet?"

"Well, work first. And then..." Paige begins, grinning when my brother dives into the details of their relationship.

The table grows lively as we start loading up on side dishes, but my focus stays on Shilo. I notice how he grabs barely a spoonful of anything, and without hesitation, I start adding extras to his plate. He scoffs softly, leaning back with his arms crossed, adorably irritated. Raising a brow at his attitude, I plop a generous scoop of green bean casserole in front of him.

Like a fucking brat, he lifts his plate and scrapes everything onto mine with a fork, holding my gaze while he does it.

Casting a glance around the table to ensure everyone's attention is occupied, I lean over until my lips brush his ear. "You've only made this worse for yourself. Now you have to eat both our helpings, doll face, or I'll spoon-feed you the same way you fed me your cock in my office."

A squeak leaves his mouth, low enough for only my ears, as a flush creeps up his neck. Swallowing hard, he switches our plates around and digs in, avoiding my gaze. Smirking to myself, I turn back to the conversation.

"So, what exactly does a Financial Officer do?" Mark asks, his sharp eyes fixed on Declan, clearly trying to decide if he's good enough for Paige.

"I handle things like accounting and risk management," Dec explains, gesturing in my direction. "Ryann, on the other hand, focuses more on hiring and internal operations."

Mark hums, his gaze shifting to me with a wry smile. "That more exciting than playing professional ball?"

Ouch.

Forcing a polite smile, I take a sip of my wine. "I wouldn't call it exciting, necessarily. More... fulfilling. I'm helping my father run a multi-million dollar corporation that'll be mine someday. As monotonous as the work can be, there's something satisfying about building a legacy."

Next to me, Shilo snorts, almost choking on his mashed potatoes, but his dad nods at me in approval.

"A family man, huh? I can appreciate that," Mark chuckles lightly. "Although, let's be honest, you'd probably have a better pick of the ladies if you'd gone into basketball."

Paige and her mother groan in unison, both throwing scathing looks his way as he shrugs.

"I'm just saying!"

"Oh, I'm not too worried about that." I huff a small laugh, gingerly cutting off a piece of meat. "I like men."

The room's atmosphere shifts instantly.

Shilo freezes, his spine snapping straight as he sets down his fork. The silence is deafening, making it painfully clear I've said something wrong. Frowning, I glance at my little doll, but his attention is locked on his father.

When I meet Mark's gaze, I find a disgusted glare that catches me off guard. He quickly schools his features, turning to Declan with forced casualness, but it's too late. I saw it. *Felt* it.

Vitriol. Judgment. Hatred.

A foot taps mine under the table, and I blink at Paige, who offers me an apologetic smile before looking away. Sheila's expression mirrors her daughter's as she gazes at Shilo, who's now poking at his plate with his head down.

Reaching under the table, I place a hand on his knee. The moment our skin touches, he flinches, pulling away sharply.

"I'm full," he announces, standing abruptly.

Mark waves him off without a glance, already deep in a discussion about politics with my brother. Once Shilo leaves the room, he takes the warmth with him, my body growing cold in his absence. I watch him quickly climb the stairs two at a time like he can't get away fast enough, and it's hard not to follow after him. The last thing I want to do here is make things difficult between him and his father, even if my instincts are screaming at me to throw him over my shoulder and carry him out like a caveman.

After finishing my meal in silence, I collect both mine and Shilo's plates. "Where's the kitchen? I'll clear these away."

"Don't you worry about that." Sheila takes them from me, patting my arm softly. "I've got these. And thank you for the wine. It was delicious."

"No problem at all, you can keep the rest."

Taking a step forward, I'm about to excuse myself for a breather when she grabs my wrist.

"Oh! Shilo must have dropped his phone when he hightailed it out of here. Can you take it to him?"

Frowning down at my empty hand, the 'phone' clearly imaginary, I flick my gaze back up to hers as she winks.

"Up the stairs, third door on the left. Thank you, dear."

Well...alright, then.

Mark doesn't acknowledge me as I leave, and while I've grown used to bigoted assholes, his disdain stings—not for me, but for Shilo. I've been out for years, faced slurs and hostility in locker rooms and boardrooms alike. It barely fazes me. But my little doll doesn't have armor like I do.

The hallway upstairs is dark, save for the faint glow under one door. I raise a hand to knock, but the sound of retching freezes me in place. It's a sound I've heard him make before, and anger surges through me. Without thinking, I push the door open.

His room is bigger than I expected, cluttered but cozy. A shelf of plants lines the window, and a curved computer monitor sits on a desk. But my focus is on the bathroom, where I find Shilo kneeling in front of the toilet with two fingers shoved down his throat.

"What the *fuck* do you think you're doing?"

Yelping in surprise, he whips around, falling sideways against the tub. "What are you doing in my room?!"

His knees draw up to his chest as I tower over him, my eyes darting to the toilet. He hasn't succeeded in purging yet.

"It's n-not what you think," he stammers, wrapping his arms around himself.

"Oh? So you weren't about to throw up everything you just ate for dinner?"

He opens his mouth, probably to deny it, but my vibrating anger silences him. His forehead lowers to his knees, thin shoulders shaking with sobs.

Suddenly, in this moment, he looks even smaller than he did two weeks ago. Like my little doll is wasting away before my eyes.

How can I even call him my anything *if I'm allowing this to happen?*

"Just...please, just go, Mr. Callahan."

Christ, even his voice sounds frail.

I don't know how to do this. I've never been the comforting type, viewing insecurities and uncertainty as weaknesses. I had to grow thick skin if I was going to survive my father. But despite my abrasive attitude, I'm not cruel. I can't leave him like this.

Scrubbing a hand down my face, I take a deep breath and drop to the floor, leaning my back against the wall.

"I saw the school pictures downstairs. And your sister mentioned bullies. Is this the reason?"

He quietly cries into his knees for a moment before nodding.

My chest tightens painfully for him. "Do your parents know?"

He shakes his head, still hiding himself from me. "They suspect something. At least, my mom and Paige do. Dad makes comments about how I need to bulk up and get muscle."

The memory of Mark's reaction to my sexuality sends rage burning through me. "He doesn't know you're gay."

Shilo peeks at me through his hair. "No. Paige told Mom, though..."

We sit in heavy silence, letting his words sink in. If his mom knows, I probably shouldn't stay up here too long. She seems like an intelligent woman; she'll put two and two together, but I don't want to leave him yet.

Gesturing toward the toilet with my chin, I level him with a stern look. "What brought this on? You weren't purging when I left for Florida."

"Do you really need to ask that?" he snaps, taking me by surprise.

My lips tighten. "I already texted you with an apology."

He scoffs, burying his face in his knees once again. "Apology not accepted. Now leave me alone."

With a growl, I reach out and yank him against my chest, spreading my legs to make room. He squeaks—a noise I can't get enough of—and I tilt his chin up.

"The reason I left in a hurry had nothing to do with your body, Shilo. If you haven't noticed, I'm very attracted to it." I roll my hips against his side, loving the way his skin flushes when he feels my arousal. "But this? What you're doing? It isn't healthy."

"I fucking know that," he shouts sharply. "I hear it enough from my therapist. I don't need it from my boss, too. It's...not something I can stop cold turkey, okay?"

His chest heaves as he avoids my gaze, and I exhale slowly before pressing his head against my shoulder. He stiffens when my fingers curl into his hair, massaging his scalp.

"Um, what are you doing?" he mumbles.

"Comforting you."

There's a beat of silence. "...Why?"

Good question.

A gruff laugh leaves my throat as I lightly pull his hair. "Stop being a brat and let it happen."

My hand kneads his nape, the taut tendons loosening after a few moments. Shilo sighs softly, nearly melting into me as he buries his snotty face into my jacket, and I smack my lips in annoyance.

"Only you can have me sitting on a bathroom floor, using my three-thousand dollar suit as a tissue."

He says something I don't catch, though I'm fairly certain I heard the words *pretentious asshole* in there somewhere. We'll have to have a discussion later about his filthy mouth. Actually, we'll have to discuss a lot of things.

We sit in silence as I rub his neck, my free arm resting stiffly at my side. There's an urge to wrap it around him, but I refrain, uncomfortable with physical affection. The fact that he's leaning against me seems like enough. When his pet pops out to watch me, I fight to hold in a shudder.

"Is there a reason you only have one rat? Don't they need friends?"

Shilo sighs, rubbing his rat's head before the vermin disappears once again into his hood. "Master Splinter is a loner like me. He has aggression issues."

"Hm."

"Does your father know?" He blurts suddenly, and I glance down at him in question. "That you're gay, I mean."

"Yes."

His face falls, like he was expecting something more. So I square my shoulders and concede, knowing what he's really asking for.

"I never actually *came out* traditionally. In junior high, I'd bring home boys for some experimental fun, and he caught on pretty quickly. All he ever said was, '*As long as you keep it quiet and still take a wife someday to carry on the family name, I don't care what you do*'. We never spoke about it again."

Shilo squints up at me, clearly taken aback. "He expects you to marry a woman even though you're not attracted to them?"

My head thumps against the wall as I gaze straight ahead, sorting through my words. "The Callahan name is very old in Ireland. We come from a long line of power and money. Unfortunately, with all that power comes certain...expectations."

"That's messed up."

"You've no idea."

Though I've managed to avoid it so far, part of me wonders if this whole ruse with Olivia is my father's way of pushing me to marry and produce heirs. Especially now, with him stepping down next year.

Speaking of which...

Pulling out my phone, I open my email to read his response to my dinner cancellation.

Ryann,

This is very disappointing. Your mother was looking forward to introducing you and your brother to her family.

I expect your presence at the Christmas party next month with a plus one.

Ronin

His threat is perfectly clear. By *plus one,* he means Olivia.

My stomach sours, Thanksgiving dinner churning uneasily at the thought.

"Your mother?" Shilo glances at my screen curiously, having read the email, and I quickly lock my phone before putting it away.

"He means my stepmother. She's his fourth wife and about a year older than you. Also, his former secretary."

His lips twist into a grimace. "Dating employees must run in the family."

Giving him a ghost of a smile, I brush a thumb over his mouth, wanting to change the subject. "Will I see you at my condo tonight, or are you still ignoring me?"

Something shifts in his expression. His face tightens as he ducks his head, pulling out of my touch. An uncomfortable weight drops in my gut when he pushes to his feet and turns away.

"I...I don't think we should continue doing that."

My breath catches as I stand, following him into his room, where he starts to pace. "Doing what, exactly?"

"S-sleeping together." Wringing his fingers anxiously, he stares at the floor.

I cross my arms with a frown. "Did you not enjoy it, doll?"

"Don't," he pleads, rubbing his sternum. "Please, don't call me that. And I enjoyed everything we did, it's just..."

"Just what?"

He swallows hard, the delicate column of his neck flexing. When his eyes meet mine, they pierce right through me. "I don't think I can do it. Separate feelings from sex, I mean. I'm not like you."

A sinking sensation spreads through me, sharp and painful, but I keep my face neutral "I told you from the beginning what to expect."

"You did. And I really thought that I could handle it, but I can't." Licking his lips, he looks away, focusing on the door. "Every time we do something, and you treat me like garbage after, it makes me feel worse. For my mental health, I think it's best if we just...stop."

His words hit like a gut punch, and my first instinct is to defend myself, but the broken look on his face stops me cold. Because he's right. I *did* treat him like garbage. He forgave me, and I was given another chance when I promised I wouldn't do it again.

But then I took his virginity in the back of my car before kicking him to the curb like a fucking prick. For the first time in my life, sex felt like it meant something, and it terrified me.

Declan was right. I only know how to use people. Just like Ronin. Like father, like son.

Clearing his throat, Shilo throws me a sideways glance, trembling slightly. "I'm, uh, actually going to be putting in my two-week notice on Monday. I'll have to retake this course next year, which will set me back a bit, but it's not too big of a deal."

"You don't have to do that," I bark, sharper than intended. Softening my voice, I try again. "You don't have to quit just because we're ending our sexual arrangement, Shilo. I won't force you into anything."

His shoulders droop at that. "I don't think I can just pretend. It'll be too hard."

"Pretend what?"

Meeting my gaze fully, I'm stunned by the sadness swimming in his pale blue eyes. "That I don't have feelings for you."

The air is knocked out of me, and all I can do is stare as I flounder for a response.

My brain tries to sort through this logically. Feelings? How is that even possible? Technically, we only fucked *once.* That first time in August didn't count, I wasn't even able to fully penetrate him.

But then it hits me how many firsts I've been for him, and it all makes sense. Of course he would grow attached. He's young. I'm the only man he's ever been with.

The only one he'll ever be with.

I quickly shake that thought away, even though imagining him with anyone else has me furious.

He's not *mine.* I can't keep him. So I need to let him go.

Running a hand through my hair, I take a step closer. "Look, you don't need to quit. If being my assistant is no longer an option, I'll find you another position."

His head tilts, purple strands falling over his brow. "You'd do that for me?"

I don't want to. But I will.

"Declan and I promised Paige that we'd help you. Callahan men keep their promises."

Jesus Christ. Dad's words bite me in the ass again.

"Okay," Shilo says slowly, expression cautious. "That would be cool. I'd appreciate that."

An awkward silence falls over us. I get the sense that he's ready for me to leave, but I don't want to go. The image of how I found him earlier, kneeling before the toilet, makes me want to push him down onto the bed and worship his body until he forgets his insecurities, but that's no longer my place. If it ever was.

I'd just make it worse.

"Come to the startup meeting Monday," I say finally, feeling hoarse. "I'll hand you over to Liza. She's in charge of our developers. I'm sure she'll find work for you."

He perks up at that, almost excited, and my petty heart revolts. "Thank you, Mr. Callahan."

Goddammit.

With nothing left to say, I nod curtly before heading to the door. My hand grips the handle, and I'm about to step into the hallway when Shilo's soft voice stops me.

"I mean it," he whispers, his gaze steady for once. "Thanks for everything."

"You're welcome."

Giving him one last glance, I shut the door behind me, making my way out of the house. Declan is still somewhere inside, but I send him a text to thank Sheila for dinner. Mark can go fuck himself.

Once inside the car, I buckle up and lean against the headrest, staring blankly out the windshield. If I breathe deep enough, I swear I can still smell the floral scent of Shilo's body wash, and the memory of what we did has my cock swelling despite the dejected feeling in my chest.

I guess it's back to bars and hookups.

As I pull away from the curb, my eyes catch on his silhouette, watching me from his bedroom window, and I can't help but think how much I *don't* want to return to that. Not at all.

Too little, too late.

Shilo

"Relax your shoulders. Sit as tall as you can, and take deep breaths."

From the back of the yoga class, I follow KC's instructions, my legs crossed and my palms pressed together. Supposedly calming music drifts from the speakers, but the heavy smell of incense makes my head pound.

"Now, let's take a moment to connect with our heart space, dropping our heads forward to stretch our necks."

Next to me, Carpenter mutters something too low for me to catch, his black beanie pulled low over his thick brows. He doesn't look thrilled to be here, but like me, he follows the rest of the class begrudgingly.

Coming to yoga wasn't my idea. Apparently, my attitude was starting to bring everyone down, so KC dragged us all to participate in his class today.

Not that I mind.

Maybe two months ago, I would've minded, but KC's grown on me. Like a fungus. Or a mole.

"As we exhale, let us open our eyes and reach our arms up toward the ceiling, letting our fingertips kiss. We'll do this twice."

Glancing at Carpenter, I whisper from the corner of my mouth, "Why does he keep saying *we*?"

He snorts softly. "My name is Legion, for we are many."

A snicker escapes me, but I cut it short when Tina throws us a chastising look over their shoulder. I've been spending a lot of time with all of them lately, especially the last few weeks since Thanksgiving. Mostly to distract myself from texting Ryann.

I haven't seen or heard from him since he transferred me to the R&D department. Not even at work.

Liza's great, she's super nice and has me running diagnostics on CalTek software, which is cool. But... she's not Ryann.

I know I made the right decision ending our arrangement, but that doesn't mean I don't miss messing up his coffee every day or inventing new ways to irritate him. I miss the things he did to my body. Wish I could say I missed how he made me *feel*, but the truth is, he didn't make me feel very good. Not after the clothes came back on, anyway.

At the front of the class, KC unfolds his legs, leaning up. "Now, we'll move onto all fours as we arch our backs into a stretch."

"His favorite position," Carpenter mutters, rolling over to his hands and knees. I'm not sure if he means yoga or something else, so I keep my mouth shut.

The stretch actually feels good on my lower back after being hunched over a keyboard all day, and the outfit KC lent me is surprisingly comfortable. The shirt hangs loosely while the pants hug all the right places. If I weren't so worried about Dad freaking out, I'd probably wear stuff like this more often. He nearly had a coronary the day Paige gave me a pedicure, and that was bad enough.

As the class goes on, my headache worsens, but I do my best to keep up, even though I'm nowhere near as flexible as KC. Carpenter notices, too, judging by the little comments he keeps making. There's a curious look in his eye when he watches his roommate, though, and I can't help wondering if he's as straight as he claims.

Not that I'm interested in him or anything. I'm not interested in *anyone*, despite KC's failed attempts to find me a boyfriend at various gay bars. Crowds aren't my thing, and I spent the whole time anxious I'd run into Ryann. I'm self-conscious enough knowing he and KC used to sleep together, I don't need to see him touching or kissing someone else.

I was so naive, thinking I could give him my body without my heart.

"Now for our last stretch," KC continues, his voice soothing. "Let's spread our feet apart and slowly bend forward, touching our palms to the floor."

I follow his lead but only make it halfway down when Carpenter whips his head toward me, his amber eyes wide with panic.

"I think I have to fart," he whispers.

A laugh bursts out of me, loud enough to distract the class. Carpenter's shoulders start to shake as he cracks up too, and then we're both losing it like a couple of middle schoolers. He wobbles on his mat, his long arms flailing as he tries to keep his balance, but he's nearly a foot taller than me and ends up dragging me down with him.

We hit the ground hard, my body landing squarely on top of his pelvis.

Wheezing loudly, he grimaces, his broad nose wrinkling in pain. I plant my hands on his chest to push myself up, my face burning.

"Crap, I'm sorry. Are you okay?"

He coughs into his fist. "No, you landed on my nuts. Get me some ice."

For whatever reason, that makes me laugh harder, especially when Carpenter admits that he hoped the sound of our fall covered the fart. Luckily, everyone's gathering their things to leave, but I'm so busy snickering that I completely miss the tall figure looming over us.

"Shilo?"

Ah, jeez.

My smile vanishes instantly at the sound of his voice, and my gaze jerks upward to meet a pair of intense hazel eyes.

Ryann. My stomach flips at the sight of him after so many weeks. He's in basketball shorts and a tank top, his muscled biceps on full display, and his neck glistens with sweat.

I want to lick him. See what he tastes like.

No. *Bad Shilo.*

His eyes shift from me to Carpenter, who's still sprawled beneath me, and the realization hits me like a slap—I'm *straddling* him. Oh, shit.

Scrambling to my feet quickly, I dip my head, offering Carpenter a hand. He groans dramatically when I help him up, one hand cupping his crotch.

"Are you alright?" Ryann asks unevenly, lifting a brow.

"No, Shilo made my balls ache."

My eyes nearly bug out of my skull as I gape at him, cheeks heating. "Wait, no, that's not what–"

"Seriously, I think you broke my dick by how hard you sat on it."

What the hell?!

Slapping my forehead, I squeezing my eyes shut to hide Ryann's reaction to those words, warm embarrassment spreading down my neck.

Behind me, KC clicks his tongue. "TMI, Carpenter. Ry here doesn't want to hear what you two do in the bedroom."

Parting my lids, I glare at his smirk, while Carpenter scoffs. He looks ready to fire off a comeback, but Tina grabs him by the arm and drags him away before he can confirm or deny anything. Panic sparks in my chest.

Ryann's jaw tightens as he watches Carpenter go, his posture stiff. When his gaze swings back to me, I'm shocked by the emotion swimming in his golden-green eyes.

"R-Ryann." I clear my throat, mouth dry. "That wasn't...Carpenter and I aren't—"

"I don't need to hear it." He cuts me off with a firm, flat tone. "It's none of my business. I just saw you across the gym and thought I'd come over to ask how you like your new position with Liza."

"Oh." Disappointment has my shoulders sagging. "Um, it's been good. She's nice."

He waits, silently prompting me to elaborate, but I have nothing else to say. When it becomes clear that's all he's getting, he nods once, running a hand through his damp hair.

"I'll leave you to it, then."

Turning on his heel, he heads back toward the weight room, and my eyes can't help but follow him, drifting down to the tight muscles of his ass in those shorts. I tear my gaze away with effort, only to find KC watching me with an accusatory stare.

He doesn't say anything, just rolls his lips and leads me to his car.

It's much later, when I'm perched on his kitchen counter and he's dyeing my roots, that he finally brings it up.

"So...what was all that stuff with Ry earlier?"

I squint at him, shrugging as I keep my focus on the TV in the living room where Carpenter and Tina are slaying zombies. "What stuff?"

KC makes an impatient noise as he dries my freshly washed waves with a diffuser. "I don't want to get all up in people's business, Shi, but—"

"Since when?" Carpenter scoffs from the couch, earning a sharp glare from KC.

"I'm not talking to you, especially after you ruined my yoga class today."

"I told you I was gassy, and you didn't believe me."

Blowing out a long breath, KC shuts his eyes like he's praying. "Straight boys are going to be the death of me."

Tina cackles, leaning closer to Carpenter and whispering something that makes him grin. KC ignores them, turning his full attention back to me.

"Something's been up with you for weeks. I figured it might have been a man situation, but I didn't know the man in question was Ryann."

I open my mouth to deny it, but the words catch in my throat when I meet his gaze. I've never been good at lying. Paige always says I wear my heart on my sleeve, and right now, I hate how easy I am to read.

Licking my lips, I glance down at my lap. "We had a...thing. And I ended it."

"A thing?"

"Yeah." My gaze flicks up from beneath my lashes. "And I know that you two had a thing, too."

The living room goes silent. KC's face twists into a grimace as he sets down the diffuser before reaching up to tug at his braid.

"It's not that I was trying to keep it from you, Shilo. After we went our separate ways, he had me sign an NDA. I'm not allowed to bring it up."

Honestly, I'm not surprised. It sounds exactly like something a rich jerk would do. Still, a part of me wonders why he never made *me* sign one.

"Well, it doesn't matter because I kind of broke things off with him."

"Why?"

The question comes from Carpenter, and we all turn to look at him.

"Like, respectfully, if I were gay, I'd be climbing that dude like a tree."

KC narrows his eyes briefly, studying his roommate, while I wrestle with my thoughts.

"He's kind of...emotionally unavailable."

"If I'd known something was going on between you two, I'd have told you that," KC says with a sigh. "Ry isn't the commitment type. He won't even let his hookups sleep in his bed."

"Figured that out the hard way," I grumble, guilt tugging at my chest. Ryann *had* warned me from the start that it would be nothing more than sex.

I just didn't plan on liking the things he said to me so much.

"Some unsolicited and probably horrible advice?" Satisfied with his work, KC ruffles my hair as he pulls me off the counter. "The only way to get over someone like him is to fuck it out of your system."

Tina laughs, tossing the controller onto the couch cushions as they stand with a stretch. "That's your advice for everything."

"And it's never steered me wrong. There's nothing a good, hard fuck can't fix."

"Christ," Carpenter mutters, shaking his head like he's trying to clear it while KC smirks.

But I don't just want to *fuck.* I want...

Well, I don't know what I want, but it's not a one night stand. That would only worsen the situation I find myself in whenever Ryann treats me like I'm precious before growing cold and distant. Giving strangers access to my body isn't going to fix that. I'm self-aware enough to know that I'd end up chasing a feeling and making myself sick when I never find it.

So I just shrug to end the conversation, mumbling my goodbyes as I grab my stuff and slip out of their apartment. Something tells me they wouldn't understand even if I tried explaining it to them. I don't fully understand it myself.

Soft snowflakes melt against the windshield as I drive home, pulling my hoodie tighter around myself to fight off the chill. The streets are quiet this late at night, peaceful. I take my time, letting the Christmas lights blur past me, their colors soft and warm against the darkness. Not for the first time, I try to find that sense of wonder everyone talks about during the holidays, but it's just not there. If I'm honest, the season has always felt depressing.

Giving gifts stresses me out, the expectations of it. I've also been told I'm hard to buy for, which makes no sense. What part of *'I want a thousand-watt fully modular power supply for my PC'* is hard to understand?

I'm not even halfway home when I get distracted, my thoughts wandering, and hit a curb. Mom's Corolla shudders violently.

"*Dammit.*" Cursing under my breath, I pull off to the side of the road and climb out, praying with all my might that it's just uneven pavement. But, of course, my prayers go unanswered.

"Are you frickin' kidding me?" I howl in frustration as I spot the completely flat back tire. Just great. God, why me?

Throwing my hood up, I blow on my cold hands and try to remember how to change a tire. Dad tried showing me when I first got my license, but I was sixteen and my attention span was kind of short. I think I need a jack. And that metal X thing. It can't be too hard.

Finding what I need after rooting around in the trunk, I glare up at the sky when the flakes turn into freezing rain. Like this couldn't get any worse.

The spare tire is heavy, but I heave it out onto the ground before focusing on the near-impossible task of jacking the car off the ground. I can admit that I'm not a strong guy, all of my muscles are in my brain, and the frickin' thing will *not* cooperate. I even stand on the lever, hoping my body weight will get it to move while my clothes thoroughly soak through, but it does no good. I'm stuck.

As I shift to jump down, the rain-slicked metal betrays me. My foot slips, and though I manage to catch myself, the sharp, rusted edge of the fender slices deep into my left palm.

"*Ouch*, frick!"

Kicking the offending tire with a furious shout, I slide back into the driver's seat, dripping wet. Blood pools in my palm, and I seethe as the sting sharpens with every passing second. It's too dark to tell how bad the cut is, so I wipe it off on my jeans with a hiss of pain, my teeth chattering violently. Reaching for my phone on the center console, I fumble to unlock it, my fingers clumsy from the cold.

Clearly, I need help, but who would be awake right now? Definitely not Dad. KC said he was going to bed when I left, and I don't have Carpenter or Tina's numbers.

Scrolling through my pitiful list of contacts, my thumb hovers over Ryann's name.

No. Bad idea.

Would he even answer, anyway? I could call Paige, but with all the preparations for CalTek's Christmas party, she's probably asleep. Maybe Declan?

Debating for all of five seconds, I hit the call button and chew on my fingernail, blood from my cut rolling down my arm beneath the sleeve.

After five or so rings, he finally answers.

"Shilo? What's wrong?"

His voice is slightly raspy from sleep, and the sound of it sends goosebumps over my frozen skin.

"Hi, Mr. Callahan, I'm sorry to wake you, but I–"

"Call me Ryann, dammit."

His grumpy growl ignites a fire in my veins, and I grin despite the burning in my palm and sopping clothes.

"Ryann. Sorry. I, uh, blew a tire on the way home from hanging out with Kansas, and I can't get the jack to work. I would have called someone else, but it's like one in the morning, and it's raining pretty hard, plus I also scraped my hand, and I might get tetanus–"

"Slow down. Where are you?"

Glancing out the window, I give him the name of the last street sign I passed.

"I'll be there in ten minutes. Stay in the car."

He hangs up without waiting for me to respond, and I stare at my dark screen, raindrops pelting the window. Warm air from the heater makes me shiver as I press a few napkins to my wound before resting my head against the steering wheel.

True to his word, Ryann pulls up beside me precisely ten minutes later, stepping out of his car just as I climb out of mine.

"What happened?" he asks, opening an umbrella and holding it above me, dressed in jeans.

"I accidentally hit a curb. I think it popped the bead."

He follows me to the passenger side, scanning the mess I've made before studying me with a frown. "Jesus Christ, you're soaking wet. Let me see your hand."

Taking it gingerly, he pulls away the bloody napkins with a grimace. "We need to get that cleaned. Come on."

Ryann starts to lead me by the wrist toward his car, his touch unbearably warm against my frozen skin, and I pull back stubbornly. "W-what about the t-tire?"

"I'll have Declan help me with it in the morning when it stops raining. You're freezing, Shilo. Let me get you dry and take care of that cut."

It's a terrible idea to get in his car. I *know* it is. But my jaw hurts from how hard my teeth are chattering, and I can't feel my toes anymore. So with a reluctant nod, I let him guide me to the passenger seat. He gently pushes me down into the warm leather, shaking out the umbrella before climbing behind the wheel. Heat blasts from the vents, filling the car with welcome warmth, and I sigh softly, sinking into his familiar scent.

He glances at me sideways. "My place is closer than yours. It'll make more sense if we go there."

Logically, I know he's right. My head tells me I should insist he take me home, but my heart has other ideas. I nod weakly and shut my eyes, curling up in the seat as soft music plays through the speakers, lulling me into a fragile peace.

I must have dozed off because the next thing I know, Ryann's nudging me awake in the parking garage beneath his building with an odd look on his face.

"You alright?"

Blinking, I nod, rubbing at my eyes before hissing as the jagged cut on my palm flares in pain. "I'm fine. Just sleepy."

His gaze lingers for a moment before he turns away. "Let's get you inside."

The elevator ride to his condo feels endless. I keep yawning, wet strands of hair clinging to my forehead as I fight the urge to lean against him for support. My entire body feels drained, utterly sapped of energy.

When we step into his foyer, I notice the puddle of water forming beneath me. Every step leaves droplets on his marble floors as we move through the living room and down a long hallway. Eventually, he leads me into a spacious bathroom. Why do we *always* end up in bathrooms?

"I'll get you something to wear. Take off those clothes and warm up." Pulling out a towel from the cupboard, he hands it to me before disappearing back into the hall. I watch him go, debating on whether I should do what he says.

Being naked around him is the last thing that should happen right now, but one look in the backlit mirror above a black granite sink has me grimacing. I look like a drowned cat, purple streaks running down the sides of my face and neck from the fresh dye KC just put in earlier.

Turning my back on my reflection, I pull off the soaked hoodie and toss it to the ground with a wet *plop* before kicking off my socks and shoes. There's no shirt underneath, so my jeans follow shortly after, and I wrap the soft towel around my shoulders to hide my torso. Luckily, it's big enough that it almost covers my balls, but it's not like Ryann hasn't seen them before.

He knocks on the door a second later, stepping inside with a pair of sweats and a University of Washington T-shirt. "They'll be loose on you, but they're dry. Come into the kitchen when you're dressed."

Without a backward glance, he leaves again, and I do my best to wipe away the streaks of dye staining my skin before pulling on his clothes. The shirt hangs down to my thighs, and the pants need to be tightened at the waist, but they smell like him. The scent has my stomach flipping, blood rushing south, and before I know it, my neglected dick is stirring to life.

Frickin' hell.

Cheeks burning, I tuck myself up into the waistband, trying to focus on anything but the fact that I'm hard from just wearing his clothes.

Once I've gotten my hair as dry as possible, I pad barefoot into the kitchen. Ryann's leaning against the counter, sipping from a steaming mug in the dim lighting. When his gaze flicks over me, something shifts in his expression, darkening briefly before he turns away. Whatever that look meant, I don't have time to figure it out.

"Come here." He turns on the sink, setting down his mug and handing me another one when I reach him. "It's chamomile. My mother used to make it for me when I couldn't sleep. Give me your hand."

Squinting at him, I take a loud slurp of the tea. "Only if you say pretty please."

His lips twitch, curving into a crooked smile. "Pretty please, Shilo, let me clean out your cut so you don't get tetanus."

Holy shit.

Shocked that he actually said it, I let him run my palm under warm water, studying his profile as he scrubs out the wound. A few days' worth of stubble dusts his chin, giving him a rugged look amplified by his messy hair.

My eyes greedily take him in, soaking up every detail. "I don't think I've ever seen you wear jeans before. It's weird."

He huffs, keeping his gaze down as he spreads some ointment on my hand. "These are probably the only pair I own. I threw them on quickly when you called. You're lucky this won't need stitches."

His gentle touch sends mixed signals to my brain, each electric pulse skittering from my palm to my toes. As he wraps the bandage around my hand, he rubs it lightly to ensure it's secure, his face so close now that his breath tickles my nose.

"Are you hungry?"

Yes, but not for food. "I'm alright. Kansas fed me."

"At least someone did," he mutters, looking down to where his hand still holds mine. The weight of his tone reminds me of what happened at the gym earlier, and my chest tightens.

"Carpenter is straight," I blurt out quickly. "At least, I think. I'm pretty sure he's got a secret crush on Kansas, but I haven't known him long enough to tell."

Ryann stills, his hazel gaze shifting to my face, unreadable. The silence stretches, and the back of my neck burns with embarrassment.

"I just thought I'd make that clear, b-because of how things looked earlier. But I'm not really into Carpenter that way...just so you know."

"I said it wasn't my business," he replies gruffly, letting go of my hand before turning away. "You're a big boy, Shilo. You can interact with whoever you want, however you want."

I've never hated the sound of my name on his lips more than this moment.

Opening a trunk near the bar, he pulls out a blanket and pillow, tossing them onto the couch. "If it's alright with you, I'm going back to bed. I'm exhausted. You can use the couch tonight, and I'll take you back to your car in the morning to change that tire."

KC's words about Ryann not letting hookups in his bed flash through my mind as I glare at the sectional, wondering how much bodily fluids might be lurking on it. I'm never sitting on that thing again.

"I'll just take the floor. Or the bathtub,"

His brows furrow up as he freezes, studying me with a narrowed gaze. "Why don't you want to sleep on my couch?"

"Cuz," I mumble, ducking my head to place my empty mug in the sink.

Within three strides, he's in front me, his fingers tilting my chin up. "Don't hide from me, Shilo. Tell me why you'd rather sleep in a bathtub."

"Because you... you've probably never fucked anyone there. And I don't want to sleep someplace where that's happened."

His lips part slightly, eyes widening as they flit between mine. I'm so uncomfortable that I focus on his ear instead of meeting his gaze. After a moment, his hand trails down when I swallow, thumb brushing gently against the hollow of my throat. He can probably feel my pulse hammering wildly, and my breath grows shallow, but I refuse to look at him.

"Alright," he finally says softly, nodding as if coming to a decision. "Okay. Let's go."

Turning abruptly, his hand falls away, leaving me cold and confused as he strides toward the hall.

"Go where?"

"To bed. Come on before I change my mind."

Excitement jolts me awake, lighting a fire under my previously exhausted feet. I hurry after him, blinking in awe as I step into his bedroom for the first time. The bed is massive, swathed in gray and black linens, under a canopy of gauzy curtains. A full wall of windows lets in the soft glow of city lights, and beyond a set of closed French doors, I catch sight of a balcony with a lounger.

"Your room is bigger than Kansas's apartment," I marvel, turning slowly to take it all in.

Ryann shrugs, disappearing into a walk-in closet that's probably large enough to qualify as a third bedroom. "Believe it or not, Declan's is bigger. He went for space while I went for practicality."

"What about *that* is practical?" Following him, I point to a crystal chandelier hanging from the ceiling.

He throws me an annoyed glance over his shoulder. "Do you mind? I need to change out of these jeans that you seem to think are weird."

Oh. Turning back around, I give him privacy as I jump onto his bed, nuzzling into soft pillows. His spicy scent is everywhere—on the sheets, on my clothes, on my skin. Something about that fact makes my brain fuzzy and my dick harder than it already was.

With a groan, I slip under the covers, sighing at the warmth just as Ryann reenters the room. He's wearing a pair of sweats now, his broad shoulders bare, and he pauses for half a second when his eyes land on me.

"By all means, make yourself comfortable," he says dryly, a faint edge to his tone.

Suddenly self-conscious, I bolt upright with a startled squeak. "S-sorry, did you mean for me to sleep on the floor? I'll move–"

"Lay back down and go to sleep," he growls, flicking off the light as he crawls in beside me.

Pulling my knees to my chest, I glance at him sideways. "Why are you angry?"

"I'm not. Go to sleep."

Grumbling softly, I flop onto my side, keeping my arms locked around my knees as I face him. "Sure sounds like it."

He puts a hand behind his head and doesn't respond, stretching onto his back beneath the covers. I can feel the warmth from his body even though he's on the very edge of the bed, still close enough for me to reach out and touch him if I wanted, but I don't. Instead, I keep my hands to myself, studying his silhouette in the dark. The curtains are open, letting in just enough light to splay shadows over his broad chest, abs rising and falling with every breath, full lips slightly parted.

I have to bite back a whimper as I squeeze my thighs from the pressure in my sweatpants.

"Close your eyes, Shilo," he sighs, and my lids fall shut even though I doubt I'll get any sleep with how horny I am. Maybe it'll eventually go away if I ignore it?

Except it doesn't. The longer I lay next to him, the more uncomfortable it gets, and I rotate around like a rotisserie chicken until Ryann eventually snarls at me.

"What the fuck is wrong with you?"

"I can't sleep," I whine, glaring up at the canopy when I settle onto my back, and he leans over me.

"Yes, I've noticed. Why?"

"It's just that I..." Trailing off, my teeth find my bottom lip as I shake my head, about to turn away.

He grabs my jaw before I can hide. "Goddammit, spit it out so that I can get some rest. It's just that you *what*?"

"I'm *hard*, okay?" Tearing my face from his grip, I flip over and cross my arms. "It's been weeks since I've touched it, and now that you're close by, my dick won't go down. It hurts."

He's quiet for so long that I think he might have fallen asleep, but then I feel the sheets rustle behind me. "Do you need to come, baby doll?"

His accent is thick, rumbling in my ear, and the whimper I've held back finally falls from my lips.

"Yes. Please."

"Mm, roll over and touch yourself."

A shiver wracks my body as I follow his command, finding his gaze intently on me when I reach under the covers to pull out my length. As soon as my hand wraps around it, I hum in relief, feeling my eyes sting with that first stroke.

Ryann reaches out to pull the blanket down, exposing me to the open air, his deep groan vibrating the bed as he watches me pleasure myself.

"Have you been holding out for me, Shilo?" He sounds pleased, taking my hand off my shaft, and he brings it to his lips with a smirk when I cry out in protest. "Has my little doll been waiting for permission to come?"

Honestly, I hadn't intended to, but I think he's right. I *like* it when my pleasure belongs to him.

"Please," I whisper, panting as he fills my palm with his spit before placing it back on my cock.

"Please, what?"

With his fingers wrapped around mine, he starts to jerk me slowly, pushing down on my hips when I try to thrust into our fists.

"Please let me come, Ryann."

"Fuck, you sound so sweet when you beg," he breathes, pumping me faster, making me feel so good that my neck arches off the pillow when I toss my head back and moan.

Slick sounds fill the room, each pass he makes over my tip sending rivulets of precum down my length. It drips onto my sack, coating my taint, hole clenching with need.

I want him inside me again, but I...can't let it happen.

So instead, I let him work me with my own fist until I'm shooting onto my shirt, painting it with cum while I turn my face into the pillow and bite. Once he's squeezed every last drop out of me, Ryann lifts his fingers to my mouth, growling softly when I open automatically and suck my release from his skin. Any remaining ounce of energy completely vanishes, leaving my body limp as I turn onto my side with a blissful smile and close my eyes.

He huffs next to me. "Your shirt is a mess."

"Technically, it's *your* shirt." Cracking open a lid, I catch sight of the bulge in the crotch of his sweats and scoot closer. "Do you want me to—"

"No, Shilo, I want to go to sleep," he snaps, rolling away from me, but I'm too tired to even care about his surliness.

"Kay." Yawning into my arm, I curl up against his back, feeling his spine go rigid. I don't move, though.

He relaxes after a while, anyway, and the warmth of his body, combined with his soft breath, has me falling into one of the best sleeps I've ever had.

Ryann

I'm drowning in smoke, the heat pressing in on me from all sides, suffocating. Flames lick at the walls, devouring everything in their path. I hear my mother's voice calling out for me, but I can't find her. I'm running, searching, but the fire is everywhere, closing in, choking the air from my lungs.

"Mom!" I scream, my voice breaking. "Mom, where are you?"

But there's no answer. Just the roar of the fire and my heart pounding in my ears. I'm too late. I'm always too late.

"No, I gasp, the word tearing from my throat. "No, please— "

A hand grabs my shoulder, shaking me, and suddenly the fire is gone. My eyes snap open, and I'm not in the house anymore. I'm in my bed, the sheets tangled around me, drenched in sweat. My chest is heaving, my heart racing, and it takes a moment for me to realize where I am.

"Ry?" Shilo says softly, his hand still on my shoulder. "I think you're having a bad dream. It's okay, you're safe."

Safe. The word barely registers as I struggle to catch my breath, my mind still trapped in the nightmare.

"It was the fire," I manage to choke out. The admission slips from my tongue before I can stop it, and I hate how weak it makes me feel. But Shilo doesn't flinch. Instead, he shifts closer, wrapping his arms around me. I don't resist—I can't. I bury my face in his shoulder, my whole body trembling as the memories flood back, relentless. "My mother, she...she didn't make it."

She never makes it.

His fingers thread through my hair, grounding me with gentle touches as he holds me until the shaking subsides. "It's okay, everything's alright."

But it isn't. The guilt twists inside me, sharp and unforgiving. It's been months since I've had the dream, but every time I do, it's ten times worse than the last. Clearly, I'm due for some form of physical release. I only dream when I'm wound too tight. Apparently, my grueling workout at the gym earlier wasn't enough.

Gradually, the tension in my body starts to ease, the tremors subsiding, but I still feel restless. Ill-at-ease. I can tell that Shilo is awake by the uneven rhythm of his breathing, and I finally pull back to gaze down into his eyes, brows pinched with concern.

"Thank you."

"Yeah." Clearing his throat, he licks his lips, searching my face. "I mean, you're welcome. Want to talk about it?"

"No."

The word hangs heavy between us, harsher than I meant it, and his face falls slightly. "Okay."

He tries to pull away, but I hang onto him tighter, suddenly desperate to forget about the weight of the past threatening to pull me back under, to forget about the loneliness I've been drowning under for weeks. God, I've missed him. I've tried to keep my distance, give him space, but when I saw him sitting on some broad-shouldered stud across the gym, I'd seen red. And then tonight, bringing him home with me, I tried to keep things professional for his sake. All of that went out the window the moment he begged me to make him come. He's all I've thought about since Thanksgiving, dammit.

Pressing my mouth to his throat, I feel his surprised squeak vibrate against my lips as I take his supple skin in between my teeth.

"Oh," he breathes softly, gripping my hair to keep me latched on, and I chuckle, sucking marks into his flesh.

With a quick roll of our bodies, I pin him beneath me, kissing and nipping until I make my way down his shirt—or, *my* shirt, as he stated—still covered with his earlier release. That gorgeous cock of his is hard again, straining in his sweats when I rub my stubbled cheek over his inner thigh. He palms himself, watching me with hooded eyes, and I caress down his legs until I have his bare feet in my grip.

"I've been fantasizing about this," I growl, planting a kiss on the sole of his foot before sucking his toes into my mouth.

He coughs in disbelief, lips hanging open and cheeks flushed, a wet spot forming on his crotch as his dick leaks for me. "W-what are you doing?!"

A deep groan is my only response, picking up his other foot to do the same, and my little doll shudders as he squeezes the base of his shaft.

"That would be the *weirdest* thing to come from," he complains, yanking his foot away, and I grin as I crawl up his body.

"It's okay to like it, baby. I won't tell anyone." Diving for his mouth, I press my cock against him before curling my fingers under the waistband of his sweats. "Can I take these off?"

"*Please,*" he nods earnestly, practically ripping them from his body to free his dick, and a chuckle escapes me at his impatience. My horny doll needs to come again.

A glance at the clock tells me I have exactly four hours before I have to be up for work. Probably earlier if I plan on having Declan help change Shilo's tire. There's no way I'll sleep again with the dream weighing heavily on my mind, at least not unless I come as well, but I shake those thoughts away as I envelop Shilo's length in my mouth.

He cries out, bucking his hips and hitting my throat, a spurt of precum layering my tongue. So fucking delicious. Sucking cock has never been my favorite—I'd much rather be the one on the receiving end—but Shilo's every reaction has me damn near addicted. His breathy moans, soft whimpers, fingers flexing on the sheets like he doesn't know where to put his hands. And I take my time with it, too, lazily licking at his shaft, pulling those sounds from him that have me aching and heavy. Much better than the quick blowjobs I gave him in my office.

Spit drips down over his sack, pooling in his hole, and I gently suck one of his smooth balls into my mouth, reveling in the way he clutches my shoulders tightly.

"Oh god, Ryann, that...I like that."

He gasps when I hum, the slight noise vibrating his sack before I give the other ball a turn, loving the fact that no one's ever done this to him before. No one but me.

"Lift your legs, doll." Helping him bend his knees to his chest, I groan at the sight of his pink pucker on display, wet and inviting. Holding Shilo's widened gaze, I slowly lower myself down, flicking my tongue out to lap at his hole, causing him to jolt and squeak in surprise. His flushed cheeks become darker, pupils swallowing the blue in his eyes as his head falls back against the pillow, throat working around a whimper.

"Feel good?"

He can only stammer in response as he pushes his ass against my face, and I use my thumbs to spread him wider. He tastes so sweet, so uniquely *Shilo.* I fuck his hole with my tongue until he starts to shake, a sure sign that he's about to come.

"H-hey, wait," he protests when I pull away, his chest heaving.

Smirking darkly, I grab onto his jaw. "Open up, baby. Stick out your tongue."

Doing as he's told, his lips part, allowing me to let a string of spit drip into his mouth.

"Swallow. See how good you taste."

"Mmm." His eyes roll back when he follows my command, and I nearly come from the sight. I need to be inside of him *now.*

Reaching into the nightstand, I kiss him deeply as I dig around for supplies, breaking away with a frown when I find only lube. Shit.

"I don't have any condoms," I murmur, and Shilo freezes, expression flattening.

Oh, no. I don't like that.

"Can I fuck you, baby doll?" Nuzzling his neck, I kiss my way up his face, nipping at his earlobe. "We can do it just like this. I'll hold you and go slow, I promise."

"B-but what about condoms?" He rasps, squirming when I lick inside his ear.

"I'm on PrEP, and I got tested before you were hired. All clear." Pulling back, I gaze down at him with a lifted brow. "And I'm assuming you are as well unless there's been someone else other than me...?"

He blinks, purple strands sticking to his forehead with sweat. "No. Only you."

The tension in my shoulders melts away as relief washes over me. It shouldn't. He's young—he should be out experiencing life with people his own age, like Carpenter, but I *don't want him to.* The thought of anyone else touching him drives me fucking mad.

"What do you say?" I kiss him gently, grinding my hips against his.

A flicker of uncertainty crosses his features, but he licks his lips and nods slowly. "Yeah. Yes."

"Shilo." Holding his face between my palms, I gaze intently into his eyes. "Don't say yes if you aren't sure. I'd never want you to feel like you can't say no."

Surprisingly, he scoffs, wrapping his legs around my waist. "I'm sure. Please, I...I want it."

We stare at each other for a few moments, and when I see nothing but resolve reflected back at me, I give him another kiss before shucking off my underwear, heart thudding in my chest. "Let me get you ready."

His hole is already softened from the way I devoured it, but he's still far too tight to take me. Using the bottle of warming lube, I work him open with my fingers, backing off his prostate every time he nears the edge of orgasm. I'm so hard it's painful, and by the time he's prepped enough, I almost sob with relief when my cock breaches that first ring of muscle. With a pop, his body sucks me in, velvet heat surrounding my length and squeezing it tight. My instincts scream at me to go hard, to pound into him until I'm spilling my load, but I promised him I'd take it slow, so I do just that.

Pressing him into the mattress, my arms hold him steady as I work myself inside him little by little. He's pliant beneath me, our tongues gliding lazily, and he moans into my mouth once I'm seated to the hilt.

"So full," he whimpers, fingers dancing down my spine as I pull out before gently thrusting back in.

Fuck, he feels too good. His thighs squeeze me tightly, hips meeting my rhythm, and my self-control hangs by a thread. I can't take my eyes off his face, all the emotions crossing his features like an open book, the feel of his breath on my cheek. His reactions tell me what he likes and what he doesn't, his lashes fluttering when I hit his prostate just right, my name on his lips. I've never fucked anyone face-to-face before, and the more I watch him, the more I understand why. It's intoxicating.

"Right there," he cries out, nails digging into my skin, the sting making me shudder as I feel my cock begin to pulse. "God, there, Ry. Don't stop."

Reaching between us, I jerk his length, needing him to come before I do. His teeth find his bottom lip as he trembles, and I take it between my own when he erupts in my hand for the second time tonight. As his hole clenches around me, I follow close behind, painting his walls with my cum, pumping him full.

Once we're both spent, I collapse on top of him, my hips still moving slowly even though my balls are drained, but I don't want to pull out yet. He feels so soft, so right. So...mine.

Eventually, though, my over-sensitive cock starts to protest. Leaning back on my knees, I watch myself slip out of his body as my release drips from his hole. On instinct, I reach out to push it back in with my fingers, causing Shilo to flinch.

"Sorry," I murmur, realizing he's probably tender, but I'm mesmerized by the sticky mess trying to escape. The thought of my cum inside him, marking him, has my dick trying to rally for round two. This is definitely something I could get used to.

Immediately, my brain has a steel door slamming shut over those thoughts, souring my mood.

I don't get attached. I don't sleep in bed with my hookups, and I definitely don't fantasize about fucking them before work so that my cum leaks out of their ass all day.

This is just a one-off. The dream muddled my senses, that's all. I'll be back to normal in the morning.

Shilo watches me as I get off the bed, heading for the bathroom to dampen a cloth. When I return, his brows are pinched with worry, but I say nothing as I quickly clean us up. He finally breaks the silence after I've grabbed a fresh shirt from my closet.

"Do you want me to sleep on the couch now?"

His voice sounds so small and defeated. I hate it. I hate that I've made him feel this way.

"No." Tossing him the shirt, I turn my back and sit on the edge of the bed. "That shirt is now a bio-hazard. Switch it out so we can sleep."

Much to my relief, he snorts, throwing the soiled shirt on the floor before nestling under into the sheets. "I like wearing your clothes. They smell nice."

"Don't get used to it. I'm taking my shirt back in the morning."

He hums contentedly, curling on his side, and I watch him for a few minutes, battling demons in my head.

I want to slide in behind him, curve my body around his, and press my face to his hair. Place my palm on his chest and sleep to the steady beat of his heart. But instead, I climb beneath the covers and face the windows, leaving my arms empty.

I can't *want.* There's no place in my life for such things, I don't deserve it. Not after what I've done. There's only Cal-Tek.

Warmth suddenly blooms on my back as Shilo once again lays against me. His arm slips around my waist, pressing his face into my skin. Making me the little spoon.

"What's your mom's name?"

Stiffening briefly, I force myself to relax. "Ava."

Holding my breath, I wait for him to launch into questions I'm not ready to answer, but instead, a yawn is his only response.

"Night, Ryann," he mumbles, caressing my abs, and I can't help the laugh of disbelief that leaves my throat.

He's so sweet. So *good.* My mere existence sullies him.

"Good night, Shilo."

I promised myself years ago that I'd never let anyone close, and now I'm practically letting someone under my skin. It's too much. These feelings burning in my chest are too much.

Now that he's in, though, I don't know if I'll be able to get him out. It's terrifying.

As his quiet snores fill the silence, soft hair tickling my shoulder, I fall deeper into this pit until only one thing becomes abundantly clear.

I know what I have to do.

Shilo

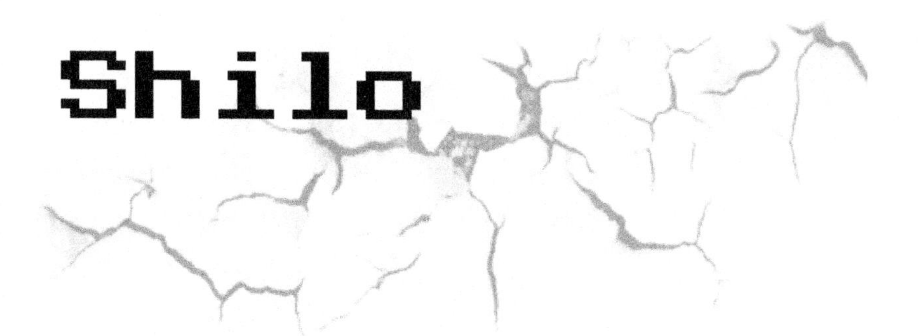

"Why do I even have to go to this stupid thing?"

"It's not stupid, Shilo." Paige throws me an exasperated glance as she leads me down a hall lined with Christmas trees toward CalTek's ballroom.

Yeah. CalTek has a frickin' ballroom. They only use it for special occasions, though, like tonight. Not only is this the annual company Christmas party, but they've also combined it with a charity event, so the place is *packed.* The dress code is also black tie required. Which, according to Paige, means I had to wear a tuxedo.

I don't even *own* a tuxedo. I wasn't even going to come, but for whatever reason, Ronin Callahan sent out an email declaring that all employees were required to attend. So here I am—dressed in a rented tux that cost way too much, my hair half up and combed out of my face. I hate it.

Mom loves it, though. She took so many pictures that I was embarrassed, all teary-eyed because I never got to go to prom. It would have been a nice moment if Dad hadn't ruined it by asking why I didn't have a date. Maybe I should have asked

Tina since KC is bringing Carpenter, but I didn't think about it until just now.

"There's a rumor going 'round that Ronin is making some kind of announcement tonight." My sister stops before a pair of double doors thrown open to reveal an ornately decorated space within. From this vantage point, I can see giant glowing ice sculptures and a lit-up tree that's gotta be at least twenty feet tall. There's violinists, too, and caterers running around with trays of champagne. Jeez.

Declan appears out of nowhere, deep red tie matching Paige's evening gown, and he sweeps her into his arms before kissing her lips. "Well, don't you look ravishing, my dear."

She giggles and I gag, which earns me a laugh as he reaches out to bump my fist.

"You look great, too, Shilo. Love the bow tie."

"Thanks," I mumble, shuffling awkwardly on my feet. It's purple, like my hair. And my nails.

Paige links an arm with each of us, putting herself in the middle as she strides into the ballroom on six-inch heels. "Come on, boys, let's get this show on the road. I need some rum cake."

Round tables draped in dark blue cloths fill one side of the room, accompanied by a bar and walls lined with food. Overhead, the largest chandelier I've ever seen glitters, its ropes of crystal cascading like frozen snowflakes. My eyes find KC immediately—he's impossible to miss in a bright pink tuxedo. Where did he even find something like that, anyway? Carpenter stands next to him, sporting a matching tie and an irritated expression, arms crossed. They both wave when they spot me.

"Gonna go see my friends," I whisper to Paige, ignoring the relieved smile on her face as I take off. She and Mom have been ecstatic that I've been getting out of the house, but I wish they wouldn't be so obvious about it.

"God, you look sexy." KC kisses my cheek, which I wipe off. "And you even match with Ry. Did you both plan that?"

Frowning, I sweep my gaze across the room in search of Ryann. "Huh? No, have you seen him?"

"Like five minutes ago with his date."

Date? My heart plummets to the floor.

It's been seven days since I fell asleep in his bed, and I haven't heard from him since. The morning after we had sex, I'd woken up practically on top of him, and we'd humped each other while making out. He ended up pushing my head down to come in my mouth before forcing me to eat breakfast and then drove me back to my car. It was stupid because, despite myself, I'd been hoping he would text me afterward, but he didn't. I wasn't even surprised. Kind of expected it.

But a *date?*

My stomach roils.

Carpenter snags a glass of champagne from a nearby server, flagging down another one carrying a tray of hors d'oeuvres. "Your guys' job is awesome. Where do I apply?"

"That's the fifth crab cake you've stuffed your face with since we got here," KC protests in disgust, and his roommate grins with a full mouth.

"Yeah, cuz they're delicious. You should try the cheese balls."

Rolling his eyes dramatically, KC turns to me. "I wasn't even going to bring him. Why did I bring him, Shilo?"

"Because you love me," Carpenter grunts, zeroing in on the dessert table.

The two of them bicker back and forth while I morph into a wallflower, leaning back to watch the party unfold. Everyone's laughing, drinking, *merry and bright,* but I feel...alone. Outcast. They all have their special person tonight, but I'm personless. Not for the first time, I wonder why I have difficulty connecting with people. Wishing my brain wasn't broken. Wishing I was normal.

"Here, try this." Carpenter's fingers shove something sweet into my mouth, ruining my wallowing, and I glare at him as I chew on the sticky substance.

"W'th hell?"

He wiggles his brows. "Good, right? It's butter mochi. Now try this one."

As soon as I swallow, he pries my mouth open again with some kind of cherry chocolate truffle, placing it on my tongue. The explosion of flavor causes an involuntary moan to leave my throat.

And, of course, Ryann chooses that exact moment to make his presence known as his familiar scent fills my nostrils.

"Evening."

My eyes snap up to where he's gazing down at me with a raised brow, looking suave as hell in a tux that probably cost a few thousand dollars. KC smirks at me, and that's when I realize that Carpenter's fingers are still in my mouth. Panicking, I do the only thing my anxious brain can think of.

I bite down.

"Ow, motherfuck!"

"H-hi, Mr. Callahan," I stammer as I swallow the treat, licking its sweetness from my lips.

Ryann briefly catches the movement before turning his attention to Carpenter, who's shaking out his fingers with a grimace. "Are you alright?"

KC snorts. "He's fine, ignore him. Who's your date, Ry?"

With a jolt, I notice that someone is standing next to him. A tall someone. With long, luscious auburn curls and an hourglass figure. A very, very *feminine* figure.

My face twists in confusion as the woman's perfectly painted smile lights up the room. She extends her hand to KC, her voice dripping with charm. "Hello, nice to meet you. I'm Olivia. Ryann's girlfriend."

His...

Wait.

KC's delicate brows slam together. "I'm sorry, I think I might have misheard. Did you just say that you're Ryann's *girlfriend?*"

Her sparkling blue eyes tighten in uncertainty as she tilts her head. "Yes, that's what I said."

A strangled noise escapes the back of my throat like I've just been sucker-punched. Whatever they say next is drowned out by the roaring in my ears. I feel someone's gaze on me, *his* gaze, but all I can focus on is the sweat gathering on my nape as my vision swims, a suffocating heat surging through me. The hors d'oeuvres in my stomach turn to lead.

Stupid, stupid Shilo. Thrown to the curb *again.*

"S'cuse me," I mumble, swallowing bile as I spin on my heel and bolt.

Someone calls after me, but I don't stop. Shoving through the crowd, I ignore the sting in my eyes as I push toward the courtyard doors. Cold air bites at my skin when I burst outside, the cheerful glow of Christmas lights mocking me. Hunching over, I wrap my arms around myself and fight the urge to vomit. If I had any idea where the bathroom was, I'd probably be there already.

A few people linger nearby, snapping photos in front of a decorated fountain, but none of them spare me a glance when I collapse onto the fountain's ledge, scowling at my reflection in the water. No matter what I do—no matter how much I change—I still can't stand the sight of myself.

In the murky depths, another face suddenly joins mine, hazel eyes I know all too well pinched with concern.

"Shilo," Ryann says quietly. "Let me explain."

I can't bring myself to look at him directly, so I glare at his reflection instead. "I thought you were gay."

He sighs heavily. "I am."

"Then what the *hell*?"

He glances over his shoulder before reaching out, his hand brushing my arm. "Let's talk somewhere quieter."

"Don't touch me," I mutter, shoving his hand away as I stand. Without looking back, I march toward a weeping willow at the courtyard's edge. Behind me, I hear the soft sound of his suede shoes tapping against the concrete as he follows.

Once beneath the sweeping branches, I cross my arms tightly and put as much space between us as I can, shivering against the biting breeze. It's dark here, the shadows swallowing Ryann's face as he watches me with his hands shoved into his pockets. Seething silently, I wait for him to speak.

"You've heard of AVA, right?" He asks, the question catching me off guard. I nod slowly, my chest tightening at the thought of how he named it after his mother.

"The program wasn't originally ours," he continues. "Another tech company owns it. My father signed a contract with their CEO to acquire the rights."

"What does this have to do with anything?"

His tone hardens. "Ronin isn't just trying to buy the rights to AVA. He wants the whole damn company. And to make the merger go smoothly, he expects me to... woo the CEO. Hence, Olivia."

My nose wrinkles as I squint at him. "Woo?"

"Charm her. Take her on dates. Get into her good graces. Whatever you want to call it."

"That sounds archaic as hell," I say slowly, letting his words sink in. "Last I checked, this is the twenty-first century. You can say no."

He lifts a brow at that. "Just like you can say no to hunting with your father?"

My lips smack in irritation. “That’s different.”

“How so?”

“Because I’m just a broke college kid, and you’re...” I gesture at him, my hand flailing vaguely. “You’re you.”

A bitter laugh escapes him. “Exactly. I’m me. Ryann Callahan, heir to one of the richest men on the West Coast and future CEO of his company. We all have roles to play, Shilo.”

Another chilly gust sneaks through the branches, and I lick my lips, exhaling a puff of visible breath. His words from Thanksgiving echo in my mind. “So, what, then? You’re just expected to... date her until she hands over the tech your dad wants? Even though you don’t like her?”

“In a nutshell, yes,” he admits, unbuttoning his tux jacket and stepping closer. He drapes it over my shoulders, enveloping me in his warmth. “Did you know my mother and father didn’t even meet until their wedding day? Arrangements like this aren’t as common in the States, but they’re still practiced in other countries. Especially among the wealthy.”

“But what about your brother and my sister? They’re together by choice.”

He sighs, his golden-green eyes sad as his hands rest gently on my shoulders. “Declan and I are close now, but it wasn’t always that way. When we immigrated here, my mother left and took him with her. We were raised apart until our teens. Dec doesn’t have the responsibilities I do.”

That explains a lot, honestly. Sweet, smiley Declan and stone-cold Ryann—polar opposites. My chest tightens for them both. Was Ryann’s mother not part of his life at all?

"But you're twins," I press, still struggling to understand. "Shouldn't the same rules apply to both of you?"

"It'd make my life a hell of a lot easier if they did. But no."

"Well..." My voice trails off as I glance through the willow branches toward the glowing ballroom. "What does this mean for us?"

Heavy silence stretches between us. I don't dare look at him until his hands slip from my shoulders as he takes a step back.

"You made it clear on Thanksgiving," he says softly, "that there would be no *us*."

"Yeah, but—" The words catch in my throat. *But then you let me sleep in your bed.* "I thought things changed."

I thought you cared about me.

Ryann runs a hand through his hair, leaving it disheveled, before crossing his arms. His white shirt stretches over his biceps, and I hate how distracting it is. "You told me you couldn't keep feelings out of the equation."

"And what about her?" I scoff angrily, my face heating with embarrassment. "Is this... whatever you have with her just going to be casual, too?"

"It's complicated." His voice is flat, lifeless—like he's already given up. No emotion, no fight. Just cold resignation. He's like a robot following orders, and I suddenly feel ridiculous for even caring. When he mutters a half-hearted apology, I can't take it anymore.

Shoving his jacket into his arms, I turn and run back inside, ignoring him when he calls after me, the weight of his indifference leaving me hollow.

Inside, Carpenter stands next to Declan, a glass of champagne in hand. I march right up to him and snatch it away without a word.

"Hey, Shilo, you wouldn't believe what—oh, okay." Carpenter stops mid-sentence, raising a brow as I down the entire glass in one go. He shares a glance with KC, who leans in, his eyes flicking toward the door behind me.

"Ry just came in through the same door you did. What's up? What happened?"

I shake my head, not in the mood to talk, and grab KC's drink, draining that one too.

I've never been much of a drinker, but there's a first time for everything, I guess.

"Slow down, Igs. You're going to make yourself sick."

Maybe that's the point.

Ignoring my sister's warning, I wipe my mouth and turn just in time to see Ryann cross the room. He pauses next to what's-her-face, leaning in to whisper something at her ear, his lips so close to her skin it makes my stomach churn. His hand rests lightly on her hip as he gives her a small smile.

And I hate—absolutely *hate*—that I wish I were her.

Don't even know who she is and I'm jealous. It's not right.

I'm about to tell Paige I'm leaving when a ripple of hushed whispers rolls through the ballroom. Heads swivel toward the back, where an older, strikingly handsome man steps inside with a young woman on his arm. His features hit me immediately—high cheekbones, full lips, and those piercing hazel eyes. My stomach knots as Paige grabs my wrist.

"That's Ronin Callahan," she hisses, tugging me forward. "Let's go say hi."

"No, wait—"

Too late. Against my will, I'm yanked through the crowd and deposited in front of the man who raised Ryann.

I don't know if it's the champagne buzzing through my veins or the memory of our heated conversation outside, but a swell of hatred has me glaring when I meet his gaze.

"Mr. Callahan, hello," Paige chirps brightly. "This is my little brother, Shilo. He just started a few months ago."

"Ah yes, the intern." Ronin extends a hand with a tight smile that's unnervingly like his son's. "Nice to meet you, Shilo."

There's something condescending in his tone, like the introduction is a chore. I don't realize I'm scowling at his outstretched hand until Paige elbows me sharply in the ribs.

Reluctantly, I grab it, muttering, "How do you do?"

But he's already moving on, parting the crowd like frickin' Moses, heading straight for Ryann and his... whatever she is. It doesn't escape my notice that he doesn't even glance in Declan's direction.

"Well, that went well," Paige murmurs dryly. She tucks a loose strand of hair behind my ear before turning back to her boyfriend, oblivious to the storm brewing in my chest.

With a huff, I grab another glass of champagne out of Carpenter's hand.

"Dude," he groans, throwing his arms in the air. "First, you bite me, and now you're stealing all my drinks? Why do you hate me?"

I ignore him, slurping down the bubbly liquid as I watch Ronin wave and shake hands like a celebrity. He treats his employees well, though, so I guess he probably seems like one to them. Not to me, though. Never even met him before today, and I already hate him.

I shouldn't have come tonight. Should have faked sick, pretended to be busy, taken Mom's car and left town. Joined the circus. The way that woman grins at Ryann like he hung the moon makes me want to scoop my eyes out.

KC suddenly grabs my arm, prying the glass from my fingers before dragging me away. "Come on, let's dance."

"Kansas, no one else is dancing. What are you doing?"

"Getting you away from nosy ears so we can talk."

That makes me snort—the concept of ears having noses. I'm feeling pretty good thanks to the alcohol, so I let him steer me to the middle of the room where he wraps his arms around my shoulders.

"Okay, so spill the tea." He leans close, whispering in my ear, smelling like freshly baked cookies. "What did Ryann say?"

"Say about what?" Honestly, he smells like banana bread. It reminds me of my grandma back in Idaho, and I love her, so I inhale deep.

"Jesus, Shilo, stop sniffing me and pay attention. We both know that man is the furthest thing from straight, so why is he pretending to have a girlfriend?"

My brows furrow as I squint at him with blurry vision. "Why do you think he's pretending?"

KC rolls his eyes so far back that I'm surprised they don't stick there. "Did you not hear what I just said? Ryann loves dick, Shilo, and there's no way he'd suddenly give it up."

Mm, dick. Me too. Ryann's dick. Ugh.

"Maybe he would," I mumble, suddenly sad and horny, but KC shakes his head.

"Something's going on, I think. Maybe with his dad. They have a bad relationship."

A scoff leaves my lips as I snag another champagne from a passing server. "Ryann doesn't *do* relationships, he says."

"My point exactly."

Hey, wait...yeah, he's right.

Maybe it's not that he doesn't do relationships, he just doesn't do them with *me*.

My gaze finds him immediately, still standing with his date as he introduces her around. I take in the fancy dress she's wearing and the pricey-looking jewelry. She seems refined and classy. Confident. Basically, everything my anxious ass isn't. Is that the type of person he's looking to spend his life with? Someone he's proud to have at his side?

"You're worse than Carpenter, swear to God." KC wrenches the glass away before I can drain it all, and I toss him a glare that he returns in earnest. "Don't give me that sass, blue eyes. I'm trying to collude here."

And I'm trying to get drunk. Other than that night at Kintsugi, I've never drank before, and it seems like an excellent way to cope with my problems right now. It's not healthy, but whatever.

Ducking out of KC's arms, I slip into the crowd, chasing after another server for more champagne. Whether he lets me go on purpose or loses track of me, I don't care. I slink into a dark corner behind the stage and start drinking, eyes glued to Ryann like a creep. Only when my glass is empty do I emerge from my hidey hole, grabbing more champagne before retreating again.

The party unfolds around me, everyone participating in a raffle and charity toy drive. By the time it all ends, prizes given out, I've probably drank too much.

No, scratch that, I've *definitely* drank too much because everything feels floaty? But I'm also increasingly irritated because Ryann hasn't turned his attention away from Oli-whatsherface this entire time. Not once has he glanced up to look for me or expressed concern for my whereabouts, unlike Paige and Carpenter, who I had to dodge when I snuck out for another glass.

It's not fair. I want his eyes on me. I want him to smile at me and touch me in public like he does in private, but what we have will never *be* public. He'll never show me off proudly. The woman at his side laughs at something he said, a full-bodied sound that's probably really sexy. Ryann doesn't laugh with her, but there's a small, satisfied tilt to his lips as she gestures animatedly. Like he's enjoying their conversation. Maybe a little too much...

I want to make him angry. Get him so pissed off that he can't enjoy his night, that's what I need to do. But how?

Scanning the room, my eyes land on my sister. She's standing with Declan, her purse slung over her shoulder. An idea, stupid and impulsive, pops into my head. It's not like me at all, but I'm going to blame the alcohol for this one, because right now I could not care less.

I weave through the crowd, my heart thumping as I reach Paige. She's too busy shoveling cake into her mouth to notice me until I'm right in front of her.

"Jesus Christ, Iggy," she chokes, jolting in surprise. "We've been looking for you! Where have you been?"

"Not feeling good," I lie, clutching my stomach for effect. "Can I grab the Tums from your purse?"

"Told you that you'd make yourself sick," she sighs, holding out her bag without question before returning to some conversation I don't care to be a part of.

Reaching inside, I grab what I'm really after before sneaking off like a thief in the night, snickering at the stunt I'm about to pull.

Ryann

Where the fuck is Shilo?

After coming back inside, he'd danced with KC briefly before vanishing completely. I haven't had the chance to search for him properly—not with Ronin watching my every move around Olivia. But I felt his eyes on me earlier, and it pissed me off that I couldn't see him.

Then, after what felt like hours, I caught a flash of purple hair near Paige. Just as quickly as I saw him, he was gone again. He's not with KC or Carpenter, either, because those two have been glued to the dessert table all night.

So where the fuck is he?

Olivia tosses her hair, nibbling delicately on hors d'oeuvres. "Well, I'm officially impressed. You Callahans know how to celebrate. My parties at Sentinel Solutions consist of pizza and soda."

Most of my smiles tonight have been fake, but this one is genuine as I glance around the room. My employees are laughing, dancing, enjoying themselves. "We like to take care of our own. Happy people make happy customers. Without our workforce, we'd still be the small tech firm my grandfather started."

"Your grandfather founded the business?" she asks, arching a perfectly shaped brow.

"Him and my father," I confirm, glancing toward Ronin, who's schmoozing nearby with his little trophy wife on his arm. "Back in the seventies, they built car radios out of a shed in Ireland. We've come a long way."

"I'll say." She winks at me, sipping her drink through a straw in what I'm sure is meant to be sultry. I smirk, playing along, even though this entire charade is exhausting.

The hum of lively conversations and clinking glasses surrounds us, but my focus keeps slipping. I scan the room again, searching for the one person who could make this insufferable evening worth enduring. But he's nowhere to be seen. And it really fucking bothers me.

"Looking for your boy?" Olivia murmurs, close enough that no one else can hear.

My jaw tightens, and I give her a stiff nod.

"I think I saw him leave about twenty minutes ago," she says, gesturing casually toward the double doors before running a hand down my arm for show. "He's upset about us, isn't he?"

Understatement of the century. Hurt would be more accurate. And he wouldn't even let me explain.

I'm about to head toward Paige to find out where my little doll has gone when my phone buzzes in my pocket, a text lighting up the screen.

Dollface:

I have a question.

My heart thuds when I read his message, and I turn away to type out a response.

Me:

Where the hell did you go?

Dollface:

Can I come?

Can he...

Glancing sideways to ensure Ronin's attention is elsewhere, I excuse myself to the restroom.

Dollface:

Please?

Me:

No. Where are you?

The only thing he sends me is a picture of the Seattle skyline from a window, and the familiar sight has me stopping dead in my tracks, eyes bugging out at the screen.

Me:

How the fuck did you get into my father's office, Shilo?

His following text is a photo of his very hard cock, dripping precum, and my own jumps to full attention. Jesus Christ.

He's in so much fucking trouble.

Me:

Stay where you are, and do not touch yourself.

Dollface:

...too late :(

Oh, I don't think so.

Quickly marching to the elevator, I scan my badge on the panel and put in a code that takes me up to the Tower. How Shilo was even able to get up there is a mystery because only four people in the entire building know that code: me, Declan, Dad, and...

And Paige.

Goddamn brat.

The ascent takes ages. By the time the elevator doors open, I'm aching. My cock is begging for some friction, so I palm it over my pants and make my way through a lounge toward the open office door.

Stepping inside, I'm greeted by the sight of Shilo sitting in my father's chair. The faint light filtering through the windows casts soft shadows across his face, purple strands falling into his eyes as his arm moves beneath the massive mahogany desk. He doesn't notice my presence, so I cross my arms and lean against the doorway, sweeping my gaze over the familiar room that never fails to put me on edge.

I've always hated this office, from the built-in bookshelves crammed with leather-bound lies to the bar cart in the corner that's seen more deals sealed with scotch than trust. It's not just the memories of tense conversations I've endured here—it's what the space stands for. Money. Power. Control.

Those things run through my veins as well, but unlike Ronin Callahan, I don't wield them like weapons to manipulate people who stand in my way.

A low whimper brings me back to the present, and I shove off of the wall to stalk toward Shilo softly. Slick sounds of him stroking himself fill my ears, the sound so fucking filthy that I almost release a groan. His pants are unzipped, tuxedo jacket draped over the back of the chair as his pale, hairless chest peeks through the top button of his shirt.

"I didn't give you permission to come."

His head snaps up, arm halting when our eyes collide.

"In fact, I specifically remember telling you not to touch yourself."

Shilo huffs, keeping a hand wrapped around his dick. "Can't help it, I think it's the champagne. Made me horny."

Judging from the way he's slurring his words, I'd say that he's probably been hiding and drinking all night. Naughty, naughty doll.

Coming around the desk, I raise a brow at him and cross my arms again. "How did you get in here? Your access is restricted."

Those gorgeous—albeit glazed—eyes dance around my face as he licks his lips and swallows nervously. "I s-stole my sister's badge. And the code was in an email you sent to Declan. Don't be mad."

"Oh, I'm not mad, doll face, I'm furious." Leaning down, I grip the plush leather arms of the chair tightly, putting my face within inches of his. "Do you know how much trouble we could get into if you're caught right now?"

A needy whine brushes against my lips as he jerks himself once. "Please, Ry, I need to come. Help me."

God, if it weren't for the fact that he's drunk right now and violating so many company policies, I'd bend him over my father's desk and pound his little hole as punishment. As it were...

Straightening, I lean a hip against the desk and gaze down at the angry, swollen head of his cock. I wish I could taste it, suck on it until he turned into a squirming, overstimulated mess. But I can't touch right now.

"You can come," I say, fighting a grin at the desperate moan that leaves his throat, "but you can't touch yourself, and neither will I. Do it hands-free."

"Huh?" His mouth drops open as he blinks down at himself. "H-how...how the frick am I supposed to do that?"

"Hmm, I suppose you'll have to get creative."

He glares at me, chest heaving as he looks around dazedly. Muttering a curse, he gets to his feet, his sticky length jabbing me in the stomach when he reaches up to undo my tie.

"What are you doing?"

"Getting creative." Once it's free, Shilo takes the tie and wraps it around his cock like a sling, shuddering when the fabric glides against it. "How expensive was this? Feels so good."

"It's Brioni silk." Fuck, the way his leaking crown looks sliding in and out of the material is obscene.

"I don't know what that means." Thrusting his hips, he lets out a filthy moan as his head falls back, and I'm so damn tempted to sink my teeth into his pretty throat. Put my marks on him, claim him for all to see.

"I...hate your...dad," he pants through clenched teeth. Something about the unhinged way he snarls those words drives me fucking crazy, like the champagne tonight was enough to obliterate his inhibitions completely.

"You and I both, doll." Everything inside of me right now is screaming for release, the urge to pull out my own cock becoming painful to ignore. Especially when he turns his body so that each thrust has his balls rubbing against the edge of the desk.

"He...I—mm, God." My little doll tenses as a rope of cum shoots from his dick. Hips slowing, he completely coats the keyboard, covering it with wave after wave of his sticky release in the hottest display I've ever seen. Crying out, he bites his lip, still rubbing himself with my tie until he's drained of every last drop, and only then do I allow myself to touch him.

My hands hold him steady as his legs give out, nearly collapsing forward, my name rolling off his tongue. His head hits my chest and he nuzzles closer, inhaling deep before sighing.

"You always smell so good, you know?"

With a chuckle, I grab the tie from his hand and set it aside before reaching down to fix his pants. "It's an imported fragrance. I modeled for their campaign during my junior year of college."

"Mm, underwear," he mumbles, swaying on his feet. "Waterfalls. Palm trees."

My brows fly up as I lower him onto my father's chair, buttoning up the top of his shirt. "Have you been researching me, doll face?"

A hiccup leaves his throat. "You look so hot in those p-pitchers. All oiled and—" Hiccup. "Muscles."

"Jesus."

He's definitely had too much to drink. And knowing Shilo, he's probably got an empty stomach as well. His lids slide shut as he slumps down, clearly ready to pass out.

"Wait for me right here. Don't move."

He doesn't respond, already asleep, his breathing deep and even. I make quick work of cleaning up the mess, including the wireless keyboard still sticky with his cum, before heading to the elevator. Once in my office, I swap it with my own, ensuring there's no trace of what happened upstairs.

A buzz in my pocket pulls my attention, and I curse under my breath at Olivia's text.

Olivia SinClaire:

Ronin's looking for you.

Fuck. He's going to be livid that I vanished during his big announcement and missed my speech. There's no fixing that now, though, so I fire off an email about a fake work emergency, hoping it'll buy me some time. Next, I text Paige to let her know I'm taking her brother home.

Ronin's fury can wait until morning. Right now, my little doll needs me.

Shilo's still right where I left him, snoozing soundly, looking adorably uncomfortable with his head bent forward at an awkward angle.

After swapping out the keyboard, I nudge his shoulder. "Come on, baby, let's get you home."

"Lee' me alone," he grumbles, weakly swatting at my arms, and I grunt as I lift him to his feet.

"Trust me, you do not want to sleep here."

He fights the whole way to the elevator, leaning heavily against me and eventually dropping his full body weight into my arms, weighing so little that it's unnerving. With a frown, I glance down at his sleeping face as the elevator descends to the parking garage. Even through the fabric of his tux, he feels too thin. Frail, almost. It makes me uneasy. From what I remember, he wasn't this small back in August. But then again, I've never held him for long. How would I know if this is normal for him?

Those high school photos I saw on Thanksgiving flash through my memory—Shilo, younger and healthier, a softness to his face that's long gone. That, paired with catching him in the bathroom, his fingers down his throat...

My arms instinctively tighten around him. No, I don't think this is normal at all.

Once we reach the car, I buckle Shilo into the passenger seat before sliding behind the wheel. But as soon as I start the engine, he unbuckles himself, shifting sideways until his head rests in my lap with a contented sigh.

I should push him off, tell him to sit upright and put the seat belt back on. Safety first, after all. But my fingers have a mind of their own, slipping into his soft strands, combing through them. I just... can't. So I let him stay like that as I drive us to his house, taking the scenic route to steal a little more time.

"Shilo, you need to wake up. We're here."

Pulling up to the curb, I gently lift him upright, and he mumbles something incoherent under his breath before fumbling for the door handle. As the door swings open, he pitches sideways, and if it weren't for my quick grip on his jacket sleeve, he would've face-planted right onto the pavement.

"Fucking hell." I yank him back, scowling when he laughs like this is some kind of game.

His head lolls, eyes glazed as he gives me a sloppy grin. "M'drunk."

"Yes, I can see that. We'll have a discussion about it when you're sober."

Scoffing, he waves off my words with a lazy hand before scooting closer. My breath catches as he shifts, and before I can react, he's straddling me, settling onto my lap.

"This," he murmurs softly. "I want this."

"Shilo, goddammit, we need to get you inside."

With a hum, he wraps his arms around me and buries his face into my neck. The feeling of his lips on my skin plus the pressure of him sitting on my crotch has my cock swelling, but I ignore it, choosing to get out of the car instead while he clings to me like a koala.

As I approach the front door, the house is brightly lit with Christmas decorations, the glow warm and inviting, but all the windows are dark. My plan is simple: drop him off on the porch, make sure he gets inside, and leave. But when I try to set him down, he clings tighter, his legs locking stubbornly around my waist like he has no intention of letting go.

Heaving a heavy sigh, I fish into his pockets, pulling out his keys to unlock the door. "Your father is going to be unhappy if he catches you like this."

"Not here," my little doll mumbles against my throat. "He's on duty. Only Mom."

Thank fuck for small miracles, at least.

Carrying him inside, I nudge the door closed with my foot. It slams harder than I intended, the sound echoing in the quiet house. I wince, but it's too late—his mother's voice calls from down the hall.

"Paige? That you?"

"S'me, Mum," Shilo shouts back, lifting his head to kiss my jaw.

"Hi, honey. There's some meatloaf in the fridge if you're hungry."

"M'not—" He starts to say, but I clap a hand over his mouth and give him a stern look as I make my way toward the kitchen. He needs to eat. Not just tonight but in general, and if no one else will force him to do it, then I will.

He licks and sucks at my palm, gazing at me from behind his lashes as I set him down on a butcher block counter. Pulling open a refrigerator covered in mismatched magnets, I spot the plastic container with his name scrawled on top and pop it in the microwave.

The kitchen is small, cozy, and I briefly take in the beige cabinets and old linoleum floors before asking Shilo where the silverware is. When he doesn't respond, I find him with his eyes closed, snoring softly. Fucking hell. Luckily, there aren't a lot of drawers, and I find what I'm looking for as the microwave dings.

Resigning myself to feeding him, I spear some food with a fork, blowing to cool it off before bringing it to his mouth. "Open up, doll."

He complies, cracking open a lid when I place the food on his tongue. "Said I wasn't hungry."

"Too damn bad. Eat."

With a grunt, he closes his eye again, wrapping his legs around my hips as he lets me feed him slowly, one bite at a time. When the container is half empty, he finally pushes the fork away, and I finish the rest myself before lifting him back into my arms.

Carrying him upstairs, I step into his room, which is noticeably messier than it was on Thanksgiving. Clothes are scattered across the floor, and the desk is buried under a chaotic pile of papers and computer parts

"Gotta pee." He lets go of me, feet hitting the ground, but when he stumbles toward the bathroom, he trips over a pair of sneakers and crashes to the floor. "Shit. Ouch."

"Are you alright?"

"Mm-hmm." When he pushes to a stand, his legs wobble, and he nearly takes out his 3D printer by falling into it. "W-why s'everything moving?"

Pinching the bridge of my nose, I sigh and grab his arm, guiding him carefully into the bathroom. Once there, he positions himself in front of the toilet and starts to undo his pants, but stops abruptly before whipping his head around to glare at me.

"Go away."

Nice try. After all that food he just ate, I'm not letting him out of my sight.

"You can barely stand, Shilo. Just go. I won't watch."

His precious face twists into a grimace. "But you'll *listen.* Sh-shut up your ears. Shut 'em up."

Huffing a laugh, I turn him around, placing my back to his chest. "Okay, they're closed. Now go."

He grumbles the entire time but doesn't fight me, and I help him wash his hands when he's done. Getting him to brush his teeth is a losing battle, so I just walk him back into his room, where he flops backward onto his bed. Fully clothed.

Without giving myself too much time to second-guess, I decide to undress him, starting with his pants since they're already unbuttoned. Of course, he's not wearing anything underneath, which does absolutely nothing to help the situation in my own slacks.

Still, I force myself to stay focused, moving on to remove his socks and shoes. Those cute as fuck toes make a brief appearance, and I can't help but glance at them before quickly shifting my attention back to the task at hand.

Next is his tuxedo jacket, which comes off easily enough, but when I unbutton his shirt, Shilo pushes me away with surprising strength.

"*No.*"

"You can't sleep in that shirt, doll face. It'll wrinkle. Let me take care of you."

He curls inward, rolling onto his side and tucking his knees to his chest, like he's trying to shield himself from the world. A flare of anger rises in my chest as I grind my molars. Not at him, but at whoever made him feel this way about himself.

"M' fine, Mr. Callahan. You can lee' me now."

"How many more times do I have to tell you to call me Ryann, Shilo?"

"Don't want to," he mutters, burying his face into his arms. "Hurts."

My brows slam together as I frown. "Hurts? What hurts? Calling me by my name?"

"Mm." With a nod, he wraps a blanket around himself, and I stand there, completely taken off guard.

"Why?"

He's quiet for a long moment. "Cuz tomorrow, this won't be real."

That's all he says. And honestly, I don't ask him to clarify because I'm not sure I want to know. Instead, I let him sleep while I tidy up his room, finding a hamper in the closet to stuff his clothes into. His rat watches me from its cage with beady eyes, little whiskers twitching.

When there's nothing left to do, I contemplate leaving. I really do. But the memory of Shilo's body pressed into my back when he slept in my bed, combined with his little snores, has me sitting next to him. And try as I might, I can't seem to come up with an excuse for why I lift his head onto my lap. I just do. It feels nice to have my fingers in his hair again. Peaceful. Relaxing.

Checking the time on my phone—and ignoring multiple missed calls from Declan and my dad—I realize it's past midnight, which means...

"Merry Christmas, doll," I whisper softly, leaning back to close my eyes. I can't remember the last time I spent the holiday with anyone. Not since Mom died. This time isn't any different; I'm not actually spending it with Shilo. I'll be gone before he wakes.

But for now, in this quiet moment, it almost feels like we're spending it together.

The elevator to my condo slides shut behind me, and I let out a long breath, rolling my shoulders to release some of the tension from leaning against Shilo's headboard for hours. I'm exhausted, my mind still buzzing with the endless list of tasks I need to get through before the AVA launch and everything that happened tonight.

As I step into the living room, ready to collapse, I freeze. There, sprawled comfortably on my new couch like he owns the place, is my brother. One leg draped lazily over the armrest, flipping through a magazine.

Fuck. So much for avoiding him.

"What the hell are you doing here?" I bark sharply.

Dec looks up, a grin spreading on his face. "Merry Christmas to you too, big brother. You missed Dad's whole retirement announcement. How's Shilo?"

"He's asleep." A heavy sigh leaves my lips as I rub my burning eyes. Asshole's only two minutes younger. "Declan, it's late. I've got a lot of work to do in the morning, and I'm tired. Can we shelve this conversation for another day?"

He swings his legs off the couch and stands, tossing the magazine onto the coffee table. "Yeah, I can tell. You look like shit. When was the last time you slept?"

I don't have the energy for this. "I'm fine. Just busy."

My twin raises an eyebrow, clearly not buying my bullshit. “Busy, huh? Or maybe overworking yourself to death?”

Walking past him, I head for the kitchen, ignoring his concerns. “I’ve got a lot riding on this, Declan. You know that.”

He follows close behind, leaning against the counter as I open the fridge and pull out a water bottle. “I’d say I get it, Ry, but I don’t. This is getting out of hand. You’re killing yourself over this AVA project, and for what? To prove something to Dad?”

I twist the cap off the bottle, avoiding his gaze as I take a swig. “It’s not about proving anything. This is important. If AVA fails, the whole company fails.”

As Ronin likes to remind me repeatedly.

Declan’s expression softens. “You know you don’t have to do everything alone, right? I’m here. You can ask me for help.”

Shaking my head, I scrub a hand down my face, scratching my stubbled cheek. “This is a project Dad entrusted to me. I’ve got it under control.”

“Yeah?” He crosses his arms, watching me closely. “Is that why you’re dating Olivia? Because you’ve got everything *under control?*”

My hand tightens around the bottle, making it crinkle, as my shoulders tense. “Olivia and I have an understanding. It’s nothing more than a business arrangement.”

“A business arrangement,” he repeats slowly, his tone laced with disbelief. “Seriously? You’re dating a woman you can’t possibly care about because Dad told you to. Do you know how ridiculous that sounds?”

The weight of his words presses down on me, and I glance away. "It's not that simple."

"Then tell me," he urges, stepping closer. "Talk to me, Ryann. I'm still your brother, remember?"

"Of course I do," I grumble irritably, feeling guilty.

For a moment, I'm tempted to tell him everything—to admit how alone I sometimes feel, how every decision I make seems like a trap, how I'm terrified of Ronin finding out the truth, and the confusion surrounding Shilo.

But I can't. I can't let Declan see how much I struggle to keep it all together, he's done too much for me already. So I force a smile, hoping it looks convincing.

"I appreciate the offer, but I'm good. Really. I've got this."

Declan's shoulders slump, and I hate the disappointment in his eyes. It feels like sophomore year of high school again, when we were strangers. "Ryann...if this is about what happened to Mom—"

"No," I cut him off, trying to keep my tone light despite the agony just mentioning her brings. "You don't need to worry about me. I'll figure it out. I always do."

He studies me for a long moment with those green eyes like hers, and I know he's trying to see through me. "You know I don't blame you anymore, right? I haven't for a long time."

My first instinct is to flinch, but I tamp it down. "Yeah. I know."

It doesn't matter that he doesn't blame me. I still do. That will never change.

"Alright."

We both gaze at one another in silence, him trying to get me to crack as I hold onto my resolve with all my might.

Finally, he breaks the stare-down, dropping his head with a defeated sigh. "If you change your mind or need anything at all, you know where to find me."

I nod, grateful for the offer, even if I can't take it. "Thanks, Dec. I mean it."

He gives me a small smile, but it doesn't reach his eyes. "Take care of yourself, okay? This company, Dad...there are more important things out there."

"Yeah," I say quietly as he heads for the elevator. "You too."

The doors slide shut, and I'm left standing in the kitchen, silence pressing around me. It's fucking lonely. Having Shilo in my bed last week felt too good, and now that's all I can think about. I used to revel in solitude, but now I want to get in my car and drive back to his parents house to curl up beside him. This whole business with Olivia has probably made sure that I'll never fall asleep beside him again, and I feel so fucking raw.

This is for the best. He deserves someone his own age who can proudly claim him, not some bitter, emotionally stunted man sixteen years his senior. I'm the one who told him to keep feelings out of our arrangement.

But as I stand in the cold, suffocating silence of my empty condo, a gnawing thought takes root.

Maybe separating feelings from Shilo was never an option to begin with.

Shilo

Christmas comes and goes like it usually does.

After waking up with the first—and definitely last—hangover of my life, Mom cooks me a greasy breakfast that I actually keep down while Dad blasts eighties holiday music. We exchange gifts once Paige gets home from spending the night with Declan, watch *It's A Wonderful Life* with steaming mugs of apple cider, and then pile into the car for a drive down Snowflake Lane to look at the lights.

All very typical for a Reed family Christmas.

What surprises me, though, is the text I get from Ryann because I'd been expecting the cold shoulder from him like usual.

Boss:

Merry Christmas. How are you feeling this morning?

Me:

Hi, Merry Christmas. I'm alright. Slightly nauseous and my head hurts.

Boss:

Champagne will do that. Take some Tylenol and drink lots of fluids.

Me:

Yes, Boss.

When he doesn't respond for over an hour, I send another message.

Me:

Thanks for last night, by the way. Can't remember much, but I think you brought me home and fed me? Unless I dreamed all of that. In which case, nevermind, and idk how I got home.

Boss:

It wasn't a dream, and you're welcome. Anytime.

I stare at that text for far too long, especially when days go by without another word. The idea that he's probably spending the holidays with his girlfriend makes me nauseous. With CalTek closed again until after New Year's, I have too much time to think about it all. Think about *him*.

I don't leave my room for a week, burying myself in building my PC just to keep my mind busy. I don't even shower until Dad threatens to toss me outside into the rain, claiming I reek. Mom changes my sheets while I'm in the bathroom, and the fresh linens make my mood plummet—they no longer smell like Ryann's cologne. The gloom clings to me until New Year's Eve, when there's an unexpected knock at my bedroom door.

"Shilo, you've got a friend here to see you. Can I let him in?"

Yanking off my gaming headset, I shoot to my feet, hope sparking in my chest. "Yeah, Mom. Who is it?"

"He said you call him Kansas?"

Deflating instantly, I slump back into my computer chair just as KC sweeps into my room, wearing a skintight golden jumpsuit that probably gave Dad an aneurysm.

He halts, gazing over my baggy shirt and pajama bottoms with pursed lips. "Well, don't act so excited to see me. It's embarrassing."

"Sorry, I just hoped you'd be Ryann. How'd you know where I live?"

"Your sister." He flops onto my unmade bed, wrinkling his nose at Master Splinter in the corner. "Since you disappeared from the party on Christmas Eve and couldn't be bothered to answer my texts, I decided to check in."

With a wince, I pull my arms inside my shirt. "Uh, yeah, sorry about that...I had too much free liquor and wasn't feeling good. Then the holiday happened..."

"It's fine, Shilo. I know I'm not the center of your universe, though I should be," he pouts, folding his arms. "But I'll only forgive you if you take me out tonight."

"Out?"

"Yes. Out. It's New Year's Eve, and parties are happening across the city. Tina and their girlfriend will also be tagging along, so chop-chop. Throw on something slutty, and let's go."

Frowning, I glance down at my week-old clothes. "But I don't own anything slutty. And I kinda want to play Minecraft instead."

KC huffs, sliding off my bed to peruse my closet. "I'm going to pretend you did *not* just say that."

There's something off about his tone, an unfamiliar edge that makes me nervous. I watch him closely as he yanks shirts off hangers sharply, definitely agitated.

Worried I might have upset one of my only friends, I ask cautiously, "Is something wrong?"

"No, Shilo, why would anything be wrong?" Giving up on the closet, he starts rummaging through my drawers. "Not that you'd know, seeing as how you've completely ignored me. Actually, you know what, yes. Something is wrong, and he wears a disgustingly sexy beanie that shouldn't make him as hot as it does."

"Ah. Carpenter." My shoulders relax, knowing that I'm not the problem.

"Yes, my infuriatingly attractive, *straight* roommate who's driving me absolutely insane," he clips, holding up my suspenders with a raised brow. "You could wear these with just a pair of pants. Nothing else. That whole nerdy twink vibe works for you."

"I'm not going anywhere without a shirt," I answer quickly.

"Fine, be boring. At least put on something tight so we can fuck."

My jaw drops to the floor as I stammer, feeling my cheeks heat. "I...w-what, we aren't...I don't like you like that, Kansas."

He sucks in a breath before throwing his head back to laugh, startling my rat. "Oh, blue-eyed boy, your face. That was beautiful. Not you and I *together*, but we are finding someone to get down and dirty with tonight if it's the last thing I do."

"But I don't want to get down and dirty." Well, I do. But not with a stranger. Just with my boss. Ex-boss?

KC throws me a pointed look, reading my thoughts. "He has a girlfriend, Shilo. You know that, right?"

Immediately, I scowl. "Yeah, but...I don't think it's real."

Ryann made it sound like it wasn't real, anyway. Just an act he was putting on for his father.

There's a brief pause where KC's eyes soften, and then he's pulling out his phone as he slowly walks over to me. "I hate to be the bearer of bad news, but this looks very real to me."

He holds it up, and I blink at the screen, my stomach sinking as an Instagram photo of Ryann and Olivia assaults my eyes. It's a post from Christmas—they're on a boat surrounded by lights, probably the Ship Festival on the Puget Sound. And he's...kissing her. Not on the lips, but still. On her cheek. The caption reads:

> Happy Holidays to the best boyfriend a girl can ask for! So glad I met you. Love you, babe.

Love? She *loves* him? When did that happen? I thought they'd just started going out.

Oh, how wrong I was because a quick scroll on her page shows multiple pictures of them together, dating all the way back to...

August. When we first met.

"I'm sorry," KC says softly. "I thought you knew. It's actually why I figured you went full hermit mode."

Burning bile rises in my throat, and I cough, quickly making a beeline for the bathroom, where I all but force myself to keep my breakfast down.

I will not do it. I won't. Doctor Iskar says it's a trauma response, and *I won't let it win.*

But it's hard. Especially when the cruel things kids used to say about me come rushing back, their words slicing through my brain like fresh wounds—comments about my body, the way I looked. I spent all four years of high school trapped in a constant state of panic. Even now, I can still feel their hands on me, shoving me to the ground in the PE locker room, laughing while I cried.

"Are you alright?"

KC approaches me, and I straighten from where I'd been hunched over the sink, meeting his concerned expression in the mirror.

"I'm fine. It's all fine."

I'm fine, I'm fine, I'm fine.

"You don't need to lie, babe." He sets his chin on my shoulder, eyes so full of pity that I want to scream.

"I really don't feel like partying, Kansas. I'm sorry."

He gazes at me for a long moment before nodding slowly. "Okay. That's fine. I'll order a pizza, and we'll play some games until midnight, then pass out. If it's fine with your parents, I mean."

Spinning around, he heads back into my room, and I follow with a frown. "They don't care, I'm an adult. But why would you want to hang out here? Why not your place?"

"I cannot deal with Carpenter right now. Let me avoid him, Shilo. If we aren't going out, here's as good a place as any."

"What did he do?"

Flopping face-first onto my bed, KC growls into the blankets. "I don't want to talk about it." After a beat, he turns his head to peek at me. "Any chance you'd let me kiss you at midnight and take a picture of it? Platonically, of course. I want to post it to the 'Gram and make certain people jealous."

I'm about to say no thanks, but his words make me pause. By *certain people*, I'm sure he means Carpenter, but...would Ryann see it, too? Would it make him jealous? Would he even care?

"I'll...think about it," I tell him, and he grins when I pull out my computer chair.

"Oh, this is *so* happening. Just don't fall in love, Shi, because that would ruin our friendship, and I'd hate to lose you."

Yeah, right. Pretty sure that won't happen because I'm already in love with someone I can never have.

Things at CalTek don't just pick up after the holidays—they explode. With IntelliCon coming up, everyone's scrambling to prepare for the big presentation Ryann's giving at the convention. He and Declan have been so swamped they even hired Carpenter as their full-time PA. KC's ecstatic about it. (Kidding—he's absolutely livid.)

Even my own duties have ramped up. Liza has me working directly with the developers on aspects of AVA since they finally let me in on the secret: it's a smart-home security ecosystem, apparently, called Advanced Vigilance Assistant. Cameras, alarms, locks, the whole shebang. Olivia owns the company that CalTek purchased the software from, I guess. Some mid-sized security firm.

I even help Carpenter with the PowerPoint he was tasked with, which was an absolute struggle—he's probably the least tech-savvy person I've ever met. Seriously, why was he even hired? On his first day, he had computer issues and texted me in a full-blown panic. I told him to clear his cache and cookies, and he thought I was telling him to throw up. *What even?*

Ryann texted me on New Years, but I never responded, and I haven't seen him since Christmas Eve. I'm still pissed about him hiding the fact that he was in a fake relationship the entire time we were...doing whatever we were doing. And I want to confront him about it, but there's just been no time with everything going on. But I think I'll get my chance because the morning they're scheduled to leave on their flight to New York, he appears before my desk in the R&D department.

"Why aren't you preparing to leave?"

I glance up with a yelp, hurriedly clicking off the YouTube video I'd been watching of one of his college games. "Huh? Leave where? I'm not off until noon."

It's been weeks since I've seen him, and he looks good. So good. I hate it.

His hazel eyes study me intently, lips thinning with disapproval. "Clearly, I'll need to talk with Liza about reading her emails. You're coming to New York, Shilo, and the plane takes off at eleven. Go home and pack a bag. I'll pick you up."

Wait, what? What the hell?

"Ryann, I can't—" But he's already walking away, so I jump up to hurry after him. "It's a week and a half convention. I can't be gone for that long!"

"And why not?" Without stopping, he raises a brow down at me. "Your classes are online, are they not? Plus, it's paid. I've added you to the project, and I'll need your assistance with that damn friend of yours that Declan hired. He doesn't know his own ass from his elbow."

Okay, well... he's got a point, but...

Almost two whole weeks?! Away from home? Honestly, I don't think I've ever been away from my family that long, which sounds really pathetic. What if something happens while I'm out there? It's New York, what if I get mugged? Or, like, lost? Like that kid in Home Alone. I'm not as bright as him, I would for sure have gotten kidnapped by those two goofy criminals. And then what? I'm not cut out for a life of crime.

Ryann sighs heavily, glancing around before cupping my cheek. "Shilo, you'll be fine. Liza and I will stay by your side, along with a handful of devs and our useless PA. Go get ready."

When his hand falls from my face, an embarrassing whine leaves my throat at the loss of contact. I want it back, want it all over me. His eyes darken before he turns away, striding toward the elevator.

"Go. Hurry. I'll pick you up in thirty."

I watch him leave, nearly panting because I haven't came in forever, and the sight of his butt in those slacks is insane. But I don't have time to think about that, I have thirty minutes to—

Wait, thirty minutes?! It takes me at least fifteen to get to the house!

Hightailing it out of there, I race home, cursing out traffic the entire time. Mom's on the couch when I burst through the door, out of breath, and I shout over my shoulder that I'm leaving for two weeks on my way up the stairs.

"What do you mean you're leaving for two weeks?"

"Can't explain, work trip, gotta pack."

I'm throwing anything I can find into a duffle bag when the doorbell rings, and Ryann's scent floods my senses when he enters my room.

"We've got less than an hour to get to the airport. Let's go."

"I haven't done laundry," I panic, stuffing what I'm pretty sure is a pillowcase into my bag on accident.

"Jesus Christ, your room is a mess again." He grabs the duffle from me, zipping it quickly as he heads for the door. "Don't worry about it, I'll send for housekeeping when we arrive. Hurry up."

Ugh, I frickin *hate* being rushed. But I follow him out, hugging my poor, bewildered mother before telling her I'll call when we land. Honestly, it's a good thing Dad's at work because he'd probably have a few strong words to say about this, and I'm glad I don't have to deal with that.

We barely make it to our gate, where Carpenter greets me with a narrowed glare. There's a brief hiccup with my last-minute ticket, but the airline sorts it out, herding us onto the plane like cattle. I end up sandwiched between Liza and Ryann, which wouldn't be so bad if my arm and knee weren't pinned against his the entire six-hour flight. He spends it glued to his laptop, anyway, doing work stuff. When I comment on him deigning to sit with us peasants in coach instead of first class, he throws me a threatening look that makes my stomach flip.

Liza and I attempt to watch her favorite movie, *Code Breakers*, but we start our descent before it's over—mercifully, because it was terrible. I tell her that, and she laughs like I'm joking.

The last time I was in New York, I was ten, and my family hated it. Too loud, too crowded, too expensive—though, as a kid, the expensive part wasn't my problem. Turns out, nothing much has changed. By the time we've crammed ourselves and our bags into the hotel shuttle, I'm already exhausted and completely overstimulated.

True to his word, Ryann stays close, even squeezing into the backseat next to me. Carpenter's on my other side, unusually quiet, and when I ask him if he's okay, I get a shrug in response. According to KC, the two haven't talked since that picture on New Year's. I still don't know what's going on between them, but I hope I didn't hurt Carpenter's feelings.

By the time we reach the Four Seasons in New York, it's already late, thanks to the three-hour time difference. Ryann leads the group to the counter in the sleek hotel lobby, while I hover nearby, wishing I had a hoodie to pull over my head. The overhead lighting reflects off the marble and glass, too bright for my tired eyes. I'm practically nodding off on my feet when Ryann's raised voice snaps me awake, arguing with the concierge.

"What do you mean there are no other rooms available? We made these reservations months ago." He glares at the poor, stuttering man, who holds up his palms defensively.

"For a party of six, yes. And we have six rooms reserved. All other accommodations are booked. I'm sorry, sir."

"How is that fucking possible?"

"Bet it's because of the Symbiotic concert tonight," one of the developers says with a shrug, and the man behind the desk nods eagerly.

"They're playing a show every night this week. All hotels in the city are full."

Ryann blows out a frustrated breath, gritting his teeth. "I don't know what a Symbiotic is, but we added another person to our party last minute. Where is he supposed to stay?"

"They're a metal band," Carpenter clarifies. "I don't mind sharing my room. Shilo can stay with me."

At this point, I'll stay anywhere as long as I can get some sleep.

Ryann eyes Carpenter coldly before glancing at me, swaying slightly against Liza. His expression softens.

"No, he'll stay with me. My room should have an extra pullout."

"Uh, about that..." The concierge coughs with a wince. "Due to the flood of reservations, our system made a mistake. All of your rooms are standard with one queen bed."

A heavy silence settles over the group, everyone exchanging uneasy glances while Ryann visibly fights to keep his temper in check.

"Fucking fantastic. Just give us the keys." Snatching the card from the counter, he grabs my bag off the floor and strides toward the elevators without another word.

"I really don't mind staying in Carpenter's room, Mr. Callahan. It's fine," I try, trailing after him.

"Shilo," he growls, punching the call button hard enough to make it rattle, "I'm not in the mood. I've got a hundred things to finish tonight before I can even think about sleeping, and we have to be up early for Phase One of the convention. Don't argue."

I don't have the energy to argue, even if I wanted to.

When we finally reach the room, Ryann drops my bag onto the bed and immediately sets up his laptop on the desk. I stand there awkwardly, shifting on my feet as I watch him, unsure of what to do. He glances briefly over his shoulder.

"Get some sleep. I'll be up for a while working on this presentation."

That's all he says before diving back into his work. Feeling dismissed, I grab a pair of pajamas from my bag and close myself in the bathroom for a shower.

By the time I step back out, he's completely engrossed, the faint glow of his laptop illuminating his face in the dim room. I'm so sleepy that I don't even bother saying goodnight, choosing to crawl under the covers instead. Within seconds, I'm out like a light, sleep claiming me instantly.

Shilo

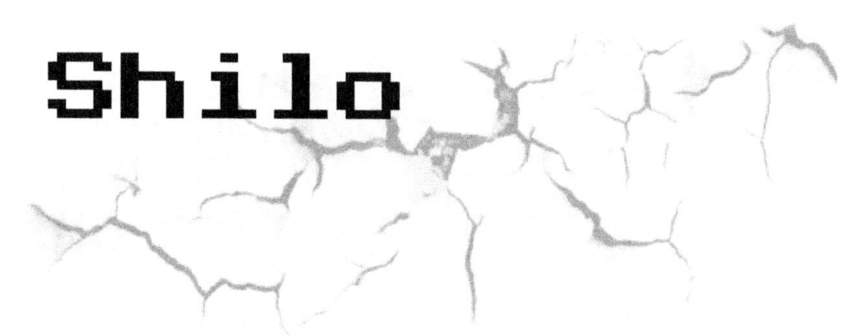

IntelliCon is massive—bigger than any convention I've ever been to.

After a quick hotel breakfast, we arrive at the Javits Center in Manhattan just before eight, and I gape at the gleaming structure as Ryann and Liza usher us inside. The place reminds me of the CalTek building, all glass and steel, towering and intimidating. As we head toward one of the auditoriums to set up, Carpenter and I lag behind, taking in the sheer scale of the event. It's mind-blowing. Hands-on workshops, showcases, VR experiences, drone races, and even robot battles stretch as far as the eye can see. Every major tech company is here, launching new products, while startups scramble to make their mark.

We pass a booth offering scholarships for whoever can build a computer mainframe the fastest, and I nearly sign up on the spot before Liza grabs my arm to drag me away. Seriously, this place is every PC nerd's wet dream, it sucks that I'm here to work. I want to *play*. Not fair.

"You'll have plenty of time to explore later," Liza laughs as I make grabby hands at the sign-up sheet. "Our presentation starts in an hour."

The auditorium is empty when we arrive, and we get to work setting up our exhibit behind the curtain while Ryann barks orders like his usual grouchy self. He didn't sleep at all last night—I know because he was still hunched over his laptop when I woke up this morning. Aside from the faintest shadows under his eyes, he looks flawless, as always. His tailored suit and gold tie look like something straight off a runway.

I, on the other hand, look like a disaster. My polo is wrinkled from being balled up in my bag last night, and my too-big slacks sag off my hips. Even Carpenter managed to clean up decently, though his trusty beanie still hides his hair. I try not to feel self-conscious, but standing next to Ryann, it's hard not to.

The presentation includes interactive demos, where attendees can test out AVA's features. Carpenter struggles with getting the laptop to screen-share, and as I step in to help, I seize the opportunity to ask about KC.

"So, what's up with you and Kansas?" I ask, keeping my tone light.

He glances at me sideways, pursing his lips as the PowerPoint finally appears on the wall-length screen behind the stage. "I was gonna ask you the same thing, actually."

"Me?"

"Yeah." Raising an eyebrow, he turns to face me fully. "If you guys are, like, a thing, that's cool. I just wish one of you had told me."

My hands freeze on the keyboard as I whip my head toward him, wide-eyed. "We aren't a thing. I don't like Kansas that way, we're just friends."

"Kissing friends?"

Well, no. Not really. The kiss was alright, I guess, but I don't plan on doing it again. There's only one person I want to kiss.

With a shrug, my eyes find Ryann across the room, studying his speech cards. "In all honesty, we only did it because he said he wanted to make someone jealous."

Carpenter's expression grows even more suspicious. "Who?"

"Dunno. He didn't say."

Probably *you*. But I don't say that. It's not my business.

Carpenter seems to warm up to me for the rest of the morning, sticking close as we help Liza and Ryann with whatever they need. The auditorium fills quickly, every seat taken, with people even lining the walls just to get a glimpse of CalTek's latest invention. When the lights dim and dramatic music fills the space, it's showtime.

Ryann steps onto the stage, commanding the crowd effortlessly. Watching him from the sidelines is mesmerizing. He introduces AVA with the kind of knowledge and passion that makes it impossible not to pay attention.

"As many of you know, CalTek started as a family business," Ryann begins intently. "Family has always been at the forefront of our core values. Not only does AVA have the most advanced camera features in the industry, but we've also integrated an AI-based fire and carbon monoxide detection system that comes standard with every purchase. Your well-being is our top priority, guaranteed."

A lump rises in my throat as I listen, struck by the weight of his words. His focus on safety, the emphasis on protecting people, shows me how deeply personal this project is to him. No wonder he's spent the last few months working himself to the bone. After everything that's happened—the nightmare he had—it's clear who he's been doing all of this for. His mom.

The crowd is captivated, and when Ryann opens the floor for questions, hands shoot up instantly. He answers each one with patience and confidence before announcing a seventy-two-hour Hackathon at the end of the week. It's open to everyone—except CalTek employees—and challenges teams to create new applications for AVA's software. The winning team not only gets bragging rights but also a cut of the sales if their app is chosen.

It's an amazing opportunity for aspiring programmers to showcase their skills. I won't lie, it sucks that I can't participate, but with all the other competitions happening here, I'll find something worth entering. So it's fine.

While our developers manage the demos, Liza and Ryann drag us into another room where they're both speaking on a panel about cyber-security and AI ethics. Carpenter dozes off halfway through, muttering something about it being boring, but I'm on the edge of my seat, scribbling notes.

The rest of the day flies by, and when it's time to pack up, Ryann gives everyone the go-ahead to explore before dinner. Unfortunately, I'm too late for the mainframe contest, but I manage to hit a crypto workshop and a Q&A on Automation. Carpenter ropes me into a virtual escape room, accidentally picking the horror-themed one. An hour of him shrieking in my ear later, we finally stumble out, laughing, and meet up with the rest of our group by the shuttle.

Everyone's there—except Ryann. When I ask Liza where he is, she just shrugs.

"He had some work to do back at the hotel, but he said to have fun."

Work? What work? Sure, he has a few more panels this week, but the presentation is done. What else could he possibly be working on? As the shuttle takes us to the restaurant, I pull out my phone to text him, but there's no reply. And without him, it feels...lonely, even with Carpenter babbling nonstop. Seriously, the guy just doesn't shut up. No wonder KC gets irritated with him.

My mood only worsens as the evening drags on. I barely touch my spaghetti, every bite making me nauseous, while everyone else buzzes about their day at the Con. By the time we make it back to the Four Seasons, I'm overstimulated and on edge. At one point, I even plug my ears when one of the devs starts belting out a show tune in the van.

When I finally reach our room, I'm frickin' exhausted. My legs ache from walking all day, and I just want to collapse into bed. But the door is locked.

Crap. I don't have a key. Leaning my forehead against the door, I knock softly, resisting the urge to lie down in the hallway and pass out. No answer.

"Ryann?" I call out, louder this time. Still nothing. What the hell?

With my stomach in knots, I pull out my phone and call his number, but it goes straight to voicemail.

"Ryann? Open up. I forgot my key." My knocking turns frantic, morphing into desperate pounding and then kicks, a panic swelling in my chest when it gets hard to breathe.

Where is he? Why isn't he answering? *What the hell am I supposed to do?*

I'm on the verge of finding Liza when the door suddenly flies open. I stumble forward with a startled yelp, straight into Ryann's arms.

"Christ, Shilo, why are you out here yelling?"

"Where have you been?!" I nearly wail, my voice cracking as I vaguely register his rumpled shirt and the messy state of his hair. "I called and called, but you didn't answer!"

His eyes widen behind the thick-rimmed glasses he wore on Halloween, and he shuts the door, gently pulling me into the room. "Hey, it's alright. Shh, I'm sorry, doll. I fell asleep."

I hadn't even noticed the tears on my cheeks until his thumbs brush them away, and I bury my face into his chest as embarrassing sobs wrack my body. "I...forgot my key, and you...left me out there."

God, I hate it when I get like this, but I can't *stop* it. I can only ride it out.

Ryann stiffens for a moment before his arms tighten around me. He carefully steers us to the bed and tugs me onto his lap. "It was a long day, and I didn't sleep last night. I should have texted. I didn't mean to upset you."

I cling to him as the tears come harder, his hand stroking my back in slow, steady circles. Memories of kids laughing at me for breaking down like this come flooding back, Dad's voice ringing in my head.

Stop being a crybaby and suck it up, son. Do you think they let you cry in the Air Force?

With a trembling hand, I wipe my nose, sitting back to give Ryann some space. He's watching me closely, but I keep my burning eyes on his chest. "Sorry."

"Why are you apologizing?" He asks roughly. "I knew I had both keys but figured I'd be awake when you returned. Don't be sorry, doll face."

His words make fresh tears well up, and I lean forward, resting my forehead against his chin as I swallow another sob.

"What do you need from me right now? What can I do?"

Sighing heavily, I slip beneath the hem of his shirt, feeling his abs clench at the contact. "T-this is good. Just let me touch you."

He pauses, just for a moment, then nods. "Alright."

My fingertips wander over his body, exploring the planes of his chest. He inhales sharply when my nails graze lightly over his nipples, and I focus there, tracing gentle circles as my own breathing steadies. His, on the other hand, grows noticeably uneven, each exhale heavier than the last. When his throat flexes with a hard swallow, I lean in, pressing my lips softly to his Adam's apple. The quiet hum he lets out vibrates against my mouth, sending a shiver through me. His cock starts to harden, and my own pokes his torso as his palms slide down to my ass. Not going to lie, I want to hump him, but I don't. And he doesn't push, either.

Moving on from his nipples, I run my fingers through the curly strands of his happy trail, causing him to groan. He feels so strong, so manly. I wish he would hold me like this more often. Which reminds me...

"You've been with Olivia since August," I accuse, not lifting my head from his neck. "Saw it on her Instagram."

Ryann goes still beneath me. "It's complicated."

I pull back, rubbing my eyes with my fists before fixing him with a glare. "You also told me there's been no one else since we started this...thing. You lied."

Those golden-green eyes flash, his jaw tightening as he weaves his fingers into my hair. "I didn't lie to you, Shilo. Sexually, I've only been with you since October."

"That's—" Squirming on his lap, I try to slip out of his grip. "That's such a bullshit thing to say."

"It's not bullshit, it's the truth." He keeps me in place, holding my body against his. "Olivia and I aren't together that way."

"I saw the way she hung off you at the Christmas party. Saw her post where she said she loved you, Ryann. I *saw.*"

A dry laugh leaves his throat. "Yes, the Christmas party where you ran away before I could explain. Then proceeded to drink yourself under the table before coming all over my father's computer."

I freeze, feeling my cheeks heat as I gape at him in horror. "I did *what?*"

"Exactly." Narrowing his gaze, he reaches up to adjust those sexy-as-hell glasses. "Then afterward, you ignored my text on New Year's Eve, and KC uploaded a photo of you two kissing. Was I wrong in assuming something was happening there?"

Folding my arms, I scowl at him from under my hair. "*Very* wrong. I don't like Kansas that way. Why does everyone keep thinking I do?"

His brows lift at that. "And you think I like Olivia that way? I'm gay, doll. She's a lovely woman, but she does nothing for me."

"So, it's all an act?" I was right when I told Kansas that I thought their relationship was fake?

He huffs, running a hand through his hair before scratching his cheek. "As I said, it's complicated."

"Oh, s-screw you." Wriggling out of his grip, I slide off the bed and march toward the bathroom, embarrassed by my obvious boner. "You're the hardest person to talk to sometimes."

Seriously. It feels like trying to reason with a brick wall.

Bare feet slap against the tile as he follows me in. I glance over my shoulder just in time to see him yank off his rumpled shirt. "What are you doing?"

"Drawing us a bath," he growls, leaning over to spin the faucet above the Jacuzzi tub.

I frown, watching him adjust the temperature, my mouth watering at the way the muscles in his back flex with every movement. "I can't take a bath with you."

"Why not?"

"Because..." My voice falters, and I bite my lip, staring down at the clothes clinging to my body.

Getting in there would mean being *naked*. And I can't be naked around him. Not completely.

Ryann moves closer, lifting my chin as he searches my gaze intently. "Shilo, we've fucked. I've had my tongue inside your asshole. I promise nothing you have under there will scare me away."

I let out a squeak, my cock jumping painfully at the memory of how good that felt, how good *he* felt. But still... the wounds from high school run deep. And he's exactly the type of guy that used to mock me—one of those locker room jocks with their chiseled muscles and perfect genetics.

Rather than voice my insecurities, I shake my head and glare at the floor, blinking back tears. Eventually, he sighs, turning off the water before sitting on the edge of the tub. A shuffle of fabric catches my attention, and I glance up through my lashes to watch as he slides his pants down, his gaze fixed on the marred flesh of his thick thigh.

"I mentioned the fire that night you slept over," he begins, eyes growing distant, "but I never told you how it happened."

Pausing, he clears his throat, absently running a thumb over the scar. "It was my fault. The fire. I killed my mother."

My head snaps up, a chill spreading through me at the emptiness in his tone. "What happened?"

"A bottle rocket," he says flatly, "given to me from an older kid down the street. I was fifteen. By then, my mom had finally gotten the US courts to grant her joint custody, and I'd started staying at her house. We were rebuilding our relationship." He swallows hard, still tracing his skin. "I thought it'd be fun to light the rocket in the garage, stupidly thinking it would just spark up and fizzle out. Instead, it shot through the house and set everything on fire."

"Ryann, you were just a kid," I say softly, moving closer to him. "It was an accident."

"An accident that took someone's life." He meets my gaze when I stop before him, his eyes softening as he wipes my damp cheeks. "My mother had been sleeping at the time, and we were told that she likely died that way. They found her still in bed. Cause of death was smoke inhalation."

At least she didn't suffer. That thought probably doesn't take his pain away, though.

His hands settle on my hips as he continues. "Declan took the fall for me. Things between us became even more strained than they already were. He moved in with us, but he was a ghost. Hardly spoke to anyone, spent all his time locked in his room. I attended a private school while he stayed in the public system. He...blamed me for what happened. It wasn't until college that we finally hashed it out and became brothers instead of strangers who just happened to share a womb."

"I'm so sorry," I whisper, my throat tightening around something heavy I can't quite swallow. "You must have been really lonely."

"So were you."

Those hazel eyes meet mine, and I glance down with a weak shrug. "I just got made fun of. Called names, pushed around. Nothing like what you went through."

Jeez, he lost an entire parent, and I'm over here having issues just because some kids were mean? What's wrong with me?

Ryann frowns, entwining his fingers with mine. "This isn't a competition, doll. That's not why I'm telling you this."

"Then why are you?"

He blinks, clearly caught off guard. Running a hand through his hair, he exhales sharply before looking away. "Because you needed to hear it."

My brows knit in confusion for a moment, but then his words from Christmas Eve resurface in my mind, and everything clicks. "The fire alarm for AVA. Olivia's the one who developed the software, isn't she?"

"Yes."

"So you..." My thumb instinctively finds its way to my mouth as I chew on my nail, studying his open expression. "You're dating her to get the rights to it. That's...that's messed up."

His lips quirk as he gently pulls my thumb out, replacing it with his own. "I was, at first. It was a scheme Ronin came up with to make the merger go smoothly, but you're right. It's messed up, which is why I told Olivia the truth. And we came up with a plan of our own."

“What kind of plan?” I ask around his thumb, sucking the salt from his skin.

“It’s just for show.” His voice grows thick as he stares at my mouth, his cock swelling in his briefs. “For Ronin. Those Instagram posts you saw of us were taken at business meetings, but she went back and changed the captions to convince him further. Just until he retires.”

“But that’s in *five months*,“ I whine, stepping back so his hands fall away from me. “Does that mean we can’t...fool around anymore?”

Surprise flickers in his eyes as he tilts his head. “You’d still want to? Even after all of this?”

“Well, it’s not real, right? You and her?”

Tell me I was right.

Ryann shakes his head slowly, watching me. “No.”

“Then, why not?” I mumble, fidgeting. “I-I mean, if you do. If you want me.”

Reaching out, he grabs the front of my shirt and pulls me close, his lips brushing mine softly. “I want you. But it has to stay a secret until May.”

“It was kind of a secret before, anyway.” Crawling onto his lap, I straddle his strong thighs and let out a contented sigh, rubbing my cheek against his. “But you have to let me sit on you whenever I want.”

“Deal,” he chuckles, his hand gliding up my back. “Now, take a bath with me, doll. After the week we’ve had, we deserve it.”

He reaches over to turn the faucet back on, and I hesitate, my fingers curling tightly around the hem of my shirt. My pulse kicks up, trembling slightly.

"The... the last time I got shirtless around people, they laughed at me," I whisper, peeking at him through pale purple strands. "It was senior year, in the locker room. I thought it was empty, so I stepped out of the shower stall with a towel around my waist." My voice shakes as the memory floods back. "Bobby Crawford was waiting with his football friends to take pictures. They called me a girl because I had moobs and tried to rip my towel off."

Ryann goes rigid as he pushes my hair out of my face.

"Did they hurt you?" he asks, his voice lethal.

A shiver runs through me at his tone. "No. The security guard came in to check the noise since it was after hours. I'd stayed late because the PE teacher hated me and wouldn't let me leave until I finished running the mile. But...a few weeks later, Bobby pantsed me at graduation. I fell over. It wasn't pretty."

It was also all over social media. But I'm definitely not telling him that.

"Shilo, I'd never laugh at you," he says fiercely, cupping my face with both hands. "You're the most gorgeous boy I've ever seen, and those little assholes were wrong. Everything about you is perfect."

His words wash over me, sending a wave of warmth from my head to my toes, and my heart lurches almost painfully in my chest. When he tentatively reaches for the hem of my shirt,

I nod slightly, letting him lift it. My pulse races as I hold my breath, raising my arms so the fabric can slide over my heated skin.

As soon as the shirt is gone, my first instinct is to cross my arms over my chest, shielding myself.

"Don't," he murmurs softly, gently prying my arms apart. "Don't hide from me, baby doll. Let me see you."

His eyes roam over me, taking in every inch of my body. I squeeze my eyes shut, too afraid to see his reaction if it's bad. In my mind, I can picture what he's seeing—stretch marks from rapid weight loss, the crinkled skin. Compared to him, so fit and muscular, I must look...less. What if he loses interest?

My breath hitches, a small, involuntary sound, and then suddenly, he's leaning me back. My eyes fly open just as his lips press to my chest.

"Ryann—"

He doesn't stop. Keeping me steady, he kisses down my sternum, his mouth moving lower, tracing a line down my stomach. When his gaze lifts to mine, I gasp, heat pooling low at the desire burning in his eyes.

"Beautiful," he breathes, flicking his tongue out to lick at my nipple. "Fucking delicious." Pulling me in, our lips meet in a searing kiss. "*Mine.*"

That's all it takes. That single, growled word has me dropping all my inhibitions as I throw my arms around him, desperately plunging my tongue into his mouth.

Without breaking away, he undoes my belt, lifting me to tug my pants off while keeping an arm possessively locked around my waist. His teeth sink into my bottom lip, not hard enough to break skin, but the sharp sting has me whimpering as my cock leaves a sticky mess on his abs.

"Fuck, I love those sounds you make," he groans, standing long enough to kick off his briefs before dragging me down into the tub.

The water overflows, flooding the floor, but he doesn't seem to care as he reaches for his pants to pull out a packet of lube from his wallet. All the while, I'm rutting against his stiff length, feeling it slide between my cheeks as I lick and bite at his shoulder, needy noises clawing from my throat.

Need him so bad.

"Shh, I've got you." Ripping open the packet, Ryann pours a generous amount on his fingers before reaching around to prod my hole, gently slipping in up to the knuckle.

A wave of relief has me melting into him when he adds a second finger, and I rock my hips in the warm water to meet his tempo, mind blissfully silent.

"There we go, that's it. I know what you need, baby."

Our mouths meet again as he stretches me, tongues swirling languidly for a long while. Apparently, I'm so turned on that I'm not doing words anymore, though, because I cry out in protest when his fingers slip from my body.

Can't think, only horny.

Eyes glittering, he nips at my jaw as he maneuvers my hips, positioning his slicked-up length at my hole. "It's been a few weeks, and I don't want to hurt you. Let's take it slow."

When I mumble something incoherent in response, Ryann leans back to gaze at me sternly. "Words, Shilo. I need to know if this this is okay."

"Y-yeah. Yes," I stammer, nodding as I lick my lips and squirm. "Just get inside of me, please."

Smiling in amusement, he gently presses in, the head of his cock breaching my tight pucker. Just like the last two times, it burns, but not as bad, now a dull ache that quickly disappears once he slides further in.

"Oh, God," I breathe against his mouth, my fingers clutching the hair on his nape. "You... it's so good. Feels so good."

A moan rumbles through his chest as he grips my waist tightly, teeth clenched and brows furrowed like it's taking all of his strength to hold back. He gives me a few moments to adjust before guiding me down until we're fully connected, filling me entirely. His cock brushes against my prostate, sending a shockwave of pleasure through my body, and I jerk forward.

"Fuck," Ryann grunts, shuddering as he holds me still. "Slow, doll face. Jesus. You're killing me."

"I don't want *slow.* I want—" Cutting myself off, I adjust my legs before rising off his length. His pupils blow wide when I slam myself back down.

"*Goddammit.*"

"Mmm." My eyes roll back at the feeling, my cock leaking between us as I do it again. Sitting on him like this feels so different, much better and much deeper. It's like I can feel him all the way in my heart, which would make me snort if I wasn't currently chasing the first orgasm I've had in almost a month.

He traps me against his chest, snapping his hips up, thrusting into me from below as bath water sloshes onto the floor. "Is this what you want? Need me to pound into you, hm? Fuck you so good you'll feel me for days?"

"Please, please, Ryann," I cry, teetering on the edge as I bury my face in his neck. "Let me come. Say I can come."

His ragged breaths fill my ears, skin slapping skin as he hits that spot inside of me over and over until I can't even wait for permission. My cock erupts between us, and I have to dig my teeth into his skin to keep from shouting. Two seconds later, he comes with a growl, movements growing jerky as he drains himself.

It's a feeling like none other, the way his length pulses as he fills me up. I want to experience it forever. Fall asleep with his dick in me and wake up that way. I wonder if he'd do that for me? Maybe he'd think that's weird.

"Don't move," he murmurs, breathless, as he slips out of me and reaches beneath us to pull the bath plug. While the water drains, he grabs a washcloth and cleans me up, pausing when I flinch at the damp material swiping across my tender hole. "Did I hurt you?"

Quickly shaking my head, I try to sit up but gasp when I spot the bite mark on his shoulder. "No, but I hurt *you.*"

He tilts his head, following my gaze, and a smirk curls his lips when he wipes away a few dots of blood. "Love marks, baby. Nothing to worry about."

Well, that's...incredibly sexy. I can't believe I bit him like that, though.

Once we're clean, he fills the tub with fresh water, adding soap before turning on the jets. While bubbles form around us, I stay on his lap, mewling like a cat as I nuzzle into him, already growing hard for another round.

"I like this position. We should do it again."

"Oh, we will," he huffs, taking a handful of bubbles to lather into my hair. "Not tonight, though. My refractory period is nowhere near as fast as yours, and you need to heal after that."

Ugh. But I guess he has a point. So I try to ignore my raging boner, taking some bubbles to give him a Santa beard while he grumbles at me.

It's nice just sitting here with him, laughing and being silly. Naked. For once, I don't feel like I need to act normal, or hide myself. He makes me feel like I can just... be me.

"So why purple?" He asks, watching me soap up his chest. "The hair, the nails. I've always wondered."

My smile falters as I stare at the bath water, a nervous flutter in my stomach. "Purple is pretty. Everyone likes purple things. Sunsets, grapes, the eggplant emoji. Well, I guess not everyone likes grapes. Some people are allergic, and that's crazy because they're probably my favorite fruit after kiwi, and I can't imagine being allergic—"

"Shilo."

Ryann cuts off my rambling, gently lifting my chin with a finger. I swallow hard when I meet his imploring gaze.

"It just...made it easier for me to look at myself in the mirror."

His eyes darken as he leans forward to kiss me, causing my heart to skip. "You're the most exquisite thing I've ever seen."

Feeling my cheeks heat, I duck my head, resting against his shoulder with burning eyes. It's been such a heavy night—first my freak out, then the conversation about his mom. Honestly, I'm drained, and a yawn escapes me as I steer the conversation somewhere lighter.

"Your modeling pictures are on my phone, just so you know. Been there a while. Found them when I Googled you after my interview."

A snort leaves his nostrils. "I figured as much during the Christmas party."

"I can't even remember that night." My voice grows drowsy as sleep tugs at my eyelids, another yawn slipping out. His lap is warm and comfortable, like I knew it would be. "I woke up, and my sheets smelled like you."

Huffing a quiet laugh, he reaches down to drain the water before lifting me out of the tub. "Let's get dried off and go to bed. Since I'm sure you didn't eat much at dinner, I'll order us something."

But I'm already so tired. My limbs feel heavy as he towels me off gently. When I raise my arms, he catches my sleepy grin, amusement softening his features as he helps me dress.

It feels good, being taken care of like this. Other than my mom and Paige, no one's ever made me feel like I'm something special. Someone precious.

And honestly? I think Ryann likes having someone to care for, too.

Ryann

The week passes in a blur of tech demonstrations, Q&A panels, and endless meetings. Interest in AVA is off the charts, our systems flooded with pre-orders, and my inbox constantly pings with emails from investors. Despite the successful launch, work hasn't slowed down—half my time is spent in the hotel room on conference calls until my eyes cross.

My life has always been this way, and for the longest time, I embraced it. If nothing else, it kept the loneliness at bay, even if I refused to admit it. But now? All I can think about is my little doll.

When Shilo's at the convention center with Liza and the devs, earning first place in some tech competition, or even just going out to dinner with the group, I fucking *miss* him. What the hell is happening to me?

We're in New York, and I don't want to spend my time stuck in the world's most uncomfortable chair, listening to analysts drone on about profit margins. I want to experience this city with him. Why am I even in this meeting? Isn't the financial shit Declan's department?

Pulling up his schedule, my jaw clenches when I see how light his workload is back in Seattle. A quick admin check confirms my suspicion: Ronin has been flooding my calendar with back-to-back calls. Of course. Another one of his tests, no doubt, to see how much I can handle, as if I don't already have enough on my plate. Don't get me wrong, Liza's been handling everything like a pro, but even I can tell she's starting to get frazzled. Perhaps it's time I take my twin up on his offer.

As the meeting wraps up, I grab my phone and shoot him a text, asking if he'll handle my next few calls so I can focus on the convention. His reply is almost instant—a thumbs up and a casual *you got it, bro* that makes me smile. How we went half our lives without speaking is beyond me because now, I can't imagine my life without him.

Taking an Uber to the convention center, I gaze out the window, my thoughts drifting to Shilo. Our conversations over the past week replay in my head, the way we've grown so comfortable with each other. My cock twitches when I think of his body writhing above me in his new favorite position—how gorgeous he is, unabashed and unafraid. How intoxicating. I've spent every night buried inside him, discussing shows or games I know nothing about just to watch his face light up. I can't seem to get enough. Fuck, I want him all the time.

A text buzzes in my pocket when we pull up to the convention center, and my stomach immediately sours as I spot a message from Olivia.

Olivia:

I'll be in Jersey tonight if you want to meet.

Me:

Why are you in Jersey?

This whole business with her is exhausting. Yes, it's fake, and even though we both know it, I hate playing pretend.

Olivia:

I've got season passes to the Giants game tonight.

That's right, she's a Jersey girl. I'd forgotten. Her company expanded to the West Coast only recently.

Olivia:

I can get you a seat in my suite if you like? We're playing Baltimore.

Well, shit. Football games aren't generally my thing, but getting the chance to watch one of the few openly gay NFL players take down the Giants? How can I refuse?

But how can I accept?

Flashing my attendee badge as I step inside the building, my mind is on Shilo—like it always seems to be. Things with him have just started to feel...familiar. Easy. The last thing I want is to rock the boat by ditching him for a night out with my fake girlfriend. Even if that's how our lives will look once we're back home, I can't bring myself to spend an evening without him.

And yet...what if—no. Bad idea. Terrible, even.

But still...

Me:

Make that two seats.

My little doll isn't a sports fan, but I've never been to MetLife Stadium, and the thought of sharing that experience with him makes the idea even more appealing.

It's Friday, and the convention is at its busiest. Fighting my way through the crowd toward the auditorium, I spot Liza deep in conversation, walking a few consumers through AVA's central hub. My eyes scan the room, frowning when there's no sign of purple hair.

"Where's Shilo?" I ask as soon as I'm beside her.

She throws me an exasperated look. "Him and that PA of yours were chomping at the bit to try some VR thing, so I cut them loose."

"Where at?"

With a shrug, she hands out a few brochures before wiping sweat from her brow, looking a little ragged. Guilt tugs at me for being so absent this past week.

"How are you holding up? Need any help?"

Liza flashes me an appreciative smile but shakes her head. "Oh no, I'm fine. Go check on your brother's girlfriend's brother. I'm sure you're protective of him."

Her comment makes me pause, an uncomfortable knot settling in my gut as I walk away slowly. Of course, I'm protective of him—but not for the reasons she thinks.

The urge to set her straight, to tell everyone that Shilo is mine, surges in my chest. But...I can't. Not until May.

Shilo doesn't answer when I call, so I follow signs pointing toward VR events. The area is packed, but it doesn't take long to spot his unmistakable purple hair up on stage. He's wearing a VR headset, and behind him, a giant projector displays what he's seeing—a Japanese-style fighting game where he's clashing swords with another opponent.

The crowd below the stage cheers wildly, and I watch in horror as my little doll slices off the other fighter's arm in a violent spray of blood across the screen.

Christ.

"Cool, huh?"

I glance over to see Carpenter smirking as another person steps up to fight.

"Not the word I'd use." *Barbaric* is more like it.

Carpenter snickers. "Shilo's pretty good. He's been leading for a while. Took me out with a slice to the stomach."

With sick fascination, I watch as Shilo swings a small baton that doubles as a katana in the game, taking down five more contenders in a flurry of dismemberment. The crowd roars their approval with each brutal victory until finally, someone manages to defeat him with a particularly gory decapitation.

Everyone boos at his defeat but claps enthusiastically when he removes his headset. My chest tightens at the sight of his wide grin as he bows, basking in the attention. The nervous, fidgety boy I met months ago is gone—this Shilo is confident, radiant, and completely in his element.

Maybe CalTek should look into video game design...

"Dude, that was sick!" Carpenter rushes up to meet Shilo, the two exchanging a fist bump. "I thought for sure you were going to win the competition, man. You really know how to fight!"

"Thanks," Shilo laughs, swiping a few sweaty strands of hair from his face. He freezes instantly when he spots me standing there.

"Seriously, that game felt so real, I thought you'd actually cut me," Carpenter says, lifting his shirt before grabbing Shilo's hand and pressing it to his abs. "You don't feel any stab wounds or anything, right?"

A low growl rumbles in my chest, and Shilo yanks his hand back as I fix my PA with a hard stare.

"Don't you have work to do?"

Carpenter blinks. "Uh, no?"

My eyes narrow, and we lock gazes until I can practically see the light bulb flicker on over his head.

"Oh, yeah. Right. *Work*. Got it. See you later, Shilo," he mumbles, waving awkwardly before scurrying off.

I turn back to Shilo, my gaze softening as he offers me a shy smile.

"Hi," he breathes, peeking at me through his lashes.

"Hi, doll."

A faint flush spreads across his pale cheeks, and he ducks his head, biting his lip. "Were you watching me?"

"Always." I reach out, gently tucking a strand of hair behind his ear. "Can I take you somewhere tonight?"

His brow furrows slightly, curiosity flickering in his eyes. "Where?"

The urge to pull him in and kiss that frown away is almost unbearable, but I rein it in. *Soon.*

"Have you ever been to New Jersey?"

MetLife Stadium glows like a beacon, the roar from the stands nearly deafening as we weave our way up to the VIP suites. Shilo's eyes glimmer beneath his hood, wavy tendrils brushing his cheeks as he takes in the sea of fans clad in red and gray.

"My dad is going to be so jealous," he murmurs, snapping a few quick pictures on his phone. The memory of his horrified expression when I told him where we were going brings an indulgent smile to my lips. But he came along anyway, just to spend time with me, and the thought makes my chest ache in ways I'm not entirely ready to examine.

I guide him into the suite, keeping a hand on his lower back as I scan the plush seats and perfect view of the field. A digital banner loops around the stadium, displaying donor names, and CalTek's logo flashes on the screen before cycling to the next. We've sponsored this place for years. How have I never caught a game before?

A glimpse of auburn hair catches my attention, and I quickly slip in front of Shilo, nervously running a hand across my jaw. "There's something I forgot to mention. These tickets weren't mine. They were given to us by—"

"Ryann, darling, how wonderful to see you."

I wince as Olivia steps forward, pressing a kiss to my cheek. My stomach sinks as Shilo stiffens, his entire demeanor shifting in an instant. He drops his head, shoves his hands into his pockets, and shrinks into himself, refusing to acknowledge her outstretched hand.

"And you must be Shilo," Olivia says kindly. "I recognize you from the Christmas party. Ryann's told me so much about you."

He mumbles something, scuffing the ground with his Chucks, and I meet Olivia's perplexed look with a tight smile. "Give us a moment, please, Liv."

As soon as she's gone, I reach for Shilo's shoulders, but he flinches away, catching me off guard.

"You brought me here to third wheel on your date?" he hisses, glaring at me from beneath his tousled hair.

I exhale slowly, keeping my voice even. "I brought you here because I wanted to share this with you. And it isn't a date. Not a real one, anyway. Olivia knows about us."

"She...?" His frown deepens as he lifts his head slightly, letting me see those gorgeous eyes. "I thought you said we had to keep it a secret?"

"Aye, but to be honest with her, I had to tell her about you." The suite begins to fill, and I guide him toward a quieter corner, resting a hand on his arm. "I meant what I said, doll. There's nothing between Olivia and me. It's all for show."

He swallows hard, slim throat flexing as he glances over my shoulder. "And this isn't, like, weird? Hanging out with us both?"

"Maybe a little," I admit, dragging a hand down my face. God, this was a terrible idea. "Do you want to head back to the hotel? I can call us another Uber."

"You'd come with me?" He seems surprised, his head tilting as he studies me.

Glancing around to ensure we're hidden, I give in to temptation and press my lips to his. "Of course I would. I'd never force you into something that makes you uncomfortable."

His tension visibly eases, shoulders relaxing as he rises on his toes to chase another kiss. "I think... I'm okay. It's awkward, but it's not real, right?"

"Right." Smiling, I grab his wrist and tug him toward one of the lounge seats near the front. "What *is* real, though, is us. And I want to experience your first NFL game together."

Olivia smiles as we approach, her gaze flickering between us. "Everything good?"

With a nod, I slide into the middle seat. Shilo's still visibly tense, his shoulders hunched, and I can't help but wish I could pull him onto my lap to shield him from the awkwardness.

Clearing her throat, she offers my little doll a grin. "Ryann tells me you're studying programming. I actually have a degree in that field myself."

"Computer engineering," he mumbles, fiddling with his hoodie sleeves as he peeks at her. "Kind of the same thing, but not."

"Oh, that's right. You deal with all the physical components while I specialize in code," she winks, and he thaws a fraction.

"Yeah, sorta."

The two exchange a few more words before the conversation fizzles out, and I send her a grateful smile for making an effort.

"I should FaceTime my dad," Shilo whispers as the players take the field, the crowd erupting into cheers. "These seats are insane."

The mention of his father makes my stomach roil, but I push the feeling aside and smile. "I bet he'd love that. It's not every day you get to see the Giants kick some ass live."

Olivia nudges me, grabbing a handful of popcorn from the bag at her feet. "True. And you get to see your Ravens lose."

I scoff, draping an arm behind Shilo's chair. "Shall we make a bet? If my team wins, you cut the royalties for AVA in half."

"Deal."

While Shilo chats with his father, I let myself get lost in the game, my eyes tracking number twenty-two as he moves through his warm-ups. Football was never my sport, but I've followed Huckslee Davis since his college days. The kid's got guts—coming out in an industry as hyper-masculine as the NFL takes courage I've never had.

Not for the first time, I wonder how different my life might've been if I were free to just *be*. If my mother had raised me instead of Ronin. If she hadn't died. Would I still be this version of myself? Or more like Declan, with his easy smiles and joking nature? And what if our roles had been reversed? If I'd been the one she'd taken with her instead?

Maybe I'd be in Huckslee's shoes, openly out and playing pro ball in Boston. Or maybe I wouldn't even have made it this far. I guess I'll never know.

A shiver pulls me from my thoughts as Shilo presses into my side, sneaking as close as he can without drawing attention. The ache in my chest tightens. If I were braver, I'd wrap him up in my arms for warmth, but I'm not. At least, not yet.

The game drags on, heading into overtime after the Giants' quarterback lands a flawless pass to tie it up. I spend most of it explaining the rules to Shilo, though he hardly pays attention, instead ogling every player on the field. When I lean down to tease him about it, brushing my lips against his ear, he flashes me a coy smile, his cheeks pink beneath the stadium lights.

"Don't worry, Mr. Callahan," he murmurs sweetly, popping that damn thumb into his mouth. "I'd much rather watch basketball players instead."

Oh, I do love this bold side of him, but he's playing with fire.

Two minutes left on the clock, and Huckslee intercepts the ball from the Giants, sprinting for the end zone. Olivia and I are on our feet instantly, shouting for opposing teams as he's tackled at the line. The stadium holds its breath—but his feet cross the boundary. Touchdown. *Game over*. My Ravens take the win.

"Bullshit," Olivia mutters, huffing as she grabs her Prada bag. I smirk, rolling my eyes.

"Don't be a sore loser. Your team played well."

"Yeah, yeah." She sighs, placing a hand on my little doll's shoulder with a warm smile. "It was nice to meet you, Shilo. If you ever want to talk computers, hit me up."

With that, she disappears into the crowd, leaving Shilo staring after her. When those big blue eyes finally swing back to me, they're laced with curiosity. "She seems... nice."

"She is," I agree, guiding him toward the exit. "I think we'll be good friends when all of this is over. She'll make a savage business partner."

He hums but stays quiet as we navigate the throng of fans pouring out of the stadium. By the time we find our ride and slide into the backseat, he still hasn't said much, and I can tell he's stuck inside that pretty head of his. I don't know what's on his mind, but I *do* know that I'm not ready to go back to the hotel just yet.

"Know any place where we can get some authentic Brooklyn pizza?" I ask the driver as he pulls into traffic.

The man grins, shooting me a wink in the rearview mirror. "You kiddin'? I got just the joint for you."

Shilo whips his head toward me. "But I'm not—"

"I swear to all that is holy, if you tell me you're not hungry, I'll force-feed you," I growl, cutting him off.

His eyes flash in defiance. “I ate during the game.”

“A handful of popcorn doesn’t count as eating, Shilo. That’s a snack. I’m taking you to dinner.”

His scowl softens, morphing into something tender. “Like a date? A real one?”

Reaching out for his hand, I press his knuckles to my lips. The gesture surprises even me, but the affection comes naturally. “Yes, like a date. Just you and me.”

He straightens in his seat, practically bouncing as he turns to watch the Brooklyn Bridge come into view. “I’ve never been on a date before.”

He’s never...

That revelation twists my heart painfully. How have I fucked him six ways to Sunday, but never taken him on a proper date? We’ve done everything backwards. Now that we’re...whatever we are, I want to spoil him. Share all of his firsts, all of his *onlys.* I want them all to belong to me.

Forty minutes later, our driver drops us at a busy pizzeria in Bay Ridge. The place buzzes with energy, live music spilling out onto the sidewalk, and a line nearly out the door. Once inside, Shilo’s eyes light up when he spots a row of arcade games lining a brick back wall, and I press a quick kiss to the top of his head.

“Go pick a game for us to play while I grab our food, baby.”

Not needing to be told twice, he’s off in an instant, making me chuckle when he stops in front of *Mortal Kombat.* My sweet little doll likes violence, apparently.

Stepping up to the counter, I place our order with extra cheese and no meat. As I move aside to wait, a deep voice cuts through the chatter, freezing me mid-thought. Turning toward the entrance, I lock eyes with Huckslee Davis as he strides into the restaurant, leaving me speechless

What are the odds?

He's even bigger in person, muscles straining against his oversized coat, blond curls damp and wild. Beside him, his boyfriend Taylor jostles his shoulder, something unspoken passing between them in an intimate glance that makes my skin tingle. I've seen them together in photos—they're all over social media—but in person? They're fucking stunning. This is an opportunity I cannot waste.

Making my way over, I stop just short of invading their space, praying I don't come off too forward as I hold out my palm. "Huckslee Davis? It's nice to meet you. I'm Ryann."

Two pairs of eyes swivel toward me, and Huckslee shakes my hand with a wide smile. "Hey there. You a fan?"

"Of you both." I nod toward his boyfriend. "I've caught your stunt bike show."

That earns me a cocky grin as Taylor runs a hand through his dark hair. "Yeah? You like that shit?"

"Impressive. Can I buy you both a beer?"

They exchange a glance before Huckslee offers an apologetic smile. "We don't drink. We're just here for the pie."

Damn. Worth a shot.

"Of course," I nod smoothly, glancing back to check on Shilo before returning to the conversation. "Would it be alright if I asked you a personal question?"

Huckslee lifts a brow, his features growing wary. "We're not interested in a threesome, sorry."

I choke on my spit, coughing into my arm. "That's not my question, but I appreciate the visual."

"Oh." He laughs along with me while his boyfriend rolls his eyes.

"You'd be surprised how often we get asked," Taylor smirks. "Huck and I don't share."

"Neither do I." My voice lowers, and I clear my throat. "When you came out in college, were you worried about your career? In football, I mean."

The question hits like a stone, the playful energy shifting as both men stiffen. Taylor's face falls slightly, and for a moment, I wonder if I've overstepped.

"I never really had a coming-out moment," Huckslee answers slowly, sliding an arm around Taylor's waist. "It sort of happened for me in high school. By the time I got to college, I was just dating men, and word spread on its own. I was never concerned about what the NFL thought because, well...this isn't what I plan on doing forever. There are more important things in my life."

"Ah. That makes sense." My gaze drifts to Shilo, showing someone his age how to play the game he picked. His hands gesture awkwardly as he explains the buttons, and the sight puts a small smile on my lips.

"What I can say, though," Taylor interjects, studying me intently, "is that hiding who you are eats away at your soul until there's nothing left. Trust me. Someone wise once told me that the people who matter already know the truth."

He flashes his boyfriend a quick wink, and I consider his words, rolling them over in my mind. "That's great advice. Thank you."

"Is he yours?" Huckslee asks, nodding toward Shilo, who's still at the arcade.

A lump rises in my throat, but I manage to swallow it down and nod slowly. "Yes. Mine."

At least in private, far from home. But what would I give to claim him out loud? To let the world know he's mine without hesitation?

Five months. That's all it'll take. Once Ronin steps down, I can finally give Shilo what he deserves.

Someone who can claim him proudly. Someone who isn't afraid.

Shilo

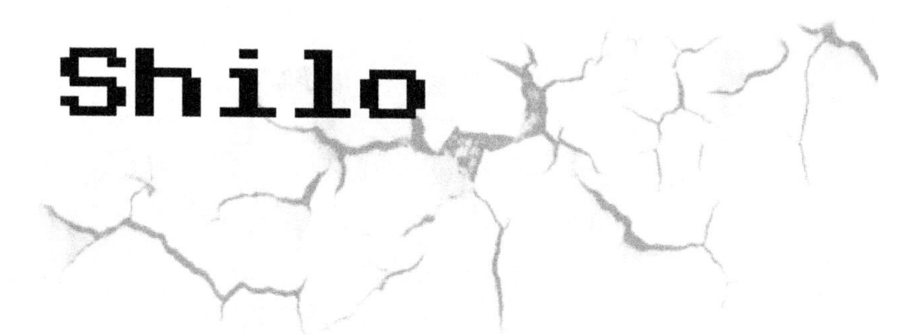

"Daaamn. I think I'd fuck you like this."

KC sets down the eyeliner he just applied to my eyes, tilting his head as he scrutinizes me. His gaze lingers until I squirm. "Seriously, Shilo, you're hot."

Tina nods in agreement beside him, and I snort, hopping off his bathroom counter. In the mirror, I take in my reflection—tight pants, a flowing crop top, shimmering skin from blush. For a brief moment, I almost like what I see. Almost.

Then my eyes land on my stomach, and the moment shatters. "I'm not hot. Do you have a longer shirt?"

"What? Why?" KC plants his hands on his hips as I eye his flat, smooth torso with a scowl.

"Because I don't look like you."

He blinks, sharing a look with Tina before dropping his hands. "No, you're small and adorable. I'm tall and scrawny."

"I don't think that's true," I mumble, poking at my side. "I've got... stretch marks."

"So?" Tina pulls up their skirt, revealing their thick thighs. "I do, too."

"And my bottom teeth are crooked," KC adds, pulling down his lip to show me. "See?"

From the living room, Carpenter chimes in, "I get zits on my ass!"

KC grins, makeup sparkling as he folds his arms. "So what should I do? Stop smiling? Should Tina stop wearing skirts?"

"Well, no," I mumble, shaking my head. "That's ridiculous. You both should do whatever you want, but I'm just...me."

Tina offers a sad smile, picking up a tube of mascara and meeting my gaze in the mirror. "We're all our own worst critics, love. And I know it sounds cliché, but beauty is more than skin deep. You're imperfectly perfect, and that's what makes you...*you*."

"Are you comfortable in that outfit?" KC checks, dressed similarly. "Like, how does it make you feel?"

I let the question settle, fingers brushing over the soft fabric as it swishes against my sternum. "I feel nice. Pretty."

"Then fuck what anyone else has to think or say. It's your birthday, and you deserve to feel pretty."

Yeah, my birthday. The big twenty-two, and instead of spending it with Ryann, the person I really want to be with, I'm heading to some college party I couldn't care less about.

Sighing, I grab my phone off the counter and reread the message he sent me this morning for the thousandth time.

Ry:

> Happy birthday, baby doll. I'd spend the day with you if I could, but we can celebrate tonight at my condo. I hope you have a fantastic day.

Of course, Ronin had to schedule some big shareholder event on my birthday which Ryann and Declan were forced to attend. With their *dates.*

He's on a date. On *my* birthday. And yeah, I'm bitter.

It's been over a month since we returned from New York, and it's been amazing. I've spent almost every weekend at his place, and during the work week, I persuaded Carpenter to get Ryann's coffee wrong just so he'd think of me. We created a routine, and it was easy to forget that this was all a secret.

Until today, when I realized he'd be standing by Olivia's side in the open while I'm still hidden. And I can't even complain because I'm the one who told him I'd be fine with it.

I'm really, *really* not fine with it.

Why do I keep doing this to myself?

"Alright, enough moping." KC tosses a makeup brush onto the cluttered counter and pulls me out of the bathroom. "We're going out to celebrate your birth, and we're going to have a great time. Maybe even find you a boyfriend."

"I don't want a boyfriend."

Carpenter chokes on the energy drink he'd been chugging when he sees us, slapping at his chest. "Holy fuck, you three look...Jesus."

KC smirks, taking in his roommate's tight shirt and jeans. "You're not so bad yourself. Almost fuckable."

"Almost?" Carpenter scowls at that.

"Yes, almost. The whole straight thing turns me off."

Tina snorts, and they start bickering as we all squeeze into KC's pink Volkswagen. Our destination isn't far—just twenty minutes with traffic—but it feels much too short when we pull up to a stranger's house swarming with people. My palms are damp, and a nervous flutter takes up residence in my gut as I watch the steady stream of bodies coming and going from the front door.

I hate parties. Why did I let them talk me into this?

Oh, right. Because, according to KC, a wild college party is a rite of passage, and he wouldn't take no for an answer. I'd rather be curled up on Ryann's new couch, laptop in hand, while he watches hot hockey players stretching on TV.

Carpenter snaps a group photo before we head inside, sending it to everyone's phones. I stare at the image for a moment, zooming in on myself. I look... good, I guess, even if I'm the shortest one in the group. Would Ryann like my outfit?

Before I can second-guess myself, I text him the picture, adding a quick selfie of my face right after. As I lower my camera, I catch KC watching me, his eyes narrowed with interest.

"What?" I blink nervously.

"Was that Ryann you were just texting?" he asks quietly, trying to peek at my phone when I hide it behind my back.

"No." Damn my squeaky voice.

"Uh-huh." He rolls his eyes and starts weaving through the crowded front porch, the pungent smells of beer, sweat, and marijuana already making me gag. "I'm not stupid, Shi. You don't have to lie to me."

Stopping in my tracks, I grab his arm, biting my lip as he spins to face me. "I didn't mean to lie. We're just... it's supposed to be a secret until he takes over for his dad."

KC tilts his head, his sharp gaze studying me long enough to make my anxiety spike.

"Are you mad at me?"

"No, not at *you*," he answers, pursing his lips. "Ryann better watch his coffee, though. I can't believe he's keeping you in the closet."

"Just for a few months," I rush defensively, feeling my cheeks heat. "Only until May. When he's CEO, he won't have to do what Ronin tells him anymore."

KC scoffs, shaking his head as he turns back around. "That sounds like bullshit to me. But hey, it's your life, Shilo. Just doesn't sound like you're much of a priority."

His words hit harder than I expect, and as I follow him into the house, I glare at the floor, trying to shake them off. I told Ryann I'd be willing to wait, but...KC has a point.

The house is fairly large, at least three stories, and heavy bass shakes the walls. I wonder how many neighbors are probably complaining about the noise. I would be.

My phone buzzes as I'm pulled toward the kitchen, and I take it out to read Ryann's response.

Ry:

I just had to sit down to hide what that picture did to me, fucking hell.

You're gorgeous. Please don't take anything off before you come home, I want to sit you on my lap and play with you.

Ah, shit. Now, *I* have to hide what *that* message did to me. Somehow. Ugh, I should have just worn a hoodie and sweats. Luckily—or unluckily—some Party Bro burps in my face when I pass by, so that takes care of the boner situation.

KC introduces us to some guy pouring shots behind the counter and with the way they're looking at each other, I'm pretty sure they've seen each other naked. Carpenter seems to think so too—his eyes narrow as he watches them flirt, his jaw tightening. His attention snaps to me when another guy standing too close presses a drink into my hand.

"Nope." Snatching the cup, Carpenter shoves it back into the guy's chest with a glare before pulling me away. "We don't take drinks from strangers. What's wrong with you?"

"I've never been to a house party before."

"Seriously? Well, fuck. Don't leave my side, then."

Tina wanders off to find their girlfriend, leaving me to watch Carpenter play beer pong. After mixing me a drink himself—presumably to ensure I don't get roofied—he demands I blow on his ping-pong balls for luck before each throw. I do it, but it makes no sense. This game is about hand-eye coordination, what does blowing on balls have to do with anything?

Eventually, Tina and their girlfriend pull me onto the dance floor, sandwiching me between them. I try to have fun, but I've never really danced before, and I'm hyperaware of how awkward I am. The pounding music combined with whatever drink Carpenter made earlier has my head spinning, and I feel more out of place than ever.

To make matters worse, KC and the guy he introduced us to have vanished, which has clearly set Carpenter on edge. His glare keeps darting toward the kitchen like he's expecting KC to reappear any second. Plus, there's no cake. Not a single slice.

What kind of birthday party has no damn cake?

Extracting myself from Tina's arms, I slip away in search of a bathroom, desperate for a break from the crush of body heat. After some wandering, I finally spot one down a dark hallway, but as I pass a group of guys huddled together smoking, one of them grabs my arm.

"What the fuck is this?" he snaps, yanking me back before I can even reach the door. The force makes me stumble, a startled yelp escaping my lips. "I don't wanna see this shit. Get the fuck out of here, fag."

My stomach plummets, cheeks burning hot at the word he just used.

"Did you hear me?" The stench of alcohol rolls off his breath, spittle landing on my face when he snarls. "Get your disgusting ass out of my sight."

Instantly, I start trembling, frozen as tears sting my eyes. Laughter erupts from his friends, spewing more words that rip open old wounds. When he takes a step toward me, I instinctively back away.

Right into a solid chest.

"There you are," Carpenter grumbles, grabbing my shoulders, and I sag against him in pure relief. "I told you not to leave my side, where'd you go?"

Drunk Asshole sneers, glancing between us. "You his boyfriend?"

Carpenter stiffens behind me, his grip tightening. "So what if I am?"

"We don't want no cocksuckers around here."

"No one wants to suck your tiny dick anyway," Carpenter scoffs, spinning us around. "Come on, Shilo."

"The fuck did you just say?"

Before I can react, my body jerks forward as Carpenter gets shoved from behind. He spins around, shoving the guy right back. "Keep your hands off me, fuckass!"

And then everything descends into chaos.

Asshole's cronies jump in, one of them landing a punch to Carpenter's cheek with a sickening crack that echoes through the hall. My screech rips through the air as another guy rears back for a second hit.

Without thinking, I lunge forward, pulling Carpenter out of harm's way. Pain explodes in my skull as someone's knuckles slam into my nose, sending me stumbling into the wall. My head smacks against it with a dull thud, and I slide to the floor as three other bodies join the fight.

Through tear-blurred eyes, I catch flashes of movement: Tina grabbing the asshole in a headlock, their girlfriend delivering a sharp kick to one of his friends' nuts. KC is on another guy's back, slapping him wildly like a feral cat. The sight would probably be really funny if I weren't bleeding all over my shirt—

Wait, I'm frickin bleeding?!

Oh, Jesus. Oh, it's everywhere.

"That's right!" Tina shouts as the three guys bolt for the backyard, brandishing a wallet like a trophy. "You better run, motherfuckers! I've got your ID!"

"Shit, Shilo." Carpenter drops to his knees in front of me, his eyes wide and frantic. "That's a lot of blood. You need a hospital."

"Ngh," I try to respond, but the blood pooling in my throat makes me gag. A garbled groan escapes as the pressure in my face builds, my eyes beginning to swell shut.

He yanks off his beanie, pressing it into my hand. "Hold this to your nose."

"Can you drive?" KC asks, panic edging his voice as he loops an arm under my shoulders. "Can anyone drive?! I think I drank too much."

"P-Paige," I manage to rasp, nausea rolling through me. My head throbs, sharp pain stabbing through my temples as my stomach churns. Bile rises in my throat, and the room spins dangerously.

KC's arms tighten around me just as the lights blink out.

Ryann

Fuck Ronin and these God-forsaken dinner parties.

One of our executives is droning on at the far end of the table, his monotone voice dragging like nails on a chalkboard. A quick glance to my left confirms Olivia's just as bored as I am, her chin propped on her hand as her eyes glaze over. Across from us, Declan and Paige look like they're one deep breath away from passing out.

Must be nice.

As the soon-to-be new head of the company, I have no choice but to pay attention, but it's hard. *I'm* hard, thanks to Shilo. Christ, he's all I seem to think about.

My gaze sweeps over the dining room in my father's manor as I try to distract myself from the picture he sent me earlier. The extravagant dinnerware gleams under a chandelier, velvet drapes covering the arched windows screaming wealth. This room has never seen warm family suppers or casual laughter, only lavish business meetings I've been forced to endure. Even as a child.

One thing's for certain—the word *frugal* has never existed in Ronin's vocabulary when it comes to personal comforts. The company, on the other hand? Different story.

"Now, about our budget for the upcoming quarter," he starts, barely sparing Declan a glance as he slides a binder over to me. "Let's discuss the areas where we can downsize."

I really fucking hate these parties. If you can even call them that. Sure, there's wine, music, and the finest desserts his live-in chef can whip up, but everyone at this table has a stick shoved so far up their asses they're practically muppets.

All I want is to get home to my little doll and kiss my way down that cute-as-fuck belly he's flaunting in his crop top.

"Is downsizing necessary when AVA's doing so well?" asks some analyst whose name I can't remember even if my life depended on it.

Ronin's cold gaze cuts to me. "I think I'll let my son answer that question."

Fucking kill me. Please.

"Our pre-orders are promising, that's true," I agree, forcing the annoyance from my tone. "We've more than made up for the overtime hours with those sales alone. However, once we launch, our Tech Support crew will—"

Paige's phone interrupts my words, blaring the Bee Gees, and her face drains of color as she fumbles to silence it.

"I am *so* sorry. Please, continue," she mutters, cheeks flushed as Ronin shoots her a disapproving glare.

My lips twitch in bemusement. She's so much like her brother. "As I was saying, Tech Support is going to have their hands full when AVA goes live, which means we'll have to allocate more hours to the budget—"

Stayin' Alive blares again, cutting me off mid-sentence. Paige huffs in frustration, excusing herself as she steps away to take the call. My gaze trails her from the corner of my eye while I try to continue, but I falter when I catch her reaction.

Her breath hitches audibly, and she goes rigid, hissing something under her breath before ending the call abruptly. When she returns to whisper into Declan's ear, her face is pinched with worry, and my gut twists uneasily.

"Apologies," my brother says, rising from his seat. "My girlfriend is having a family emergency we must attend to. Excuse us."

Family emergency?

Ronin waves them off with a curt gesture, looking only mildly inconvenienced. But my concern spikes as I push to my feet, my thoughts immediately jumping to Shilo.

Before I can take a step, a hand grips my arm with painful force, yanking me back.

"Where do you think you're going?" Ronin asks sharply, his calculating eyes—so much like mine—pinning me in place.

"I just want to make sure everything's alright." *I need to check on Shilo.*

Ronin's lips curl into something resembling a smirk. "Your concern for your brother's girlfriend is admirable, but we aren't done here. Sit."

His voice is firm, leaving no room for debate, and the weight of every gaze at the table presses down on me. My throat tightens as I slowly sink back into my seat, my heart pounding so loudly I can barely hear anything else.

Olivia's knuckles brush mine under the table, her worried gaze searching my face in question. Shaking my head, I pull out my phone to send Shilo a text.

Me:

Declan and your sister just left claiming a family emergency. Is everything alright?

Five minutes pass with no answer, the message still unread. A heavy weight settles in my stomach, the pulse in my ears drowning out conversation around me. Getting antsy, I shift in my seat until I can't take it anymore, deciding to give him a call.

But it goes to voicemail. Twice.

Me:

Shilo, pick up the phone.

I need to hear from you.

My father leans toward me imperceptibly. "If company concerns are of no interest to you, perhaps I should give this position to someone else?"

Goddammit.

Clenching my jaw, I shove my phone into my pocket and force myself to focus, or at least pretend to. I barely register the conversation, offering vague answers when prompted, my mind in a panic. Every second stretches endlessly as I wait for the buzz of a notification to ease the growing dread in my chest, thinking up one bad scenario after the next.

Where is he? What if something happened? What if he's been hurt?

The thought hits like a punch to the gut. I'd never forgive myself.

Fuck, I shouldn't be here. It's his birthday, for Christ's sake, and instead of celebrating with the boy I love, I'm dealing with fucking *work matters—*

All at once, the air is sucked from my lungs, leaving me breathless. The realization crashes over me like an icy wave, chilling me to the bone.

Love. *I love Shilo.* And I haven't even told him.

Minutes drag into an hour. Supper ends, and Ronin invites everyone into the drawing room for drinks. The moment we're dismissed, I slip away, pulling out my phone to call Declan.

No answer.

What the fuck is going on?

"Is it your boy?" Olivia's voice startles me as she approaches quietly from behind.

"I don't know." I exhale sharply, running a hand through my hair. "No one's answering their phones."

He needs to know. I have to tell him how I feel.

Just as I pull up KC's number to call for information, my phone buzzes with a message from Declan.

Finally.

Dec:

I thought you should know that we just picked up Shilo from the hospital...

There's more to the message, but I don't bother reading it. Fear drives me as I take off for the front door, my movements frantic. Why the fuck was he in the hospital? What happened?

"Ryann, wait for me!" Olivia's heels clack against the marble as she follows close behind. We're nearly to the foyer when my father steps out of the drawing room like a villain in a bad thriller.

"Where have you been? We've got board vacancies to discuss."

"We're leaving," I snap, yanking Olivia's coat from the hook before grabbing my own. "Paige's brother was hurt. I need to make sure he's okay."

"I fail to see what that has to do with you." Ronin steps closer, his full height matching mine as his lips curl in disbelief. "You've got responsibilities, boy, or did I make a mistake entrusting this company to you?"

Rage ignites in me, burning white-hot. "There are more important things than the company. Family might not matter to you, but I won't make that same mistake. Declan needs me."

He scoffs, sneering harshly. "Don't insult my intelligence. We both know it's not your brother you're worried about."

Blinking, I take a step back, briefly stunned into silence.

"I have cameras everywhere," he continues. "Especially in my office. Don't think I didn't see why you rushed off on Christmas Eve."

My chest tightens, fury warring with disbelief. The thought of him seeing Shilo that way, witnessing something so private, so *ours*, makes my blood boil. Beside me, Olivia glances between us, her face pale.

Ronin moves closer, a threatening gleam in his eye. "Take one step out that door, and you can kiss your career goodbye. That boy, too. I'll make sure neither of you works in the tech industry again."

Swallowing hard, I clench my fists. "You don't have that kind of pull."

His cruel smile twists deep. "Don't I? With that video, the boy would be lucky to get a job anywhere on the West Coast again."

My vision goes red, and I pull back my arm, ready to land a punch. Before I can make contact, Olivia catches my wrist, holding firm.

"Then they'll both work for me," she interjects, meeting my father's glare with one of her own.

He laughs darkly. "Did you forget we have a business arrangement, little girl? CalTek owns you."

"Not yet, you don't." Olivia adjusts her coat coolly before tugging me toward the door. "The merger isn't official until Spring, and Sentinel Solutions doesn't tolerate blackmail. I'm sure my board of trustees will be *very* interested in your less-than-ethical business practices."

Ronin sputters, his face trembling with rage, but I smirk as the front door closes behind us, the sight far more satisfying than it should be.

"Technically, I still own the rights to AVA," Olivia hisses, stomping toward my car. "And I'll be damned if I let it fall into *his* hands."

Before she can reach the passenger door, I pull her into a crushing hug, feeling the weight lift off my shoulders. "If I were straight, I'd kiss you for that."

She tosses her head back to laugh. "If I liked men, I'd let you."

We both grin as we slide into the car, but the moment fades when I pull out my phone to finish reading my brother's message. With every word, my blood runs colder.

Shifting into gear, I tear out of my father's driveway, racing across the city toward Declan's condo as fast as my wheels can take me.

Shilo

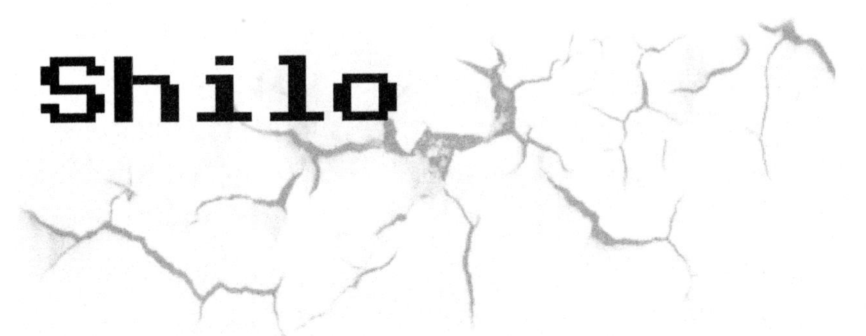

"Seriously, what the fuck is *wrong* with you?! A house party?"

My sister's angry voice makes me wince, too loud for my pounding head and aching neck. I squint at her from the hospital bed, my face feeling like someone took a sledgehammer to it. Across the room, Declan stands stiffly in his suit, shifting uncomfortably.

"I thought you were smarter than this, Shilo," Paige hisses, hands on her hips. If I could glare, I would, but my bruised eyes hurt too much. Also, I can't breathe through my nose, and I have a concussion, which sucks.

"What did I do wrong? Those homophobic assholes started it, not me." Luckily, my nose has been numb since the doctor reset the bone, but there's packing inside my nostrils to help the fracture heal.

Ugh, I wish Ryann were here. He's making an important speech tonight, though, and I don't want to jeopardize his job. It's important to him.

I just wish I were, too.

She rubs her forehead, exhaling sharply. "Mom and Dad are gonna flip their shit when they find out. They don't pay all that tuition money for you to get drunk at parties."

"*Party,*" I correct, groaning when I sit up to reach for my shoes. "One party. You know, for my birthday?"

Her eyes soften slightly, guilt flickering across her face as she comes around the bed to help me. "You're right, Iggs, I'm sorry. I just couldn't believe it when your friends told me that you got into a fight. That's not like you."

I didn't exactly *get into a fight* but I don't bother correcting her because what's the point?

Declan clears his throat, breaking the tension. "If you ask me, those guys deserved whatever your friends did. And with the ID Tina got, I'm sure the cops will find at least one of them."

Oh yeah, and *that* had been exhausting—giving statements to the police while the doctor waited for my nose to numb up. What a great birthday this has been.

If this is what twenty-two feels like, I don't know why Taylor Swift wrote a whole song about it. This frickin *blows*.

Once the doctor discharges me, Declan and Paige help me to the car. I grimace at my reflection in the window—the bloodstained crop top, the mascara streaks down my cheeks, the swollen, bruised face. I should have stayed home. Should probably stay home every night from now on, just to make sure this never happens again. And this outfit is stupid. I don't even know why I let KC convince me to wear it.

As they drive away, I rest my head on the seat and pull out my phone to check my messages, swiping away the apologies from my friends to read the texts from Ryann.

Ry:

Declan and your sister just left, claiming a family emergency. Is everything alright?

Shilo, pick up the phone.

I need to hear from you.

There are two missed calls as well, but I clear those away, blinking back tears.

I don't want to worry him, and I don't want to ruin his night. But God, I *really* wish he was here to hold me right now. I feel so stupid, so worthless. I wish I were just...someone else. Someone not me.

Actually. You know what? No.

The thought slams to a halt as KC's words from earlier echo in my head, making my chest ache.

So, should I stop smiling? Should Tina stop wearing skirts?

The fight wasn't my fault. I shouldn't be punished for just *existing*. I'm not the one with the problem—that asshole was. Everyone who ever made me feel this way in high school was the frickin problem!

The car slows as we pull up to the house, and Paige gets out to help me from the backseat.

"You don't need to come in with me," I mumble, ducking my head. "Sorry I ruined your night."

She huffs, throwing an arm around my shoulders as we climb the porch steps, leaving Declan waiting in the car. "You didn't ruin anything, Iggy. I'm just glad something worse didn't happen."

I guess she's right. But what *did* happen still hurts.

Worst. Birthday. Ever.

Thankfully, the house is dark when we step inside, and Paige pulls me toward the stairs.

"I'll help you wash your face, get you all set before I go—"

"What in God's name are you wearing?"

We freeze in place, my stomach dropping as my eyes dart toward the dining room. Dad sits at the table with a cup of coffee, his wide gaze taking in the bloodstained crop top and tight pants. My blood runs cold when my sister quickly steps in front of me.

"Dad, we thought you had work tonight," she says, her voice shaking.

"Got off early to surprise my son for his birthday, but apparently, he's been out doing God knows what." He stands abruptly, the harsh scrape of the chair against the floor making me flinch. Fear anchors me to the spot as he steps closer, my pulse racing. Logically, I know Dad's never laid a hand on us, but the memory of those guys at the party has my nervous system in overdrive, every instinct screaming at me to brace for impact.

He stops in front of Paige, his furious gaze narrowing on me over her shoulder. "Is that makeup on your face, boy?"

"Mark, why are you yelling?" Mom hurries down the hall, gasping audibly when she takes in my battered face. "Sweetheart, what happened to you?!"

She rushes forward, her hands reaching out to touch my face, but I wince, the numbness starting to fade and the pain setting in.

"Some guy beat him up for what he was wearing," Paige explains, glaring at our dad, whose lips curl back.

"What did you expect? He looks like a fuckin' queer!"

"*Mark,*" Mom scolds sharply, but the rest of her words are drowned out by the heat rising in my chest.

"Because I *am* queer!" I shout before I can stop myself.

Dad's features twist with anger, red like a cherry about to pop. "What did you just say?"

My throat tightens, and swallowing hurts thanks to the splint in my nose, but I force myself to stand taller. My shoulders square as I step out from behind Paige. "Dad, I'm gay. I've always been gay, and I didn't deserve to get my nose broken just for walking by. I didn't do anything wrong."

A heavy silence follows, the atmosphere shifting as I watch my dad's expression morph from stunned outrage to disgust.

Shame has me opening my mouth to apologize, to take it all back, but he speaks before I can get the chance.

"Get out of my house," he says quietly, so low I almost think I misheard him.

"B-but Dad—"

"I said *get out!*" he roars, the sheer force of it making us all jump. "I will not tolerate this under my own damn roof."

He storms off through the house, his footsteps echoing like thunder. Mom and Paige chase after him, but I don't follow. I can't.

My legs feel like they're made of lead, rooted to the spot as stinging tears spill over my already raw cheeks. Choked noises claw their way up my throat, a desperate, ugly sound I can't control.

He...kicked me out. *My own father kicked me out.*

I'm homeless. Where am I supposed to go? How will I finish school? What am I supposed to do?

"Igs, hey." Paige's arms wrap around me, careful not to press against my battered nose. "Shh, it's alright. He just needs some time to process. It'll be fine."

"*It's not fine,*" I wail into her shoulder, my chest heaving as it feels like it's collapsing inward. "He hates me."

Mom joins us, pressing a tender kiss to my temple. "Oh, my sweet boy, your father does not hate you. He's stubborn and set in his ways, but he loves you. He'll come around, I promise."

But her words don't halt the sobs wracking my body. It probably isn't good for the concussion, but I can't seem to stop. They hold me tightly, Mom wiping my face with gentle hands while my sister tries to console me.

A knock at the front door finally pulls us from the moment, and I look up to see Declan awkwardly standing on the porch, his brows furrowed with concern.

"Everything alright?"

"It will be," Paige answers firmly before glancing at me. "Can Shilo stay with us at your condo tonight?"

He nods immediately. "Of course."

"But I don't want to," I whisper, my lip trembling. Declan's condo isn't the place I want to be. I want to be at his brother's. With *Ryann.* But I don't have a key, Ryann's busy, and I refuse to jeopardize his career by calling him.

"It's just for the night," Paige growls, stomping up the stairs to grab some things from my room. "Until Dad gets his head out of his ass!"

Mom takes my hands, her eyes soft. "You don't have to go anywhere."

"But Dad said—"

"I know what he said," she cuts me off, gently pushing strands of hair from my face. "I will never put my children on the streets, and your father can answer to *me* if he has a problem with that."

"This is his house, though," I mumble.

"Oh, I *dare* him to kick me out. He wouldn't have the balls."

Her eyes flash, and despite everything, I choke out a laugh—only to immediately wince when my head throbs in protest.

"I think... maybe I should go. Give him some space."

"He'll come around." She presses a kiss to my cheek just as Paige reappears, my duffel bag slung over her shoulder. I follow her out, but turn back to Mom in the doorway before stepping off the porch.

"Tell Dad I love him," I say, swallowing hard. "And... thanks for coming home on my birthday."

Her smile is sad but warm as she pulls me in for one last hug. "I'm so proud of you, Shilo. Just want you to know. We've raised a fine young man."

"Thanks, Mom. Love you."

Sliding back into Declan's car, I take one last look at the house before it fades into the distance. The pain in my head mixes with a heavy numbness, tears threatening to spill as panic claws at my thoughts.

Paige says everything will be okay tomorrow, but what if it's not? What if my dad never wants to see me again, all because of something I can't change?

Closing my eyes, I let the hum of the engine lull me to sleep, even though my heart aches for something else. Someone else.

I wish it were Ryann's arms instead.

Ryann

We make it to Declan's within the hour, his high-rise silhouetted against the Aurora Bridge. Unlike my penthouse, Declan opted for a sprawling two-story unit on the ground floor, and the second we're buzzed in, I'm pounding on his front door.

"Jesus, Ryann, what the hell—" My twin starts, but I push past him, heading straight for the granite staircase.

"Where is he? The guest room?"

"Yeah, but I think he's asleep."

Ignoring him, I take the steps two at a time, bypassing a wide-eyed Paige before throwing open the guest room door.

Shilo squeaks in surprise, scrambling to sit up in the king-sized bed that swallows his small body. Rushing to his side, my heart breaks at the dark purple swelling across the bridge of his nose.

"Who the fuck hurt you?" I demand, my blood boiling as I gently cup his face, wiping away the tear tracks on his cheeks. "Who did this, baby?"

Christ, he looks terrible, and it's all I can do to keep from vibrating with rage.

"S-some drunk assholes at a party," he mumbles, taking hold of my wrists. "Carpenter, Kansas, Tina, and their girlfriend defended me."

Goddammit. Remind me to give all of them raises. Hell, I'll *hire* Tina and their girlfriend just to give them raises.

"Who was it?" Leaning in, I try to kiss him softly, but my hands shake with unspent violence "Give me names. I'll fucking murder them."

He lets out a wet laugh, crawling into my lap, his skin warm and clean from a fresh shower. "The cops have an ID. I filed a report."

"You think I'm joking, but I'm not." Wrapping my arms around him, I bury my face in his hair, hating myself for not being there when he needed me. For putting work first, *again*. I'm so fucking tired of always putting work first. He needs to know how I feel.

"What are you doing here?" he whispers, his breath warm against my neck as he clings to me. "Didn't you have a meeting?"

"That's not important. Nothing's important tonight except you." I lean back, taking a deep breath before saying what I desperately need him to hear. "I love you, Shilo. So damn much."

His blue eyes fill with fresh tears, his lips parting just as Paige's voice makes him jump.

"*What the fuck is happening?!*"

Shilo freezes, ducking his head as he grips me tighter, like he's afraid I'll let him go. Over his shoulder, Paige stands in the doorway, completely outraged, and I toss her a cool glance.

"I'm holding my boy. What does it look like?"

"Your...?" Her nostrils flare, dark eyes flashing as she marches toward us. "My brother is not your *boy!* He's your employee! And too fucking young for you. Get away from him!"

"Paige, no." Shilo slides off my lap, placing himself between us. "Leave him alone. It's not what you think."

"He's almost as old as Dad, Shilo!" she snaps, and I bristle in annoyance. For the record, fifty is *very* far off, thank you. Not to mention, she's dating *my* brother, who's the same age as me.

"And I'm old enough to make my own decisions," he counters, his chin jutting out stubbornly, fists clenched at his sides. "I know I'm... not normal sometimes. But that doesn't mean I'm dumb."

Paige huffs, folding her arms as she glares daggers at me. "I know you're not dumb, Iggy, but this is wildly inappropriate—"

"I'm an adult, aren't I? Old enough to know what I want?" Turning back to me, Shilo sits on my knee, threading our fingers. "And what I want is Ryann. I don't care what you think about it."

Her jaw works as she studies us, clearly irritated. Then her laser focus shifts to Declan, who's lingering by the doorway awkwardly.

"Did you know about this?" she demands.

Dec's eyes widen, his mouth opening and closing like a fish out of water.

"Oh, you and I are *so* having a conversation," she growls, storming over to grab him by the shirt before dragging him away. His bedroom door slams so hard I wince.

Fuck. I hope my situation didn't just blow up his.

Olivia grimaces before stepping into the room, stopping a few inches from the bed. Her gaze lands on Shilo, and her expression softens. "Well, I'm glad to see you're safe. Ry here was worried about you."

Shilo ducks his head, hiding behind his hair. "Yeah."

My shy boy.

I tilt his chin up, pressing another delicate kiss to his lips. "Why don't we drop Olivia off at her apartment so I can take you home?"

He squints at me through swollen eyes. "Home? Like your condo?"

"Yes, baby doll. That's now your home because you're staying with me."

Shilo is quiet the entire ride home, his head down and his responses mumbled, even when Olivia wishes him goodnight. By the time we step into the elevator, he's still hiding behind his hair, his emotions locked away.

I keep him pressed to my side, my thumb rubbing slow circles on the back of his neck as I fight the urge to demand words from him, to tell me what he's thinking. After what he's been through tonight, he needs patience. Not pressure.

"Sit, and I'll make you something to eat," I tell him softly, pressing a kiss to the top of his head as I guide him to a stool at the center island. He doesn't argue, doesn't push back, just rests his chin on his folded arms and watches me silently as I move around the kitchen.

Grilled cheese and soup is about the best I can manage. If my little doll is going to live here, I'll need to learn how to cook a decent meal.

When I set the plate and bowl in front of him, the sight of his bruised face as he lifts his head sends a fresh wave of anger surging through me. My fists clench against my thighs when I slide onto the stool next to him, fury simmering beneath my skin. Once the cops find whoever did this, I'll make damn sure they regret it, I swear.

Shilo barely touches his food, pushing the soup around with his spoon and ignoring the sandwich entirely. Sighing heavily, I reach out to gently pry the spoon from his hand.

"Open up, baby."

He scowls when I lift the spoon to his mouth. "I'm not a baby."

"No, you're my boy, and I'm going to take care of you. Let me do this."

His pupils dilate, blowing wide as his lips part in surprise. I take advantage by guiding the spoon onto his tongue, and he lets me feed him until the bowl is nearly empty, never dropping his gaze. There's so much trust in his eyes that my chest physically aches.

"I'm still not calling you Daddy," he grumbles around a piece of grilled cheese, finally breaking the silence.

I can't help but grin. "You can call me anything you want. You're still mine."

His breath catches as he swallows, delicate throat flexing with a nod. "Yours."

The word sends warmth flooding through my bones, stirring a fierce protectiveness in my soul. He's mine. And I'll do whatever it takes to keep him safe.

"Let's get ready for bed."

After cleaning up the dishes, I find him in the bathroom, perched on the counter. Smiling in amusement, I grab a toothbrush and scrub his teeth for him, laughing at the horrified look he gives me when I use the same brush for my own.

"Need I remind you where my tongue has been?" I chuckle, spitting into the sink. "We've shared far more than mouth germs, baby doll."

His face flushes pink, and he mutters something under his breath, making me smirk. Once we're finished, I strip us both naked before we climb between the sheets in our bedroom.

"I've been thinking about this all day," Shilo groans in relief, melting into my hold. "Would have rather been here than that stupid party."

"The feeling is mutual," I huff, ignoring my rapidly filling cock as I gaze down at him. "Tell me what happened today."

He grimaces, burying his face in my chest before flinching when the action bumps his nose. "Ow, frick. This sucks balls."

"No more hiding, Shilo. Talk to me. I want to know what's going on in your head."

Several moments pass as he gathers his thoughts, and then he scoots up slightly to throw a leg over my hip. "Okay, but c-can we...can you get inside of me first? I want to feel close...is that weird?"

Shaking my head, I kiss him softly, feeling his hardness poke at my stomach. "Not weird at all, baby. I need you."

A whimper leaves his throat when I reach over to grab the lube from the nightstand, and I spread some over his pucker before working him open with my fingers. Our kisses are slow, barely touching tongues, his cries of pleasure soft and breathy. When he's ready, I pour more over my cock before gently sliding into him, his tight hole so fucking warm that I have to force myself to stay still.

God, he feels so good, so right. Absolutely perfect.

With a contented sigh, he rubs his forehead against my shoulder. "Kansas dressed me up for my birthday. I thought I looked okay."

"You looked so damn sexy." My hips jerk involuntarily. "That picture had me hard in a room full of execs. I almost embarrassed myself."

He snorts, making his hole flex around my cock, and I groan as my balls start to ache.

"Well, anyway, the party started off fine, I guess. Carpenter told me not to leave his side and not accept drinks from strangers."

Another point in Carpenter's favor. Turns out, the useless PA isn't so useless after all.

Shilo continues. "But then it got hot and too loud, so I went to find the restroom for some air, and that's when those assholes found me."

As he recounts what happened, my anger builds with every word, softening inside of him. I have to bite my tongue to keep from snapping when he shares the things his dad said. It's official—I hate Mark Reed more than I hate my own father.

"He said I deserved it because of how I dressed," my little doll whispers against my neck, his voice catching, and I press a soft kiss to his temple.

"No one has the right to hurt you, Shilo. For any reason. You're allowed to feel comfortable in your own skin."

"I know. I've just..." He swallows hard, his blue eyes searching my face. "I've been teased my whole life about how I look, but this time it was for my sexuality. Feels like it'll never end sometimes."

My heart breaks as I pull him closer, wishing I could take all of his pain away. "I want to tell you it gets easier, hearing the comments and slurs. But it doesn't. People will always have opinions about how we live and who we love. But those opinions are about *them,* not you."

I cradle his face, making sure he's looking at me. "Don't hide away or try to change, baby. You're perfect just as you are."

He nods slowly, chewing on his thumbnail thoughtfully. "Are you gonna get in trouble for leaving your meeting early?"

"Very much so. Ronin fired me on the spot." Blowing out a breath, I run a hand through my hair. "But it doesn't matter. Nothing matters but you."

His brows slam down as he tries to wriggle away, the movement bringing my cock back to life. Letting out a low groan, I grab his hips to keep him still.

"No. Y-you can't do that, Ryann, this is important! You gave up your dreams to work at this company. You can't throw it all away for me."

"I'm not throwing anything away, hush."

He continues to struggle in my grasp, but the way his teeth sink into his bottom lip tells me that he's doing it on purpose, the naughty boy. His dick is leaving a sticky mess all over my abs.

"Shilo, listen to me. Nothing is more important than making sure you're safe. I promise I'm not going to lose my job over it."

Those beautiful eyes widen as he gently rolls his hips against me. "But you said Ronin fired you."

"He did." Meeting his rhythm, I thrust into him slowly, already close to spilling my release. "Don't worry about me. The only thing I want to focus on tonight is making you come so you can sleep."

The tip of my length tags his prostate, causing him to cry out as his fingers dig into my biceps. "Doctor said I'm not—oh, god. Mmm. I'm not supposed to do any strenuous activity. C-concussion."

"We don't have to be rough." Kissing the top of his head, I continue to slide in and out of his slick hole, keeping my pace as soft as possible. "Just close your eyes and let me make you feel good."

"Ry, please," he whimpers, and I reach between us to stroke his cock.

"I've got you. Always."

Our lips touch in sensual, heated kisses, the moans coming from his mouth drawing me closer and closer. When I lightly suck on his tongue, he comes apart, walls clenching as his cum splashes between us, and I follow him over the edge.

Neither of us moves when I've filled him completely, our kisses slowing as my little doll grows warm and pliant against me.

"So what are we gonna do now?" He murmurs, barely conscious enough to form the question.

Wiping us down with a discarded shirt, I tuck the blankets around him. "One day at a time, baby. We'll take it one day at a time."

He hums lightly, nuzzling into me. "I love you too..."

My breath catches as I freeze, my arms instinctively tightening around him. His soft, quiet breathing fill the room, and I swallow hard against the lump rising in my throat.

Besides Declan, no one's ever said those words to me. Not since my mother died.

Clearing my throat, I press a tender kiss to his forehead, careful not to bump his nose. Shiloh deserves the world, and I'm going to make damn sure I give it to him.

Ronin's sharp gaze holds mine from behind his desk, both of us staring each other down. Early morning sun streams through the windows, the clear break in weather as positive a sign as any. To my right, Declan shifts uncomfortably while Olivia sits confident and poised to my left. Tension thickens the air.

That's right, asshole. I brought backup.

"As previously stated," Olivia says again, tapping the folder sitting untouched on my father's desk, "these are our terms over at Sentinel Solutions. You'll find a revised contract and statements from my lawyer. I can have him here in five minutes if need be."

"And what if CalTek were to reject these terms?" Ronin asks coldly.

I toss him a smile to match his tone. "Then your sons and AVA will do business elsewhere. Namely, with Olivia."

Dec's breath stutters a bit, but he sits up straighter, squaring his shoulders as he nods in solidarity. It didn't take much convincing for him to agree to help me, but it *did* take a massive amount of bribing to get him to face off with our father at my side. The two have never had a close connection, and

Ronin downright intimidates my brother, if I'm being honest. The fact that he was even given a position at this company was mere courtesy, at best, which makes my request outrageous, I'm sure.

"Your grandfather and I built this company from the ground up," Ronin nearly snarls, lips curled in distaste. "I won't sit idly by and watch this nonsense tear it apart."

"It's not nonsense," I counter through clenched teeth. "Declan has shown he's more than capable, and it would allow us to expand in ways we can't if the company remains under a single leader. We each have our strengths—"

"And your brother's strength is wasting time on frivolous projects while you handle the real work. CalTek needs a single, strong leader. Not a divided front."

Declan reels back in his seat, taking offense as he should. "Those *frivolous projects* have brought in significant revenue and innovation. I'm just as invested in the company's success as Ryann. This isn't about division, it's about playing to our strengths and ensuring CalTek's future."

"I've always trusted you to lead this company, Ryann," our father interjects, not even glancing at his other son. "You were raised for this. Declan lacks discipline and focus. He's too impulsive."

Years of lies burn on my tongue, and I try to keep from lashing out in my twin's defense. "That's why we balance each other out. I'm asking you to consider what's best for the company's growth, not just what fits the traditional mold. We're stronger together but in different ways."

Ronin's eyes narrow, and for a moment, I think I see a flicker of consideration. But it quickly vanishes, replaced by familiar dismissal.

"I won't allow it," he states flatly. "This company needs stability, not an experiment in shared leadership. If you can't see that, perhaps you're not ready to lead."

Fuck. But who can say that we didn't try?

"Then this conversation is over." Olivia picks up the folder calmly, her movements graceful as she rises to her feet. She offers me her arm, and I follow her lead, Declan trailing silently behind us.

But before the door closes, I stop.

Because if I don't say what's burning inside me, this moment will replay in my mind every night that I close my eyes. And I *refuse* to waste any time in bed thinking about anything other than Shilo.

Turning back, I hold my father's gaze steady. "I gave up everything for this company. My social life, years of freedom, my college dreams. All at your behest. No one has been more dedicated to CalTek than I have. All I've done since I was fifteen is strive to make you see my worth. But I'll never measure up to your expectations. Neither will Declan."

"Either make your point or get out of my office," he growls, his eyes already back on his monitor.

And that's when I realize I'm done. Done with the lies, the hiding, the fear.

It's now or never.

Taking a deep breath, I glance at Declan, who gives me a small, unsure nod. Then I pull tight the final thread we should have tied years ago.

"Declan wasn't the one who started the fire. I was."

That gets Ronin's attention. His gaze snaps back to mine, but I don't back down.

"He took the blame because he knew how important your approval was to me, and it ruined our relationship for years. I'm done putting you above him, above myself, or anyone else. Perhaps you'll think about that kind of loyalty the next time you consider handing this company over to strangers."

His glare hardens, his eyes flicking back to the screen, but I've already said what I needed to say. I take one last look at him—not as a father, but as a man I never hope to become.

Then I turn and leave, stepping into the elevator with Declan and Olivia.

She squeezes my arm reassuringly while Declan lets out a shaky breath and leans heavily against the wall. As the elevator descends, I feel lighter than I have in years.

Like I'm finally free.

"I hope we just made the right choice," Dec murmurs, running a hand through his unruly curls.

I smirk, clapping him on the shoulder. "Give it a week, and we'll be back at our desks. Dad was calling our bluff."

His green eyes swing to mine, wary. "How do you know?"

"I was raised by the man my entire life. I know how he operates."

Unfortunately, I used to operate the same way. But not anymore. I've learned there are more important things than work.

Like my little doll, who's currently chatting with his sister at the security desk, completely unaware of my presence.

He looks relaxed, his nose less swollen, and absolutely *edible* in a sweater that hangs off one shoulder. The marks I'd kissed into his skin last night are on full display, faint but unmistakable.

I want to scoop him up, press him against the nearest wall, and make more. But he's on the clock, so I'll have to wait. It doesn't stop my mind from running rampant with visions of sitting him on the security desk and worshiping his cock, though.

"So, this is real, then?" Declan asks quietly, following my gaze toward Shilo. "You and him? Is it worth it?"

My throat tightens with emotion as I watch my little doll throw his head back in laughter at something Paige says. He ducks behind his hair, flushing awkwardly when the other security guards glance his way. A shy smile crosses his lips before he turns back to his sister, and my breath catches.

He's beautiful. Bit by bit, he's coming out of his shell.

"Oh yes," I murmur. "Very real. And very worth it."

Olivia chuckles beside me. "Once he graduates, let me know. I'd love to have him join my team."

"You're poaching my workforce now?" I throw her an annoyed glance, and she grins back.

"He's not technically yours anymore, right? You no longer work here."

Well, that's just ridiculous. "He'll always be mine."

Always.

Paige's cell goes off, blaring the Bee Gee's once again before she answers. Her expression falls when she glances up, catching sight of the three of us standing there. She says something into the phone, her tone clipped as she rounds the desk to approach us, and Shilo's eyes light up when he notices me. He follows his sister curiously.

"I'm *so* sorry about this," Paige groans with a grimace. "The big guy upstairs just called to ensure I escort you three out."

Declan scoffs, incredulous. "Wow. I shouldn't even be surprised."

He really shouldn't, and neither should I, but it stings all the same.

"What happened?" Shilo asks, searching my face with a frown, and I lean down to kiss him—just because I can.

He gasps in surprise before chasing my mouth when I pull away, his wide eyes locked on mine. I swipe my thumb over his lip, unable to stop the smile tugging at the corners of my mouth.

"I'll tell you at home over dinner."

Home. Where Shilo will sit beside me on the couch, curled up in my arms. Where he'll sleep next to me in bed. Where he belongs.

"Okay."

We map each other's features in silence, neither of us willing to break the connection, until an irritated sigh interrupts the moment.

"Stop defiling my baby brother and get out," Paige growls, her nostrils flaring.

My lips twitch as I fight the urge to smirk. She hasn't warmed up to the idea of Shilo and me, not since he admitted I was the guy he picked up in August. I'm sure she thinks her brother deserves better, and she's probably right. But I'll spend the rest of my days proving her wrong.

With one last heated glance at my little doll, I brush my fingers over his as Paige ushers us toward the front doors. She plants a quick kiss on Declan's cheek before waving us on our way.

Once we reach my car, I turn to my brother and pull him into a sudden hug, catching him off guard.

"Thank you, Dec, for standing by me. For helping. I know you've always offered it, but... I've been a stubborn ass."

Declan laughs, returning my hug tightly. "You *are* a stubborn ass, and it's about time you noticed." He pulls back, studying me with a severe but affectionate look. "I know things were rough between us starting out, but I'll always stand by you, Ry. I'm sorry there was ever a time when I didn't."

Emotion clogs my throat, and I clear it with a rough cough, clapping his shoulders before stepping back. "I'll give you a call if I hear anything from Dad."

We say our goodbyes, and as I settle into the driver's seat, I take a moment to assess my mental state.

I feel... surprisingly optimistic for someone who's just been fired. Almost giddy, even. It's a strange, foreign feeling, but not an unwelcome one.

"So, you said to give Ronin a week." Olivia's voice breaks my thoughts as she pulls a tablet from her bag, her fingers flying across the screen. "What will you do in the meantime?"

"Good question."

For the first time in years, there's no work waiting for me. No reports to write, no conference calls to attend, no endless deadlines to meet. My week is wide open—my entire life, actually.

And I know exactly what I'm going to do with my freedom.

Shilo

Three Months Later

Leaning against the cold metal bleachers, I stuff my hands into the pockets of my hoodie, my gaze fixed on the basketball game unfolding in front of me. The sharp squeak of sneakers on polished wood echoes through the gym, blending with the rhythmic thud of the ball against the court.

Obviously, sports aren't really my thing, but tonight, none of that matters. Tonight, I'm here for Ryann.

It's been three months since he joined the Adult Rec League, and this is their first game of the summer. He's been practicing hard, ever since Ronin agreed to let him split his duties with Declan—*yeah, that actually happened.* Co-CEO's. The change has been unreal.

The game is intense, the scoreboard flickering with numbers I don't understand, all eyes glued to Ryann's movements. Especially mine. Even on the court, he's in control.

"Hot damn," KC breathes beside me, fanning himself dramatically as he scans the players. "I might have to start coming here if the men look like *that.*"

Carpenter just rolls his eyes in response.

Ryann dribbles the ball down the court, his powerful legs carrying him past defenders. My heart jumps as he pulls up for a shot, the ball arcing through the air before swishing cleanly into the net. The crowd erupts into cheers, including my friends, but my focus stays on Ryann's small, satisfied smile as he jogs back to his team's side, warmth flooding my chest.

Watching him like this, I'm both ridiculously proud and kind of turned on, if I'm being honest. *This* is the Ryann I love, the man who can command both a boardroom and basketball court like nobody's business.

As the game winds down, I find myself getting more into it, even cheering a few times when he makes an impressive play—though I quickly duck inside my hood afterward. But I know he notices. I can tell by the way his eyes find mine in the crowd after every shot.

The final buzzer sounds, and Ryann's team emerges victorious. The players gather at the center of the court, clapping each other on the back, their faces flushed and glowing. Ryann's hair is damp with sweat, his grin wide and carefree, more relaxed than he's been in months. Seeing him in basketball shorts was a shock at first, so different from the tailored suits I'm used to, but now I love this side of him.

He seems more authentic, more himself.

More mine.

Once the team begins to disperse, his gaze sweeps over the bleachers until it locks on me, a look passing between us. He jogs over, still catching his breath but smiling crookedly in a way that has my stomach fluttering.

"So?" He prods, his voice slightly hoarse as he runs a hand through his damp strands.

"You're so hot," I blurt out, the words tumbling from my lips before I can stop them. With heated cheeks, I duck my head. "I-I mean, you were amazing out there. Incredible."

He laughs loudly, sending a shiver down my spine. "Thanks, doll. I'm glad you came."

Haven't yet, but I'm about to.

"Wouldn't have missed it."

Reaching out to squeeze my hand with a wink, he leans down to kiss my lips. "I have to debrief with the team and shower, then I'll take you to dinner."

Yeah, so that's a thing now. Dates. *Plural.* He's been making up for lost time, and he's fed me so much over the past few months that I actually fit into my pants now.

I'll admit, the day I had to work a little harder to button my jeans wasn't great... but with Dr. Iskar's help—and Ryann's—I'm learning to love myself, flaws and all. Not one hundred percent, but I'm getting there. It doesn't hurt that Ryann treats me like something precious every single day.

As we leave the gym, KC falls into step beside me, twiddling his fingers at the players we pass. "Think Ry will introduce me to his team?"

"I don't know, maybe?" I glance at him, trying not to laugh. "Which ones do you want to meet?"

He smirks. "All of them. At the same time. Preferably naked."

Carpenter mutters something under his breath, but we ignore him like usual, heading toward the concessions near the pool. It's not until I slide into a seat and pull out my phone that I notice Mom's message waiting in my inbox.

Birthgiver:

> Hey, sweetheart. Your father asked if you could come to dinner this weekend so that you both can talk. He misses you.

I blink at the text for several seconds, my fingers hovering over the screen as I think of how to respond. I haven't seen or spoken to my dad since the night he kicked me out. Every time I went home to grab clothes, schoolwork, or my rat, he was conveniently on duty.

The whole time my nose was healing, he never once reached out to ask if I was okay. That hurt—honestly, everything he said that night still hurts. But I've moved past sadness. Now, I'm just pissed off. According to my therapist, that's natural.

Spending a few minutes typing and deleting responses, I listen distractedly as KC and Carpenter bicker over what constitutes acceptable pool attire. My side warms as Ryann slips in beside me, the leathery scent of his soap flooding my senses.

"What's got that frown on your face, baby?" he asks, dropping a soft kiss on top of my head.

Sliding my phone toward him, I show him the message. "My dad wants to see me."

His hazel eyes meet mine, flecks of green swirling in golden pools. "But do *you* want to see him?"

"I..." My voice trails off. Do I? "What if he just says more mean things?"

"Then we'll leave," he smiles, squeezing my hand gently.

I squint an eye at him. "*We?*"

"You want to go alone?"

Okay, fair point. He's got me there.

But...

Dropping my gaze, I fiddle with the pop socket on my phone, suddenly feeling awkward. Even though Paige knows about us now, my parents don't.

"Are you gonna come with me as my boss, or my friend, or...?" I let my voice trail off, my cheeks heating.

Ryann reaches out, tilting my chin up with a finger as his eyes search mine. "Is that all we are, doll face? Just friends who fuck and live together?"

KC gasps dramatically, reminding me we have an audience witnessing this painful display.

Leaning toward Carpenter, he whispers, "*They were roommates.*"

Carpenter gives him a confused look. "So are we."

"Never mind, straight boy, you don't get it."

"Shilo?" Ryann prompts, drawing my attention back to him.

I squirm, shrugging. "I dunno. Boyfriend sounds weird, doesn't it? Like..." I flounder for a second, trying to find the words. "You're so much more than that."

It sounds dumb, but it's true. I can't explain it.

A slow smile spreads across his face, crinkling the corners of his eyes as his thumb grazes my lips. "How about 'partners'?"

Grimacing, I shrug again, resisting the urge to suck his thumb into my mouth in front of my friends. "Still sounds weird, but I guess."

"Like you're a bunch of cowboys," Carpenter quips, pointing finger guns at KC. "This town ain't big enough for the two of us, *pard'ner.*"

His attempt at a Southern accent is atrocious. Downright embarrassing. KC stares at him blankly before turning back to us.

"'Partner' is good. It's all-inclusive. Gets the point across. I still think 'boyfriend' is super cute, but yeah, it's an odd term for Ry. He hasn't exactly been boyfriend goals, has he?"

"Thanks for the insight," Ryann says dryly, sarcasm lacing his tone. "I do so appreciate your opinions on my relationship."

"As you should." KC winks at me before grabbing Carpenter by the shirt, yanking him to his feet. "C'mon, Carpenter, darling. Let's give these lovebirds some space. Great game, by the way."

As they leave, I take advantage of their absence, gently biting down on Ryann's thumb. His sharp inhale sends a rush of heat through me, his gaze darkening.

"So, is that a yes to supper with your parents this weekend?"

I mull it over, mentally listing the pros and cons.

I do miss my dad. We may have never liked the same things, but I miss his advice, his jokes, his wild stories from work at dinner. He's still a part of me. But can I handle hearing him say again that I deserved to get hit for being myself?

At least Ryann will be there this time. And Mom. Between the two of them expecting the worst, maybe it won't be as bad as I'm imagining.

After several minutes of silent debate, I groan, letting my forehead thud against Ryann's broad chest.

"Fine. We can go. But I'm bringing Master Splinter for moral support."

The familiar scent of Mom's cooking squeezes my chest as we step into the living room Friday night. It's been months since I've had it, and while Ryann's attempts at making us food are sweet, they don't compare. Call me a Mama's Boy—I don't care.

Holding Master Splinter against my chest like a shield, I crane my neck over Mom's shoulder as she greets us by the stairs. My stomach twists with nerves, despite the pangs of hunger I'm still getting used to. Eating regularly has been an adjustment. After years of ignoring hunger, it's like my body is waking up, always demanding to be fed. Something about *getting my groove back,* or so my therapist says.

"He's out back," Mom says as I glance nervously around the room, her gaze flicking to Ryann's hand on my hip.

"Mom, uh..." I cough, feeling hot and sticky despite my loose tank top. "I know you've met him before, but I wanted to reintroduce Ryann as my... partner."

That's going to take some getting used to.

Mom's eyes light up, and she pulls Ryann into a hug before he can even extend his hand. He grunts in surprise but hugs her back, smiling indulgently.

"So *you're* the reason my Shilo has been so much happier," she teases, grinning up at him, and he tosses me a sideways glance.

"I'd like to take all the credit, but I'm certain his friends have a lot to do with it."

"Meh," I shrug, though it's probably true. KC, Carpenter and Tina have become my biggest supporters, even if they drive me nuts half the time.

Mom cups my cheek, her expression warm. "Your father is grilling steaks. Why don't you go outside and say hi? He's been so excited to see you."

Swallowing hard, I give her a tight nod and head toward the back door, Ryann close behind. Mid-evening sun bathes the small backyard in golden light as we step onto the porch, Dad's favorite band, *Boston,* playing softly on the radio while he whistles along at the grill. He hasn't noticed us yet.

I'm frickin nervous. The last time I saw him, he kicked me out and told me I dressed like a queer. My outfit today—silky tank top, tan cinch pants, and jeweled flip-flops—is probably not what he'd consider "manly." Ryann bent me over the counter this morning when I came out wearing it, though, so at least *he* likes it.

My hair is also long enough to curl under my chin, which Dad never tolerated when I was in high school. He always demanded *pressed and neat.*

Yeah, this was definitely a bad idea. In fact, we should probably escape while he's distracted and make up an excuse. Tell him Master Splinter has the flu, and I wouldn't want to make anyone sick. Humans can catch the flu from rats, right? Or was that the plague? Whatever it is, my rat has it, and it's *contagious.*

Spinning around, I'm about to grab Ryann and make a run for it when Dad catches the movement from the corner of his eye. We freeze, staring at each other, but he recovers first, laughing nervously as he scratches his ball cap.

"You startled me," he says, running his gaze over me. I brace for disgust or judgment, but all I see is... relief. "It's good to see you, son. You look... healthy."

"Thanks," I mumble, setting Master Splinter on my shoulder. An awkward silence stretches before Dad clears his throat.

"Mr. Callahan, nice to see you again. Wasn't expecting ya."

Ryann's arm slips around my waist, pulling me close. "Likewise."

His tone is even, but I catch the subtle way he bristles over being called *Mr. Callahan.* If I wasn't so anxious right now, I'd probably giggle.

Dad glances between us, stunned, before turning back to the grill, his neck slightly pink. "Food'll be done shortly. Make yourselves comfortable."

So we do. Ryann leads me to the outdoor table under an umbrella, a light sprinkle cooling the air. His hand rests on my thigh, possessive yet comforting, and I lean into him as we make small talk until the steaks are ready. He's become super affectionate over the last few months, and I'm not complaining. Like, at all.

Mom eventually joins us with her pasta salad, sliding into the seat next to Dad as he gestures at the spread of food.

"Alright, folks. Dig in."

The homesickness hits hard as we all start to eat, making me sad. I don't feel like my usual self here—like I'm walking on eggshells, waiting for the other shoe to drop.

Ryann fills my plate first, piling on pasta and veggies before serving himself. When there's one steak left, Dad frowns.

"Not feeling like steak today, son?"

My first instinct is to lie, tell him I'm just not hungry like I've always done. But Ryann brushes his fingers down my arm reassuringly, and I lick my lips before shaking my head.

"I, uh, don't really like meat."

There. It's done. Wasn't so hard.

Dad blinks, his frown deepening. "Since when?"

"Since forever."

He studies me, a multitude of emotions crossing his features before he huffs and tears into his food. "Wish ya would have said something, but I'll never say no to two steaks."

That's it. That's all he says. No lecture about men needing protein or how I need to bulk up. He just accepts it and moves on, which is...surprising. And not at all what I was expecting.

Mom smiles, nudging my leg under the table. "Shilo and Ryann are dating. Did they tell you?"

Dad grunts, shaking his head around his food. "No, but I figured it out."

A beat of silence passes as we all eat.

"And...?" My mom prompts, elbowing him in the side. "What do you have to say?"

"Christ's sake, Sheila, can we at least get through the meal?" Dad reaches up to rub the back of his neck, looking uncomfortable but not upset. He's never been good at expressing emotions, but thankfully, I always had Mom and Paige for that.

"It's okay," I say quickly, squirming in my seat. "You don't have to say anything."

"No, it's not okay. Your mother's right, I have things to tell you. Just let me get my words together." He stares off toward Mom's lilac bushes, gathering his thoughts. "The day you were born, Shilo, I was so proud to have a son. So excited. Your grandfather raised us with a firm hand, and all I could think was '*man, I can't wait to give this kid everything I never had.*'"

"You did," I rush out, not wanting him to think I'm ungrateful.

"But there's more to being a parent than just giving you things," he continues, swinging his gaze to mine, and I'm shocked to find it glistening. "I got so stuck on who I thought you should be that I didn't give you the choice to be who you *are.* The words I said to you were inexcusable, and I'm sorry, son."

"Dad, no." My eyes water before I know it, and I leave my seat to give him a hug. "You were a good dad, the best."

Call me weak, but no kid wants to see their parents cry. And now that we're both crying, Mom joins in, making this situation ten times *worse.*

"I'm the man of this family, and I was supposed to protect you," Dad says, wiping his eyes. "I failed you, kid. Will you give your old man a chance to do better?"

With a nod and sniffle, I back up until Ryann pulls me onto his lap. "I only ever wanted you to be proud of me. To accept the fact that I'm not like you."

My dad huffs. "No, you're not, and thank God for that. You took after your mother. It doesn't matter who you are, you're still my son." Pausing, his face twists thoughtfully. "Or, uh...daughter, you know, if that's what you decide."

I choke on my spit as Mom smacks him on the shoulder in outrage. "Mark, he's *gay*, not trans!"

"Christ almighty, I'm trying here, woman!"

Despite how offensive that comment was, a laugh bubbles out of me. It was such a Dad thing to say.

As long as he's willing to try, *actually* try, then I don't mind correcting him when he gets it wrong. Because, let's be honest, he probably will. A lot. But if he can listen and change, accept me for who I am, that's all I can ask for.

Ryann holds me close while my parents bicker, his lips brushing my hair. "You alright?"

Master Splinter nibbles on my hair, drawing my attention, and I reach up to pet him with a smile. "Yeah. I'm fine."

This time, I mean it. I really am. I don't think I've ever been better.

He smiles brightly, making my stomach flip when he nibbles on my ear. "I love you, doll. I'm so proud of you."

His praise has me clenching my legs as I cough into my arm, fighting with my dick to stay soft. If I get hard in front of my parents, I'll simply pass away. I swear.

"Well, anyway," Dad grumbles, giving Mom an affectionately exasperated glance before returning to us. "Introduce me to your boyfriend, Shilo. Formally, this time."

"We actually prefer the term partner," I tell him, sliding off Ryann's lap so they can shake hands. "Dad, Ryann. Ryann, Dad."

"As long as you treat him right, we'll have no issues," Dad says, eyeing Ryann sternly, who smiles at me with a wink.

"Oh, I plan on it. For as long as he'll have me."

I'm pretty sure it's the other way around—Ryann can have me for as long as he wants, and as many times, too. I don't say that out loud, though.

As I bite back the urge to mumble something completely ridiculous, I catch Ryann's eye and realize it doesn't matter.

Even if I did, he'd still look at me like I'm the best damn thing that's ever happened to him.

And I feel exactly the same way.

Epilogue

Shilo - One Year Later

"Stop fidgeting, you look fine."

"I know that," I mumble, running my free hand down the front of my soft pantsuit, the other warm and secure in Ryann's grip. "I'm not worried about that. I'm worried about falling on my face."

Ryann raises a brow, looking suave in a loose button-up as he tucks a strand of ash-brown hair behind my ear. "If anyone else but me pulls your pants down, they'll get a lengthy hospital stay and permanent feeding tube."

Snorting, I pull on my robe and graduation cap as I roll my eyes. Seriously, who decided it was a good idea to make us all look like wizards? Why is this robe so long? I'm *definitely* going to trip.

Husky Stadium buzzes with excitement, and after one last kiss on Ryann's lips, I join my classmates in line, all of us bouncing on our feet to accept that degree. It's been a wild year. Not only am I getting my Bachelor of Science in Computer Engineering, but I'm starting my first full-time job on

Monday at CalTek. As a software developer. And not just because my partner is the joint CEO.

I spent the last twelve months proving myself to Liza, taking the lead on projects, helping wherever I could. I earned this position, and I'm honestly pretty proud of myself. I also get to work from mine and Ryann's condo twice a week. She offered to make the position fully remote, but after spending so much time getting to know the other developers, I decided I didn't need to. I actually *wanted* to hang out with them at work. I guess they're not so bad.

As we take our places beside the stage, my gaze sweeps the crowd, finding my mom and Dad first. Paige and Declan, newly engaged, stand beside them, along with KC, Carpenter, and Tina. The three of them graduated last year, and they'd dragged me to Kintsugi to celebrate. We have a whole LAN party planned tonight since they know crowds aren't my thing—just us, our computers, and League of Legends. I can't wait.

Last, my eyes catch Ryann's, and my stomach flutters as he smiles at me from across the stadium. Almost two years now, and he still makes me feel like I'm on a roller-coaster every time I look at him. We've got our own plans for later after I finish hanging out with my friends, and I can't wait for that either. It's going to involve lots of nakedness and lube. Massive amounts of lube.

The line starts moving, and UDub's dean announces names alphabetically. Before I know it, my time is up.

"Shilo Reed."

For a split second, I freeze. But then adrenaline kicks in, and I'm walking up to the stage, trying not to look weird as I avoid the hem of my robe. Mom's joyous scream hits my ears over the audience, and I shake hands with the dean—who's probably forgotten my name already—before grabbing my diploma quickly.

As I turn to face the crowd, I spot Ryann waving at me, and I try to be cool when I wave back, but fail miserably. I probably look like a five-year-old who just saw Santa.

Stepping carefully, and probably way too slowly, off the stage, I approach my seat, sighing in relief.

I didn't even trip. Nothing embarrassing happened.

Honestly, with how much I worried about it, the whole thing feels anticlimactic.

Once all the names are announced, we stand and toss our caps, though I don't toss mine very far. That shit was expensive as hell, and KC stitched my name on it with intricate patterns of computer code. I want to keep it forever.

And with that... it's done. I'm a college graduate. Holy smokes.

Since I attended classes in person for my final semester, a few of my classmates pat me on the back, and then I'm swept up into a crushing hug by Dad. Mom follows, planting kisses on my cheeks that make me groan in embarrassment, passing me down the line of family and friends until, *finally*, I'm in Ryann's arms.

"I'm so proud of you, doll," he whispers with soft kisses. "I love you so much."

"I love you, too."

He holds me tightly, and I melt into his familiar touch, feeling grounded. I hope this feeling never ends.

"My little Iggy is all grown up," Paige sniffles, snapping photos on her phone. "Remember when you made me hold your hand during your college tour?"

Carpenter punches my shoulder, barking out a laugh, and I scowl at my sister.

"Now he'll never forget that. Thanks."

He grabs my hand, cradling it to his chest with a grin. "Poor, sweet Shilo. Need me to take you to the bathroom? I can aim it for you."

"I don't think so," Ryann growls, snatching my hand back, and KC whistles.

"This possessive side of you is hot, Ry. I need to find *me* a man like that."

Now Carpenter's the one scowling, and Tina's cracking up.

Declan pulls Ryann off to the side as I suffer through a round of pictures that Mom wants to scrapbook. She makes me pose with Dad and my sister, makes me hold up my degree, and even makes me throw my hat again. My friends crowd around me for a photo, and I yelp when Carpenter grabs me from under my arms to hold me up like frickin' Simba.

When I try to run off, they yank me back, and I'm about two seconds away from losing it before my mom wipes her eyes, offering me a shaky smile. "Alright, now let's take a few with Ryann."

Okay, *now* we're talking. She can take pictures of us all day.

His body heat warms my side, and I turn to hug him, but freeze when he drops down onto one knee in front of me. Those hazel eyes hold me captive, his lips curved into a smile as he pulls out a velvet box.

"Two years ago, you took a chance by picking up a stranger from some seedy bar and then followed him up to his penthouse," he starts, grinning when my dad coughs awkwardly.

"That guy was an asshole," I blurt, brain completely offline as I try to understand what the hell is happening right now.

Ryann huffs, reaching out to grab my hand. "Yes, he was. But you gave him another chance when he hired you as his intern and then continued giving him more when he messed up again."

My chest is so tight I can hardly speak, my eyes stinging. "Sounds like that guy messes up a lot."

"He does." Ryann squeezes my fingers before letting go, and when he opens up the little box in his palm, my breath catches in my throat. "I can't promise you a perfect man, but I can promise that I'll spend every day being the best man I can be for *you.* Because I've been waiting my whole life for you, baby doll."

I can't breathe, my heart pounding so hard everyone can probably hear it as I stare at the silver ring nestled in velvet. Ryann's eyes search mine, vulnerability flickering in their depths, and it hits me all over again just how much this man means to me. How far we've come.

He pauses, taking a deep breath before continuing. "Shilo, you're my best friend, my partner, my everything. I want to spend the rest of my life making you feel as loved as you've made me feel. So, what do you say?" He smiles crookedly. "Will you marry me?"

I'm too overwhelmed to respond, emotions rushing in like a tidal wave. But then I see the look on his face—so open, so loving—and the only words that make sense come tumbling out of me.

"Am I getting a promotion?"

He chokes out a laugh, slipping the ring onto my finger as everything around us fades away. It's just him and me, two broken people with nothing in common who somehow make each other whole.

I don't know how we got here, but I'm not questioning it. Not fighting it. His jagged edges might not match up with mine, but that's what makes us perfect. Beautiful.

Human.

Everyone around us erupts into cheers, my mom and Paige ugly crying. Even Dad wipes a tear from his eye.

Ryann stands, pulling me in before kissing me dizzy, and in this moment, I feel it—the beginning of our forever.

I'm glad he's cool with cats because I'm *so* getting him one tomorrow.

The End

Afterword

Thank you so much for coming on this journey with me! As we come to the end of *Pretty Broken Doll*, I'm reminded of how much I've loved these two. Shilo's battle with self-image has been a central part of his story, the way he struggles to accept himself is something I know resonates with so many of us. And then there's Ryann, whose relentless drive to meet his father's expectations caused him to lose sight of his own dreams. His struggle to let go of that pressure and reclaim his own path is about learning to live for yourself.

Both of them come from different worlds, but love found a way to weave through their cracks and connect them. They had nothing in common on the surface, but beneath it all, they shared the need for acceptance—for someone to see past their flaws and love them *despite* or even *because* of those flaws.

I hope this story conveys the core message that even in our darkest moments, even when we feel like we don't fit, love finds a way.

To every reader who has made it this far, thank you again for believing in these characters. For rooting for them, and spending time with their messy, broken, and beautifully imperfect love story. I hope it reminds you that you don't need to be whole to be worthy of love.

Stay beautifully broken.

Love always,
Bree Wiley

PS: For those curious about the football player and his stunt bike boyfriend, Huckslee and Taylor, you can read their story in Finding Delaware on Amazon and Kindle Unlimited.

Acknowledgments

To my alpha and soulbestie, Giselle, for being the best supporter I could ask for. You're amazing! I couldn't have done this without you <3

Joe, love of my life, partner in all things, I adore you.

And most importantly, to my betas, for taking Shilo and Ryann into your loving arms to make sure their story was told the way it should be. Kristal, Brianna, Anya, Danielle, Cici, Lavender, and Kayla. I appreciate all of you!

Content Warning

The following list contains spoilers, so if you're the type that prefers to go in blind, please skip to the first chapter. Both MC's are consenting adults over the age of 18.

- Depictions of eating disorder and body dysmorphia.
- Puking.
- Mentions of childhood bullying.
- Bigoted parents.
- Homophobia and homophobic slurs (not between MC's)
- Mentions of parental death due to house fire.
- MC with mild burn scars.
- Sixteen year age-gap between MC's
- Violence against an MC due to homophobia (not between MC's)

- Light D/s themes
- Orgasm denial
- Light foot fetish, including toe sucking.
- Spanking
- Cock-warming
- Light spitting

About The Author

I'm a US resident who can be found cuddled on the couch with my partner and our black cat, Norman Bates. Mostly, I'm a homebody but I do enjoy getting lost in the woods. I love romance, fantasy, science fiction, and every horror video game ever made. *Pretty Broken Doll* is my second novel.

Let's be besties! Scan the code below for my author links!

Printed in Great Britain
by Amazon

57619803R00205